THE PROM GOER'S INTERSTELLAR EXCURSION

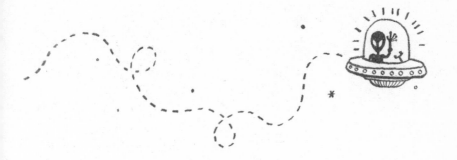

THE

Prom

GOER'S

Interstellar →

EXCURSION

CHRIS McCOY

Alfred A. Knopf · New York

Text copyright © 2015 by Chris McCoy • Jacket hand-lettering/illustrations © 2015 by Julie McLaughlin

All rights reserved. Published in the United States by Alfred A. Knopf, an imprint of Random House Children's Books, a division of Random House LLC, a Penguin Random House Company, New York.

Knopf, Borzoi Books, and the colophon are registered trademarks of Random House LLC.

Visit us on the Web! randomhouseteens.com

Educators and librarians, for a variety of teaching tools, visit us at RHTeachersLibrarians.com.

Library of Congress Cataloging-in-Publication Data
McCoy, Chris.
The prom goer's interstellar excursion / Chris McCoy.—First edition.
p. cm.
Summary: Minutes after the prom and she says yes, eighteen-year-old Bennett Bardo of Gordo, New Mexico, asks Sophie Gilkey, his dream girl, to the prom and she says yes, and Bennett catches a ride across the galaxy with a band of misfit musicians to find her.
ISBN 978-0-375-85599-3 (trade)—ISBN 978-0-375-95599-0 (lib. bdg.)—ISBN 978-0-375-89711-5 (ebook) • [1. Alien abduction—Fiction. 2. Extraterrestrial beings—Fiction. 3. Bands (Music)—Fiction. 4. Adventure and adventurers—Fiction. 5. Dating (Social customs)—Fiction. 6. Interplanetary voyages—Fiction. 7. Humorous stories.] I. Title. • PZ7.M478414457P
2015 • [Fic]—dc23 • 20130458

The text of this book is set in 11-point Simoncini Garamond. • Book design by Stephanie Moss
Printed in the United States of America • April 2015

10 9 8 7 6 5 4 3 2 1 • First Edition

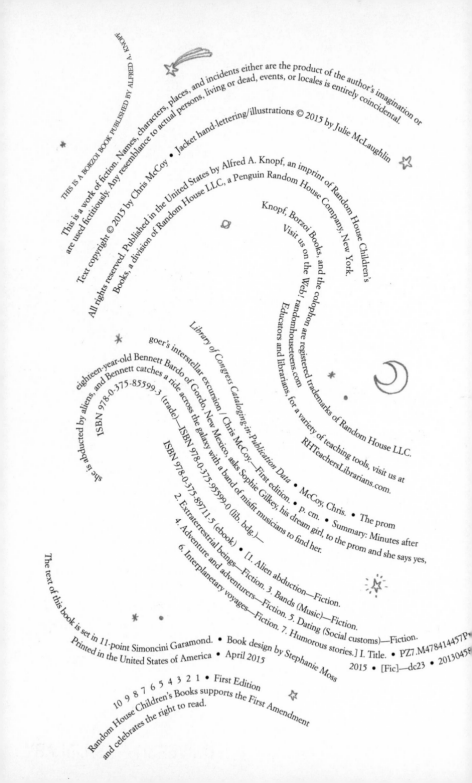

FOR MR. OZUG

PROLOGUE

I can't believe it has gotten to this point.

I am a worthless, ramen-eating, day-sleeping, I-think-I-wore-these-boxers-yesterday-but-I'm-not-even-quite-sure pile of dirt right now. Eighteen broken years old. Damned to live with my parents for the next few decades, then inevitably go stark mad and spend the rest of my life searching the New Mexico desert for the Fountain of Youth in the hope that it will allow me to relive my empty years that have slipped away.

I wish I could have jettisoned my brain when I was wait-listed by Princeton. Given it to somebody who might have used it correctly. College was the only reason I needed it, and now I'm not even going. I *would* just offer it to a research lab and tell the scientists to hook up all the electrodes and wires they want to it, if I wasn't worried about some remnant of my consciousness lingering behind. Living as a Brain in a Jar probably wouldn't be much different than living as a depressed human in my childhood bedroom in this burned corner of the American Southwest, but better safe than sorry.

As you might have guessed, I am in a fetid place mentally right now. Damn you, Princeton. Damn you, getting abducted by aliens, though that was technically my fault.

That's what happened, by the way. I'm going to be writing about it quite a bit as we go forward here, so forgive me if it feels like I'm not giving you enough information up front. It's all coming. I understand that you might find the "teaser" nature of this prologue aggravating—I don't particularly like it as a literary device myself—but I wouldn't be writing this story at all if I wasn't having a mental breakdown, so I thought it might help if you had some initial context.

The air outside is as hot as a Tesla coil, I'm desperately lonely because Sophie is gone, and I can't find a job because everybody in town views me as a potential criminal with whom one should never make eye contact. Children point at me. Old ladies gasp. I am utterly alone. Just my guitar, a yellow legal pad, and a story that I feel like I should get down on paper in case this breakdown persists and the doctors at the mental hospital where I end up need some evidence of why they cloistered me away, for their case files. Maybe I'll read these pages over when I'm done, just to think about Sophie. To keep her fresh in my mind, though I can't imagine a time when she wouldn't be in my thoughts. She's always, always there.

I'm Bennett Bardo. I don't know why I need to introduce myself if there's a distinct possibility that I'm the only person who is ever going to read this manuscript, but hey. Is this what having a true psychological meltdown feels like? I can't *believe* I'm giving myself a writing assignment on top of this depression. I can't believe anything, but then again, there's also nothing I *wouldn't* believe anymore, because of my recent experiences. Reality and unreality have broken down in my mind. Dogs are cats, squares are circles, tunnels are bridges, forks are spoons. What's wrong with me? Let's do this. Pen to paper, pen to paper. Try not to stab yourself with the pen. Okay, let's go.

SUNDAY

My hometown of Gordo, New Mexico, is isolated in the middle of the desert, roughly two hours from Roswell, which is best known for being ground zero for a 1947 flying saucer crash rumored to have been covered up by the government. The popular belief among UFO enthusiasts and conspiracy chasers and people whom until recently I would have considered to be paranoid schizophrenics is that the U.S. Air Force recovered the remnants of the saucer, as well as the bodies of a few dead aliens, and then whisked the evidence away to Area 51 in Nevada for research. Never been, can't tell you if it's true.

I can't stand my town. In every direction, it's nothing but sand and rocks and the occasional horned toad shooting blood out of its veiny eyes—they actually do that—and this horrid landscape is a significant part of why I wanted to go to Princeton. I've never seen a tree-lined campus, or experienced snow in winter, or had to layer my clothing to keep warm, or had the chance to wear interesting reindeer-printed scarves. I've barely ever had to own a *jacket,* and certainly never one stuffed with goose down or some such functional, heat-preserving lining that cradles my body like a soft mother koala, holding me, loving me.

The fact that Roswell is so close to my hometown is something of a saving grace. Even if Gordo is terrible in all ways—and it is—it's interesting to live near a spot where an event as bizarre as a UFO crash might have occurred. In keeping with the UFO element, I own a telescope that my father brought home from a yard sale years ago, and for a long time I used it every night to search for strange lights, though I never saw any. Millions of stars up there, not a lot of aliens. I kept looking, as you do. What else is there to do in life but look.

The Gilkey family has lived next door my entire life. Mr. Gilkey was my childhood dentist, but in my opinion he did a less-than-remarkable job capping my two front teeth, which I broke after Rollerblading over a sewer grate when I was nine. They're still a bit crooked, and I feel like they could be whiter, but that's probably just my insecurity talking. Mrs. Gilkey was my third-grade teacher, and taught me how to multiply and divide numbers. In retrospect, I should have paid more attention during the arithmetic part of her class, given my imperfect SAT math score eight years later, which was no doubt an important factor when it came to Princeton's decision to put me on the wait list instead of throwing open its sacrosanct doors and letting me in.

Sometimes I have a hard time wrapping my head around the value of math and physics, because I know I'm never going to create a new theorem, or discover a new law of motion, or be honored for figuring out the last digit in pi. Because I know I'll never be able to push the field of study forward, it always just seems a bit like advanced regurgitation to me. Which isn't to say I'll be able to make any sort of significant contribution to any other academic discipline either, but for some reason, math hangs me up.

Finally, the Gilkeys' daughter, Sophie, was my unobtainable crush, the most attractive girl I had ever seen. Long black hair. Vintage dresses. Cool belts. Great shoes, always. Shiny. Though I wouldn't consider myself a fashionista by any stretch of the imagination, it's hard not to appreciate her eye for detail. Sophie is destined to be a famous actress, or appear on the covers of upscale lifestyle magazines, or marry the leader of a European nation, though in all honesty it will probably have to be a minor country like Macedonia or Luxembourg, because the one thing Sophie has working against her is that she isn't very tall, and over the years, newspaper photographs have indicated to me that world leaders like *statuesque* women. Sophie is more of a small, beautiful woodland creature with the soul of a guerrilla commando.

In our senior yearbook, Sophie was voted *Most Likely for*

Everybody to Still Be Thinking About in Ten Years—a category that, in my role as yearbook editor in chief, I created for the sole purpose of being able to run another picture of her. She swept all the nonacademic yearbook superlatives—*Most Attractive, Best Smile, Most Stylish.* And *Worst Case of Senioritis,* which likely had to do with the fact that—I'm not joking about this—*she owned a motorcycle* and seemed more eager to get out of our desert wasteland than anybody in the school, myself included. I may have desperately wanted to leave, but I wasn't able to outwardly *express* this desire as well as Sophie did. Nobody could.

The only yearbook superlative I won was *Most Awkward,* a category I didn't realize the rest of the yearbook staff had plotted to include in the final edition behind my back, as a prank. It was a cruel stunt, to be sure, but in the interest of professionalism and to show I was a good sport, I dutifully ran a picture of myself. I had the photo editor take the snapshot while I was sitting down so the yearbook wouldn't permanently record how gangly and almost pipe-cleaner-ish my body had become. Even my parents thought I was looking strange, and I noticed they rarely took photographs of me anymore, though maybe that happens naturally as one gets older and the cuteness of childhood dissipates with every tick of the minute hand.

Please allow me to break from my story for a moment to talk about my parents. Though I love them very much, I'm not going to mention them too often, for the simple fact that they weren't *around* for what happened to me.

During that fateful week when my life changed, my mother

and father were on vacation, spending several days trekking across a remote part of northwestern Vietnam, and had left me to my own devices, knowing full well I didn't have enough friends to throw a party or get into any serious trouble. Their leaving me behind shouldn't be seen as a reflection of their parenting skills, but rather as a new embrace of international travel, combined with the fact that cheap tickets had fallen into their laps via an American Airlines promotional deal. They had actually left me alone the year before, when I was seventeen, while they traveled to Chile, and I had used the time as a chance to work on my music all over the house and eat quadruple-layer nachos.

Because my parents were in a far-flung region of some Southeast Asian jungle, they weren't able to check in by telephone, which meant—simply put—that what happened to me couldn't have occurred at a better time, if being killed *at least* once in deep space can be considered a good time. But I'll get to that.

Anyway, I loved Sophie, but I barely knew her. I'm not sure anybody did, at least in our high school. At the time this all took place, our graduation was approaching—at the end of May, for the record, for the sake of narrative grounding—and our prom was one week away. From what I had ascertained through the rumor mill, Sophie was going to prom with a twenty-one-year-old linguistics student from the University of New Mexico. While I didn't approve of their age difference or the fact that they were at different points in their lives, she was eighteen, so in the eyes of the law, their dalliance was legal, if a little sketchy.

I was planning to spend prom night in my bedroom, crafting a song cycle about loneliness on my acoustic guitar, though I knew I would never finish it due to my permanent case of malignant, chronic, soul-crushing writer's block, which I suppose made the fact that I was trying to complete a song *cycle* even lonelier. I knew I wouldn't even manage to get *one* song done, never mind an opus. But ambition is important.

I honestly didn't understand what kind of crumbling sinkhole I had in my brain that prevented me from being able to finish something as outwardly accomplishable as a three-minute song. I constantly had hundreds of ideas firing through me, I had dozens of little pieces of paper containing fragments of lyrics scattered around my room, I had tape recordings of riffs that I thought might lead to something interesting . . . but as soon as I tried to start putting it all together, I seized up.

I've never been to a psychiatrist, but if I had to self-analyze, I'd postulate my failures had something to do with the fact that my guitar had always been my *escape*. I'd come home from school, I'd do my work, I'd fantasize about getting out of New Mexico, and I'd play music to calm myself down. Routine.

But if I actually *finished* a song, it might mean I would feel the obligation to put that song out into the world, which would open me up to criticism, and if people then *rejected* my work, my guitar might no longer feel like such a vacation for me. This psychological labyrinth meant that every time I would get *close* to finishing a song—I could have the melody polished, the lyrics down, and nothing left to complete but the bridge—I would abandon it as not good enough, and move on to the next one. All that I had to show for my years of composition was hundreds of orphaned ideas sitting around in the gray matter of my mind, biding their time in the hope that someday I would get up the confidence to do something with them.

Anyway, the working title of the never-to-be-completed song I planned to compose on prom night, in lieu of dancing, or touching a girl, or feeling momentarily handsome, was "Sophie and Me Up in Those Trees," though I knew that appellation was likely to change during the songwriting process, because there was no good reason that Sophie would ever want to hang out with me in a tree. The whole scenario didn't seem believable.

I have to say, it's strange to grow up next door to a girl, see her jogging around, share a bus with her—though Sophie was always in the back with the beautiful people, while I was in front trying to forge a conversation with the driver because nobody else wanted to talk to me—listen to your parents talking to her parents about the two of you when they got together for cocktails, be completely in love with her, and have no clue what she's like as a human being.

I know Sophie better now, so I'm going to do the best I can to describe her here. She will never again be as fresh in my mind as she is in this moment, and I want to remember her in Technicolor detail. I will relay our conversations as well as I can recall them, I will attempt to do justice to how *profoundly* excellent a human being she is, but I'll tell you up front that I'm probably going to fail, because she has always seemed beyond me, and still does in many ways, even after everything and all of it.

Forgot something. Before I go on, here's what I look like, in case you'd like to know. Even though I'm eighteen, I only recently hit any sort of real puberty, and I've been growing taller without putting on sufficient weight to counterbalance my new height, giving me the appearance of one of those long, thin needles witch doctors stick into voodoo dolls. I think my face is fairly well proportioned—I don't suffer from the affliction of having one eye higher than the other or some such asymmetry, and since I've never been in a fight and I'm terrible at sports, my nose has never been broken and is unremarkable but straight. I currently lack the testosterone to grow a beard, but the hair on top of my head grows wildly, in waves that are impossible for me to do anything with except occasionally hack down to a less offensive height.

Anyway, on that Sunday when everything came together and then was obliterated so swiftly, it was early evening and I was looking through my telescope at the sky, checking for meteors. There was no activity in the south, so I swung the telescope to the west, and in the middle of that sweeping motion, I caught the briefest glimpse of Sophie kneeling in the Gilkeys' driveway, where she was fixing her motorcycle with a wrench. And she was *crying*.

To be clear, I have always made a point of not using my telescope for the purpose of peeping—I'm not sure if I would consider my teenage years a great success, but at the very least I've made it through them without ever turning into a stalker—so I *promise* you that the lens of my telescope landing on Sophie was purely accidental, and that I only looked at her for the minimum amount of time it took to determine with certainty that she seemed to be having a mini-meltdown.

It was shocking. I had never seen Sophie cry. For my whole life, she had been like this godlike representative of the concept of cool made human and sent to earth to unwittingly torment me simply by existing in the same place at the same time, which was not her fault and not something for which I could reasonably hold her responsible.

But there, next to her motorcycle, she seemed to be having a legitimate *break*. Tears. Eye gunk. Snot. Sweat. A weird splotchy patch on the side of her neck. I watched her put down her socket wrench and bury her head in her hands, which were *shaking*. It was strange to observe her when she seemed so alone, so I stopped. I might have been a bit of an outcast, but I tried to not be creepy, which I don't think is such a radical code by which to live one's life.

Because I had nothing planned for that evening—I'd already spent a few hours with my guitar, failing to finish a song, creating nothing, improving the world in no tangible way—I decided to walk over to Sophie's house to investigate. While she and I weren't close, we were neighbors, and checking on her seemed like a neighborly thing to do.

When I got to her driveway, she was still crying, her automotive tools scattered near the front wheel of her motorcycle.

"I . . . saw you crying," I said. "Are you okay? Hi, by the way. This is already weird that I'm here, isn't it? Crap."

She looked up at me, face wet, bubbles of spit collecting at the corners of her mouth. Still beautiful.

"Your house is a quarter mile away," she said. "How could you *possibly* see me crying?"

Should have mentioned: Sophie and I are *technically* neighbors, but our houses are *far* apart. A formidable distance. Her family owns a few acres, and my family has a large "lawn" filled with cacti and dirt. It was justifiable for her to point out that there was no way I would have been able, from my house, to see her with my naked eye.

I came clean.

"I'm sorry," I said. "I was looking at the sky to try and get out of my head for a bit, and I moved my telescope, and I saw you. I wasn't trying to spy."

"So it wasn't intentional?"

"I have a sense of personal boundaries, and the only reason I came over here is . . ."

I paused.

"I don't know why I even came here," I said. "I didn't think the decision through."

"It's fine," she said. "You're here. You're easy to deal with."

Hearing Sophie say that stung for some reason. *Easy to deal with*. Sure, I wouldn't have wanted her to consider me some sort of Jack the Ripper–esque black angel connoisseur of death, but it was hard to hear there was *no* aura of danger around me at all. Nobody wants to be considered totally nontoxic.

"So . . . ," I said.

"So, yeah?"

"I'm here . . . if you want to talk about . . . anything. I guess that was what I was thinking."

I wanted to shut my eyes and walk backward and reverse time so I had never walked to the Gilkeys' driveway in the first place. There was no reason for Sophie to tell me anything, ever. We weren't actual friends, I had no right to be looped into her personal business, and though I thought I was being chivalrous—or something like that, I'm not sure what—I was making a fool of myself.

"I'll leave you alone," I said.

She wiped her eyes and ran her hands through her hair.

"You can stay for a second if you want," she said. "You're already here."

"Do you want to talk about what happened?"

She sighed.

"There was a guy I was supposed to go to prom with. Rich."

"The linguistics student."

She paused and gave me a look of *what the hell?*

"How do you *know* that?" she said.

"Everyone at school knows your boyfriend's name," I said. "It's common knowledge that you're dating a college student."

"You're kidding," she said. "Everybody in the school knows that?"

"It's maybe the *only* thing anybody knows about you," I said. "You're mysterious."

She rubbed her eyes. "I can't stand high school."

"What happened with Rich?"

She shook her head, irritated. "It turned out he was dating a girl from his department at the same time he was seeing me, and now he's driving with her to Mexico instead of taking me to the prom. Some hotel in Baja. I checked it out online. It's nice."

"Look on the bright side. Maybe they'll get kidnapped," I said.

"I wouldn't want to prolong things by wishing something like that," she said, wiping her eyes. "I'd prefer if they were just sucked out to sea or if a volcano exploded underneath them."

"Are there many volcanoes in Mexico?"

"There's one called Las Tres Vírgenes halfway down the Baja coast, but I don't think they're traveling that far. Plus, it hasn't erupted since 1746."

I did not know that.

"So . . . that means you broke up," I said.

"*Yes,* we broke up," she said. "Do you think that I'm going to stay with someone who takes *another girl* to *Mexico*?"

Sophie was *single.* My heart leaped, though there was no reason it should matter to me that Sophie was back on the market. She had already technically opened up her dating life to the adult world, which was filled with guys with jobs and money and limbs that were proportional to their bodies. There was no way I could compete.

Sophie picked her socket wrench up off the ground and

anxiously rapped the pavement with it, looking down, lost in her head.

"It's so stupid," said Sophie. "I know I shouldn't *care* about prom, but I feel like it's something that's going to come up in conversations for the rest of my life. Neither my mom nor my grandmother went, and they both regret it. I don't want to be telling my grandchildren about how I stayed at home that night watching *Pretty in Pink.*"

"Good movie, though."

"Great movie," she said. "I don't know. I just want to go. It's as simple as that."

I wanted to go too. No matter how socially disastrous my high school career had been, I was still part of my class, and I felt like attending would provide some sort of cap to the four years I had spent rotting in a concrete building. I looked at prom like an open-casket funeral—I wanted to take one last glance at what I was leaving behind so I never had to see it again, and I figured it would be a more tolerable memory if all the people I couldn't stand were at least well dressed.

"Is there . . . anything I can do to help?" I said.

"How would you help?"

"I don't know," I said. "I had an instinct that was the sort of thing you're supposed to ask a girl who is crying two feet away from you."

"I'm not crying."

She wiped her cheek with the sleeve of her jacket. Then she stared at me for a moment, working something out in her brain.

"I do need help with *one* thing," she said.

"Name it."

"I need a ride to my mechanic. My bike won't start, which means I can't get out of here."

"Where's your mechanic?"

"Roswell."

"Roswell is a hundred and twenty miles away," I said. "Why would you have a mechanic out there?"

"He's the best," said Sophie. "Can your truck make it that far?"

I peered back in the direction of my distant house, where my 1986 Chevy pickup was sitting in the driveway, looking like it was on the verge of snapping in half, which was the normal vibe it put out into the world.

My truck is a death trap. A hole in the passenger-side floor goes through to the undercarriage, a problem my father had solved by covering the hole with a piece of plywood on which he had spray-painted the words *REMOVE AND ACTUALLY DIE*. The interior lights randomly turn blood-red, as if receiving electric signals directly from hell, and I'd covered the rotting steering wheel with a zebra-patterned sleeve so I don't have to physically touch it, which imbues the truck with a safari feel. It needs thousands of dollars of repairs, but my parents had apparently decided to roll the dice with my life because they had had crappy cars in high school too. I think they saw driving a piece of junk as a rite of passage, and they knew if I had a beat-up truck, I wouldn't be able to travel far.

I had very little confidence the truck would make it to Roswell, but if it was going to fall apart, I figured it might as well deteriorate while a beautiful girl was riding shotgun. The thought of our pictures appearing side by side in a newspaper obituary was appealing in a morbid way. I liked the idea of readers wondering, *How was a guy like that able to get a girl like her?*

"My truck can make it to Roswell," I said, trying to sound nonchalant, as if this was something I helped attractive women with all the time. "I'll pull it around and you can throw your motorcycle in the back."

"I don't think I'll *throw* the motorcycle," she said. "I've seen your truck and I'm not sure it could take the impact."

"Fine, hoist it gently into the back."

Sophie thought about this.

"*Hoist* is a weird word, don't you think?" she said.

"It's because it sounds like *moist,* which is always the first word people bring up when you ask them what word they hate."

"Nobody ever talks about *foist,* though."

"It's because *foist* is a verb, so it's harder to picture."

"Transitive verb."

If the verb was transitive, that was news to me. I'm terrible at defining parts of speech. To this day, I have no clue what a gerund is, and the thought of having to pick a quantifier out of a sentence gives me full-body shivers.

The more I reflect on all the things I don't know that I probably should know, the more I think I understand Princeton's decision.

"Very true," I said, pretending like I knew what I was talking about. "Transitive verb."

"Do you have the same opinion of *goiter* that you do of *foist*?" she said.

"*Goiter* is really bad," I said. "It sounds like something a duck might say if it was choking on a fish. I don't even think I know what a goiter *is*."

"It's when the thyroid gland starts to swell up because of an iodine deficiency," said Sophie.

"I can't believe you know that."

"If I know a word exists, I like to know its meaning," she said. "How about this: *foist some ointment on my moist goiter.*"

I almost gagged. "I feel like you could go around saying that sentence and just make people throw up on the spot."

She laughed. Sophie has a laugh that sounds a bit like an earthquake followed by a bunch of rumbling aftershocks: "*HA . . . hehhhhhhhhhh.*" Strange. I've always found the fact that her laugh is so bizarre to be comforting. It's nice to know she isn't perfect, even though she is.

"Be right back with the truck," I said.

I ran to the house to get my pickup. I may have been sprinting. I may have even leaped a hedge.

Sophie was keeping a white-knuckle grip on the passenger-side door handle. Every time we hit a pothole, the truck's steel frame screeched and groaned like a steam locomotive from the 1800s.

Aside from its profound structural problems, the biggest issue with my truck is that the radio is broken, which is a conspicuous hardship for somebody who listens to as much music as I do. The vehicle's cassette player is somewhat functional, though the only tape I have is the original cast recording of *The Phantom of the Opera,* to which we were listening.

"Sing once again with me . . . Our strange duet . . . ," said the tape.

"I never pegged you for a musical theater person," said Sophie.

"We bought the truck used. This is the tape that came with it, and I can't get it out."

"And as a result, you *happen* to listen to it all the time."

"The tape player automatically turns on when I start the truck. Try to get it out. I promise you, the Phantom of the Opera isn't going anywhere."

"That's the way the Phantom works," said Sophie. "He lingers maniacally."

"But misunderstood."

"Yeah, definitely misunderstood."

Sophie hit the eject button on the tape player. Nothing happened.

"Told you it didn't work," I said. "I know nothing about engines or carburetors or transmissions, but I know about my tape player."

"You should buy a huge boom box at a thrift store and drive around with it. That way you could listen to anything you want, and it would look kinda badass."

"I don't go to thrift stores," I said. "I have a problem with the smell of old blankets."

"Really? I buy all my clothes at thrift stores. It gives me the sense of being constantly in costume, which helps with living in the middle of nowhere."

"In what way?"

"If I'm wearing somebody else's clothes, I can trick myself into thinking this isn't my life."

Made sense.

"I can't wait to get out of New Mexico," I said. "*Look* at this place. It's like some dystopian event happened and we're the only survivors."

Outside, scrubby green bushes dotted the dead brown landscape. Power lines buzzed endlessly. Wind turbines stood motionless in the distance, starting to cool after a day of spinning in the sun.

For a while, Sophie and I made small talk. She asked if I knew where I was going to college. I told her my first choice was Princeton, but I was on the wait list, which felt like a hopeless situation. She told me the wait list was still pretty good—better than a straight-up rejection—and asked if I had any strategy for getting off it. I told her I was thinking of trying to find religion, or maybe looking up some minor god to whom nobody else was praying and asking it to help me out.

"My suggestion is you try Utu, Sumerian ruler of the sun," she said. "I always liked that particular deity."

"You're putting some *deep* knowledge on display there."

"I like arcane information," she said. "It makes me feel like less of a cookie-cutter human being if the things in my head aren't the exact same things that are in everybody else's. I never in my life want to have a conversation about a reality television program."

"What about being on one?"

"My deepest nightmare."

"Nobody would ever consider you a cookie-cutter human being," I said.

"What do you like to do outside of school?" she said. "I don't know anything about you, except that you play music."

". . . You know that I play music?"

"When you plug in your amplifier, I hear you playing guitar in your house," she said. "Do you have a microphone too? Because sometimes I think I even hear you singing through the amp."

"Yes, I have a microphone."

"Maybe *that's* what can set you apart from everybody else when it comes to getting off the wait list. You should send Princeton a *Sgt. Pepper*–style concept album about how much you want to get in."

My stomach twisted. The thought of Sophie hearing me playing guitar—hearing me *singing*—was petrifying. I never even sang if my *parents* were in the house. I only practiced when I knew I was alone. I had never realized my unfinished songs would drift outside into the street and be carried to Sophie on the treasonous desert wind.

"I'm not sure Princeton wants me to send them a playlist of my crappy songs," I said.

"Your songs aren't crappy at all, but you should finish one sometime. I've noticed they always seem to cut off in the middle. I'd love to hear a whole one someday."

I didn't know how to respond. I had used her *name* in my songs before. I glanced over to see if she had a look on her face that might indicate she was aware that I sang about her, but she was playing with the tape deck again, trying to get the *Phantom of the Opera* cassette to come out.

"So where else did you apply to college?" she said.

It was time to feel stupid again.

"Princeton was the only place I applied," I said.

"You're *kidding.*"

"I genuinely thought they would accept me. In retrospect, it wasn't my strongest idea."

"*Thousands* and *thousands* of students don't get in. Just looking at the percentages, you're out of your mind."

"My grades were basically perfect," I said. "My SAT scores were at the low end of Princeton's average, but I thought they would at least put me in the mix. I guess I figured that I wanted it so much there was no way they would say no and just leave me here."

Sophie whistled, a long, thin *whoooooo.* "Wow. I've never heard of anybody applying to just *one* college. I mean, if only one college in the world existed, it would make sense, but, y'know . . . there are quite a few."

"Subconsciously, I think I must want to be stranded forever in the desert," I said. "Where are you going to school?"

As soon as the question passed my lips, I regretted asking

it. Here I was talking about how I was worried about Princeton, and I didn't even know if she was *going* to college. Sophie wasn't in any of my AP classes, I never saw her in SAT test prep, and she didn't do any extracurricular activities, as far as I knew. On weekends, she usually just disappeared with her motorcycle—to see the ex-boyfriend, presumably, which probably isn't something you can really highlight on a college application. In the same way she seemed to be beyond popularity, she seemed to be beyond academia.

"I didn't mean to assume you were going to college if you're not, which is a perfectly fine choice," I said. "Lots of people who don't go to college become entrepreneurs or artists or captains of industry. . . ."

"I'm going to Princeton," she said.

"What?" I said.

My mouth went dry.

"I'm going to Princeton. I applied early action and I got in. The letter came in December, I think."

A cold wind blew through my car, though it was ninety degrees outside. Somewhere in the distance, I heard a chorus of hyenas laughing. The *Phantom of the Opera* cast recording suddenly grew louder—*Past the point of no return . . . The final threshold . . .* I clicked it off. We rode in silence. I saw a dead coyote on the road. It looked like the vultures had already gotten to it.

"How did I not know about that?" I croaked eventually, because I had to say something.

"I didn't tell anyone," said Sophie. "It's nobody else's business."

"That's . . . a great accomplishment," I said. I was sweating. I could feel the synapses in my brain misfiring, yelling at each other to form coherent thoughts.

"Thank you," said Sophie.

"You know, I read somewhere that Princeton doesn't typically accept two students from the same school," I said. "Especially if it's a public school like Gordo High. Did you know that? Did *yooooouuu* . . ."

The dryness in my mouth went up to my brain.

"Are you okay?" she said. "You just made a sound like you were having a stroke."

There were two more dead coyotes up ahead.

"*Enough* with the dead coyotes," I said, or maybe yelled. My motor functions were scrambled. The emergency lights were on in my head, and there was no engineer coming to save the day.

"There does seem to be a lot of roadkill around," said Sophie. "You're turning pale. Maybe we should pull over. . . ."

"Just feeling a little light-headed," I said. "One question—if you had the academic credentials to get into Princeton, how come you're not in any of my classes?"

"If you study the AP review books hard enough, you don't need the classes, so I only took the tests."

"You only took the *tests*?"

"I got a bunch of fives. Look, I don't want to talk about this. I know how it probably soun—"

"What about the SAT?"

"When I was fifteen, I scored high enough on it that I never had to take it again. We really don't have to discuss—"

My tongue tasted like antifreeze. My body was trying to poison me from the inside out.

"What about extracurricular activities?"

Sophie looked at me and sighed. I could tell that I was making her feel awkward, but I had no conscious control over my tongue, and the questions kept coming. It's rare enough that Princeton accepts one student from a public school. But *two*—it almost never happens. I could see the letters of my name plummeting off the wait list onto the admission office floor, then being swept away by an Ivy League janitor, who in my mind was wearing tweed.

"For the past year, I've been doing these long-distance mud runs two weekends a month with the guy I was seeing, which I guess the Princeton admission office thought was interesting," she said. "I actually won a bunch of them. I don't think there's anything particularly unique about it. I just like to run. They said maybe I could be on the track team, but I'm not sure how much of a team kind of person I am. That's why I liked the mud runs. I'm pretty good at dealing with obstacles one on one."

Sophie frowned.

"But I guess the prom *and* the mud runs won't be happening anymore," she said. "I don't want to have to see my ex every time I go to a race. I hadn't even thought about that part of things."

Abruptly, the engine of my truck began rattling, which jolted me out of my thoughts. I was surprised the vehicle had made it as far as it had—we had almost reached our destination and the ride had actually been smooth, like the truck was holding out as long as it could to give me a chance to talk to Sophie. This was the first time my vehicle was transporting a living, breathing girl in its cabin. It must have been as excited as I was at the beginning of the journey, and as disappointed as I was now.

"What's that *sound*?" said Sophie.

"Just the engine," I said. "Hold on."

My truck stalled and rolled onto the shoulder. For as far as I could see in either direction, there were no cars on the road. A tumbleweed smacked into my door, rolled around my front grille, and blew away across the empty landscape.

"Is this . . . bad?" said Sophie, staring at me. "Because it seems bad."

Her concern was understandable. To someone who didn't understand my truck, I could see how the situation would seem bleak—smoldering temperatures outside, miles from civilization, dead coyotes all around us, their bones bleaching in the sun.

"The truck stalls all the time," I said. "We'll be back on the road in ten seconds."

"So this isn't a breakdown?"

"Nah, this is just the truck taking a breather. Watch."

I rubbed the bottom of the steering wheel three times and whispered to my truck: "I love you."

I turned the key, and the engine started.

"*That's* how you get the truck to go? You stroke the wheel and whisper that you love it?"

"Sometimes it gets insecure and needs to know that it's appreciated."

"*HA . . . hehhhhh . . .*"

Hearing her laugh again, I decided this was the moment to be a good sport, which is what I *should* have done from the beginning.

"In all seriousness, that's great about Princeton," I said. "I'm jealous and I'm concerned it gives me less of a chance of getting in, but it's a huge achievement, especially being from this area."

"Thank you," she said. "I'm sure you'll get off the wait list."

We passed a sign: *ROSWELL—7 MILES.*

"Though I have to say, if you're smart enough to get into Princeton, I can't *believe* you couldn't find a mechanic in Gordo. You probably could get whatever you need done at Jiffy Lube. This is an insane journey."

"I have a confession," she said.

"Confess."

"I don't have a mechanic in Roswell. I wanted to drive around to clear my head."

"You're kidding."

"I'm not."

"Is your bike even *broken*?"

"Yes, it's broken, so this isn't such a *huge* lie. I'm sure we *will* find a mechanic in Roswell, at which point I'll technically have a mechanic in Roswell. But I needed to check you out. Prom is in one week. I have no date, and I need one."

My body tensed.

"Bennett, let's try this again. *Prom* is in one week. I have no date. And I *need* one. I don't have any other options here, except for you. For all intents and purposes—and, looking at the landscape where we are, maybe even for real—you are the last man on earth."

There was a difference between suddenly having an opportunity to ask Sophie to prom and actually *doing* it. I *wanted* to go to prom with Sophie—every guy in high school wanted to go to prom with her, to go anywhere with her—and I've loved her forever, but I had never considered the logistics of having to *ask* her. I had barely ever made *eye contact* with a girl before that day, let alone asked one out to a social engagement.

Sophie was staring at me, annoyed. The few muscles I have in my underdeveloped body were involuntarily seizing up with fear.

"*Bennett,*" she said. "You're *literally* the last guy in school without a date. I've made calls to see if there was anybody else. I considered hiring a male escort, but all the good ones are in Santa Fe. You need to *ask me* if you want to go."

"What if you say no?"

"I won't say no."

"How do you know you won't say no?"

"It's *my* brain, it's *my* mouth. I would know if I was going to say no. *Bennett. Road.*"

I was steering the truck into the oncoming lane. Never had I been so distracted.

"Fine," I said, steeling myself. "Sophie. Will you go to prrrrrr . . . proooooooooo . . . with me?"

"You said *prrrr* and you said *prooo* but you didn't say *prom*."

"*Prrrr . . . ooooooooo . . . mmmmmmm.*"

Sophie puckered her mouth skeptically. I could feel her looking me over, up and down.

"I don't know," she said. "How do you clean up?"

"You *told* me you wouldn't say no."

"I *didn't* say no. I said, 'How do you clean up?' I want to make sure you look good in a suit. Those prom pictures are arguably more important than the dance."

I thought about this.

"I've never had to clean up before," I said. "I wore a suit to my grandfather's funeral, but I was five, so I don't remember making any definitive style choices. I think I wanted to wear a top hat at the time, but I wouldn't do that for this particular occasion."

"I could help find you something to wear, but it has to be *good*. I spent four hundred dollars on my dress. If you're going to rent a suit, it can't look cheap."

"You spent four hundred dollars on a dress? What does it look like?"

"You'll see."

"I will?"

"Yeah, you will."

"So that's a yes, then."

"Bennett, *yes,* I'll go to prom with you. You're not great with subtext, are you?"

And suddenly there were no more dead coyotes on the road. I was going to prom with Sophie Gilkey. I wasn't sure whom the Gods of Dating were messing with more—me or Sophie. Someday she would without a doubt look back on going with me as a hastily made rebound decision, but right now—in my truck—she was *smiling.*

I couldn't tell if the grin was because she was happy to go with me or because she was simply relieved to be attending, but whatever it was, I'd take it.

"You realize you're going ninety-six miles per hour, right?" she said.

I looked down at the speedometer—she was right. My car had never gone above *fifty* before. I took my foot off the gas and eased on the brake. I could smell burning metal. Prom. Sophie Gilkey. The impossible had happened.

ROSWELL—3 MILES.

It took us thirty minutes of driving through the flat, repetitive neighborhoods of Roswell—a grid of one-story houses and straw-colored lawns—until we found a mechanic who said he could fix Sophie's motorcycle in time for us to make the return trip to Gordo that evening.

The mechanic was a dirty, scrawny man named Dusty who

was drinking a Rolling Rock when we found him. He had greasy overalls on and a golf-ball-sized Adam's apple that leaped around as he spoke.

"If you give me two hours, I can fix the bike," he said.

"Is there any way you could get it done faster?" said Sophie.

"You're lucky I'm doing it for you at *all*," said Dusty. "I was about to close up shop and hit the pipe. Yeah, the crack pipe, you don't have to ask. We've all got our vices."

"Two hours will be fine," I said.

"Is there somewhere we can go in the meantime?" said Sophie.

"Coffee shops and the like close down early," said Dusty. "Lotsa people hang out in the parking lot of the 7-Eleven, but I'm not allowed to go there anymore, personally. Got a little rowdy too many times, and they got my picture on the wall behind the counter. Decent photograph, though, my hair looks good. If I was your age, I'd head out into the desert and suck down a few beers. Lotsa stars out there to look at."

"I've never drunk before," I said under my breath to Sophie.

"You've never drunk before?" said Sophie. "How did you avoid it at parties?"

"I was never invited to parties, so pretty easily."

"Never drank?" said Dusty. "Man, I started boozin' when I was six months old. Mama used to put Four Roses in my sippy cup to get me to go to sleep. Easiest way to drink, if you ask me, sippy cup."

My reason for abstaining from alcohol throughout high school had been logical. I had thought that even recreational drinking would screw up my academic career, and therefore my chances of getting out of Gordo.

But now that high school was a couple of weeks from being truly over and I hadn't gotten into the college I'd been working toward my entire life, I wondered, what had been the *point* of not partying? What had it earned me? If I didn't find a way off the wait list, next year I'd probably be living in an abandoned building with vagrants and prostitutes and runaway convicts anyway. Might as well get a head start on it now.

"Where could we get beer?" said Sophie.

"You can buy it from me if you want," said Dusty, opening up a small refrigerator that had shelves packed with bottles of Rolling Rock. "Ten dollars a bottle."

"Ten dollars a bottle?"

"Where else are you going to get it, bein' in high school and stranded out here like you are?"

"I have five dollars," said Sophie, pulling a crumpled bill from her pocket. "What do you have?"

I checked my wallet. "Ten."

Dusty grabbed the money.

"Fifteen dollars means one and a half beers coming right up," he said, taking a bottle out of the fridge and handing it to Sophie.

"Where's the half?" I said.

Dusty shoved the bottle he had been drinking from into my hand.

"There's your half," he said. "But I suggest you wipe off the top. I've been battling a *nasty* case of tooth funk. My dentist doesn't even know what it is—he looked at it under a microscope and the closest thing he could think of was the Ebola virus, but he said that normally kills you in a few days, and I've been living with this for *years*. So I figure I'm good. Now be careful out there in the desert. Lotsa biting snakes and angry animals and stuff that's even weirder than that."

"Like what?"

Dusty smiled, showing his fungus-colored gums. "Stuff that ain't from here," he said.

What happened over the next hour or so is a strange combination of that first, intoxicating half beer of my life and deep emotional trauma.

Here's what took place. Sophie and I walked into the desert, drinking our beers, making sure to keep sight of the lights of Roswell on the horizon so we didn't get lost.

We got involved in a heavy discussion about whether a rhinoceros or a small dinosaur would win in a cage fight. I picked small dinosaur. She said rhinoceros, which I thought was ridiculous because I figured the rhino would be at a natural disadvantage since it had to be on all fours, while the dinosaur could use its sharp claws to strike down on the rhino. Sophie pointed out that I hadn't specified what *kind* of dino I was picturing, and that when I said *small dinosaur,* she pictured a single small raptor. Thinking about it that way, I agreed that a rhino would probably have the upper hand. Armored hide, heavy body mass. Made sense. Sophie won that argument.

We finished our one and a half beers and placed the bottles at the base of a twisting cholla cactus. Initially I felt bad about littering, but then I saw a case of empties lying on the other side of the cactus, which made me feel better. This was clearly a party cactus, accustomed to alcoholic beverages.

The combination of walking and drinking gave us headaches at about the same time. We felt dizzy, so we looked for somewhere to lie down. I wasn't expecting Sophie to be as lightweight a drinker as I was, but she said she had never been much of a wild woman, despite her motorcycle and her appealing I-hate-high-school image. She'd had a few beers at random parties, and that was it. It was hard to run great distances through mud with a hangover, she explained.

We walked until we found a flat rock that was big enough for us to rest on, and that was how we ended up on our backs, side by side, staring up at the stars, waiting for our mutual nausea to pass.

"How do you feel?" said Sophie.

"Spinny," I said. "How many stars do you see?"

"A billion."

"I'm seeing two billion. Guess that means I'm having double vision."

"*HA . . . hehhhhhh . . .*"

"I like your laugh."

"People think it's weird."

"It sounds a little like what would happen if you shot a blimp with a rifle—this loud *bang* followed by a long *wheeeeeeze.*"

Sophie whacked me in the chest.

"Gagh," I rasped, trying to catch my breath in the wake of the blow.

"Whoa," she said. "Sorry. That was supposed to be more of a playful hit."

"It's okay," I exhaled, seeing spots of light. "I'm thin, so I think my lungs are close to the surface. How did you learn to *hit* like that?"

"Kickboxing class. I was toning my arms for prom."

"It's working," I said. "I think you'd beat both the dinosaur and the rhino together in a cage match. In ancient times, you would have been the toast of the Colosseum. Y'know, if they had dinosaurs then."

"Sophius Maximus of Carthage."

"Sophius Aurelius of the Praetorian Guard."

"HA . . . hehhhhhhh . . ."

I had almost finished catching my breath when Sophie rolled over on the rock and kissed me, and it was gone again.

The gesture was inexplicable. One moment I was recovering from a blow that had left me dazed and emasculated, and the next moment was the best of my life. I had no idea what I was doing, so I just tried to copy her lip movements and maintain consciousness—it wouldn't have looked very dashing to faint from the profundity of the moment and fall off the rock. I closed my eyes so she wouldn't see them rolling back into my head.

The only thing that went through my mind was that Sophie smelled like a sugar apple, which is a fruit from South America my parents had recently been bringing home from the local organic food market. They're strange-looking things, like hard artichokes. Maybe her family had been eating them too. Looking back, I wish that wasn't what I was thinking about during my first kiss, but I guess the brain always does what it wants.

Then the kiss was over, and she was staring at me from one inch away.

"What was that for?" I said.

"To apologize for punching you. And also to see if you're a good kisser, which is important in a prom date."

"Am I?"

"You're a natural."

"You know my reputation."

"*HA . . . hehhhhh.* Yeah, it's all the girls talk about. I guess I'm just another in your list of conquests."

"Not to interrupt the mood, but can I tell you something?"

"What?"

"I think I'm still seeing lights from when you hit me."

"That's weird. I see lights too, if you're talking about those ones near the Big Dipper."

Sophie pointed at a group of dots in the sky. There were six total, spaced in two parallel sets, all of them moving together.

"Why would *you* be able to see lights if you were the one who hit *me*?" I said.

"That is an excellent question."

"Maybe the beer had some kind of drug in it."

"Dusty did say he enjoyed crack cocaine."

"Are the lights getting closer?" I said. "It seems like they're getting closer."

The lights grew larger.

"That *really* doesn't look right," said Sophie.

"We should head back."

"We should *absolutely* head back."

We climbed off the rock and began hustling toward Roswell, but the town was just a speck in the distance. I looked over my shoulder, and the glowing dots were not only *closer* but *brighter,* as if the object behind us had flicked on a set of stadium spotlights. The lights warmed the back of my neck, which confirmed my growing suspicion that this was bad.

I grabbed Sophie's fingers. *"Run."*

"I can run faster if you let go of my hand," she said, jerking her arm away. She was right—as soon as she was free of me, she went into another gear and was *gone,* and I saw how it was entirely possible for her to have won all those mud runs. She was a jackrabbit, zigzagging around cacti, leaping crevasses in the ground, sprinting out hundreds of feet in front of me in just a few seconds.

Which was how the thing chasing us got her alone.

The sensation of heat on the back of my neck went from warm to *scalding,* and then—BOOM—an explosion of sound knocked me to the desert ground. I felt an object accelerate above and I covered my head, but the object passed quickly, because it wasn't interested in me.

"Bennett," I heard Sophie yell.

I was on the ground, half deaf, slightly drunk, and the length of a football field from Sophie, when the UFO came to a stop.

At first, to my eyes, it didn't seem like much of a UFO at all—it looked more like a dog-catching wagon the size of a small boat, hovering ten or so feet off the ground. Painted on its side in neon blue were stick figures that reminded me of the man and woman symbols found on the doors of restaurant bathrooms, and where there would have been wheels on a normal wagon, there was a set of white, glowing skids.

Because the UFO was hovering low, Sophie was staring straight *at* it rather than *up* at it, which a million movies had told me was the typical way that the soon-to-be-abducted confronted UFOs.

For a moment, neither Sophie nor the UFO did anything. She knew she couldn't escape, and the UFO seemed to be waiting to see what she was going to do.

A small cannon emerged from the side of the van. There was a murmuring sound, and the cannon shot a cloud of red and pink confetti in front of Sophie.

She looked at the confetti a beat, then dropped to the ground and began rolling in it like a feline in the throes of a catnip binge.

"So . . . good . . . ," I heard her moan, rubbing the confetti on her face, grinning and laughing like a crazy person. *"HA . . . hehhhhhhh. HA . . . hehhhhhh . . ."*

The UFO descended to the ground, barely scattering the dirt beneath its landing rails. A door opened on the side of the ship—though there were no clouds of gas or any dramatic light emitting from it, another tenet of UFOs I thought was pretty standard-issue—and two creatures nonchalantly hopped out, carrying a cage.

The creatures weren't anything I could have anticipated—no big black eyes and skinny limbs like in *Close Encounters of the Third Kind,* no muscles and dreadlocks like in *Predator.* Though one was larger than the other, they were clearly of the same species, and both were wearing white lab coats and seemed to be carrying clipboards. They looked like screwed-up Vikings, for lack of a better comparison. Blunted horns grew out of their skulls, above foreheads that were shiny and golden. Their bulbous noses sat slightly off center in the middle of their faces, beneath tiny eyes. They had thick bodies with heavy red fur sprouting out from under their lab coats, and their feet were swollen and exposed.

They calmly walked over to Sophie, who continued to roll around in the confetti, throwing it in the air and letting it rain down upon her like she was a child at a party, paying them no attention. She was rubbing the stuff over her body, putting it in her hair, tasting it, unfazed by the fact that a couple of enormous alien roughnecks were studying her, the smaller one making marks on his orange clipboard.

All right. At this point, you're probably wondering why I didn't rush toward the aliens and pull Sophie out of there. It's something I think about all the time too. Now that I've had some distance from the moment, the only way I can explain it is that the suddenness and the *unreality* of the situation overwhelmed me, and I was stupefied. My brain felt like it had detached from my nervous system, my heart felt like it was no longer pumping blood, and all I could do was watch. I guess there are a lot of ways that I could try to explain what I was feeling in terms of my physiology, but everything boils down to the fact that I was staggeringly afraid.

When the Vikings were done making their notations, one of them grabbed the side of Sophie's face, took out what looked like a label gun, and—*pppffft*—clipped a tag through her ear, which snapped her out of her strange feline state.

"OUCH. What the—"

She was about to protest further when she looked up into the faces of the aliens and let out the most piercing, extended yell of pure terror I had ever heard. I won't try to replicate it here.

The aliens covered the holes in the sides of their heads and looked at each other like *can you believe this?* They were visibly annoyed with the volume of Sophie's screaming. When she paused to take a breath so that she could yell again, the larger Viking took out a syringe and injected her with a liquid that knocked her unconscious, after which the smaller one picked her up by the back of her neck, tossed her into the cage, and threw the cage into the van.

The duo climbed in behind her and shut the door, and with that, the van lifted into the air, hovered for a moment, and then—*WHOOSH*—disappeared into the sky in a streak of gold light, upward and out of sight.

The desert was silent. From the moment we saw the UFO to

Sophie's disappearance, the abduction had taken five minutes, tops. If that.

I heard a ringing. Sophie's cell phone was stuck in a crevice between two rocks. I answered.

"Hello?" I said weakly. All the air had left my body, and I felt like I was about to pass out.

"Hey, this is Dusty at the garage. Your motorcycle is ready."

"Be . . . right there."

"Holy crap, man, that beer must have hit you hard. You sound messed up, hombre."

Bizarrely enough, back at the garage, Dusty didn't seem concerned that he had seen *two* high school students walk out into the desert together but only *one* return.

"As long as somebody pays me a hundred for my work, I don't care who goes missing," he said. "For another hundred, I'll help you bury her."

I had $146 dollars in my bank account—money left over from my eighteenth birthday—so I paid Dusty's fee with my emergency-only debit card and hit the road with the motorcycle in the bed of my truck.

My first instinct was to call somebody for help, but I quickly realized that was unrealistic. It wasn't as if NASA had a 911 hotline you could dial to report abductions: *"Hey, this is Bennett Bardo. Listen, the girl I've loved since I was five years old was just snatched up by a couple of deformed Viking dogcatchers—no,*

I don't know if they were actually Nordic, I'm just making a comparison—and I was wondering if you could send up a shuttle to get her back. They sprinkled some confetti on her and she lost her mind. So you'll handle it? Thanks, appreciate it."

If Sophie didn't turn up, her parents would file a missing-person report, police would come around asking if I had seen her, and eventually somehow it would be revealed that she and I had walked out to the desert as a twosome and I had returned as a onesome. I was fairly certain my excuse that she was taken by aliens wouldn't hold up in court.

I considered my options. I could try to make a run for the Mexican border, but given I didn't know anybody in that country, didn't speak Spanish, was still technically not yet a high school graduate, and sunburned easily, I didn't see a future for myself as a bandito in Juárez. In the opposite direction, Canada was two days away, but my truck would never make the trip, and I didn't have enough money for gas. Going back to Gordo meant inevitable arrest and jail time, but I also couldn't stay here in Roswell, unless I wanted to Dumpster dive for sustenance and sleep in my truck. Just trying to avoid the situation would make me look even guiltier when I was eventually apprehended.

Driving my truck nowhere, I took lefts and rights aimlessly, obeying the speed limit so I didn't draw attention to myself, watching the broken center traffic stripes disappear under my wheels like a drumbeat.

I was worried about Sophie. I couldn't imagine the terror

she must have felt when she looked up and saw the extraterrestrials above her, and I almost hoped that she was still unconscious so she didn't have to deal with the dread of seeing Earth disappear beneath her without knowing where she was being taken. I hadn't been able to deal with the fear of the aliens myself, and they weren't even interested in me.

Half of me was sick with worry about her, while the rest of me was consumed by the cold outrage of being *so ridiculously close* to going to prom with *Sophie Gilkey,* and then having her snatched away. I had waited all of high school for a break—which I *thought* was going to be an acceptance to Princeton—but instead, the universe had presented me with a chance to be with the girl who had occupied my thoughts since I was old enough to start thinking about girls, and then, in a very *literal sense,* the universe had taken her from me. I stared at the Big Dipper, and it looked like a huge bucket of crap about to tip over and spill onto my head. I was *pissed.*

I had no choice. I had to go after her. I had to help her. If she had been abducted, I could find a way to get abducted too. I wasn't going to let a bunch of aliens ruin the one good experience I'd had in eighteen years. If I was in space, I wouldn't have to explain to *anybody* where she went, nor would I have to talk to the cops. I wouldn't have to figure out what to do with her motorcycle. I wouldn't have to assume a new identity or learn Spanish. I wouldn't have to give her up.

It was time to get her *back.*

Because in my haste to get on the road with her I had left my phone at home, I used Sophie's to try to figure out how to offer myself as bait. In twenty minutes of electronic sleuthing—and I have to say, I was surprised by the wealth of information out there on the subject, God bless the digital hive mind—I found four common factors in alien abductions:

The abductee usually drove a truck. Most of the time, it was the driver of an eighteen-wheeler who stepped out of his big rig on the highway, stared up into a strange light, and—*shloop*—was sucked up into the ship. But it also seemed pretty common for aliens to target guys in pickups, which was a lucky break for me, considering my mode of transport.

The abductions normally took place along deserted roads late at night or in the very early morning. Roswell was in the middle of nowhere, so that prerequisite had taken care of itself. All I had to do was drive three minutes in any direction and I would be as exposed and kidnappable as a newborn, though I realize that's perhaps not the best analogy.

The abductee was usually at least a *little* bit of a redneck. The redneck culture of my hometown was one of the things that I was desperately trying to escape—on any weekend afternoon, you could hear the roar of distant all-terrain vehicles booming off the desert floor—but I thought I could fake the part by ripping my shirt, putting on a trucker hat, and focusing my thoughts on Friday night football, about which I had never, ever given a crap.

Finally, to get the aliens' attention, it seemed to help to have a physical ailment to set you apart from other individuals— something interesting that extraterrestrials might want to check out, a curiosity for them to write about in their research papers.

I reasoned that if they had already passed up the opportunity to abduct me once, my gangly body wasn't enough to satisfy this requirement, so I'd have to figure something else out.

I had no idea why Sophie had been taken despite falling into *none* of the categories above. Maybe they were intrigued by her for intangible reasons that they didn't fully understand. I could relate. She had my heart too.

After a stop for supplies—I'd never been so happy to see a twenty-four-hour pharmacy, though the counter guy gave me a strange look when he saw what I was purchasing—I was in my truck driving back and forth on the outskirts of Roswell, wearing an *I Got Crabs in Maryland* trucker hat while waving a set of crutches out the window. I'm not sure why a store in New Mexico would have a selection of *I Got Crabs in Maryland* hats, but I can only guess that a cargo shipment went to the wrong state, luckily for me. To complete the hillbilly effect, I smeared some chewing tobacco on my teeth—my first-ever heretofore forbidden purchase as an eighteen-year-old—which gave me enough of a head rush that I felt totally unself-conscious as I screamed out the window at the empty sky.

"*Come on!*" I yelled. "I'm slow and not too intelligent and I *know* you're up there. I already saw you once *tonight.* Come back and get *me.*"

Nobody came to get me.

"*I'm here!*" I yelled. "I *will not* fight you. I would *maybe* ask for some leeway when it comes to any sort of body cavity research, but if you need a couple of examinations for your files, I'm *cool* with it, as long as you tell me where Sophie is."

Silence.

"All right. I'm not even going to use the word *probe,* because I'm sure you're sick of the association. We're all sick of it, and I don't mean to stereotype you. But whatever you need to do, you can *do.* Just don't leave me *down* here."

A pair of white lights shot out behind me.

Right away, I cursed myself for offering the extraterrestrials such personal full-body privileges, but once I realized my tactics had been successful, I felt good for having cracked the alien code. If it was this simple to get abducted, I could probably start an extreme-adventure travel business and make a decent profit. Maybe *that* was what I would do with my future instead of Princeton. Be a self-made man. An entrepreneur who looked at the stars.

I heard the *whoop* of a siren.

It was a police car.

I pulled my crutches inside the truck and watched in the rearview mirror as an obese cop squeezed out of his car and waddled over to my window.

"Boy, what the living hell are you doing out here alone at this time of night?" he spat. I looked at the nameplate pinned to his chest—*Officer Welker.* "You high? Do I need to give you a Breathalyzer?"

"I'm sorry, sir," I said. "I was stargazing."

"Stargazing by driving on a deserted street in the middle of the night? Where's your telescope?"

"I don't have one with me, but I do have one."

"People disappear out here all the time, you know," said

Officer Welker. "It ain't safe for you to be doin' this, driving around like an idiot."

I was trying to disappear, I thought to myself, but all I said was, "Yes, sir."

"I suggest you make yourself scarce. I'm only letting you go because I like your hat. Maryland crabs are the finest in the world. My wife and I honeymooned in Baltimore, had the time of our lives. But if I see you or your truck again tonight, I *will* find a reason to arrest you, and in jail you *will* stay. You got that?"

"Going straight home," I said, starting the truck. "Thank you for letting me go."

The police car rode my bumper to the main road before splitting off and speeding away in the opposite direction. I considered returning to the boondocks for another try at getting abducted, but then I thought, *What's the use?* The aliens had already decided not to take me once. Nothing I did was going to get them to reconsider.

I was discouraged, and my blood sugar was low. I felt twisting pains in my stomach. I'd been so distracted by the Sophie situation that I had forgotten to eat. I tried to remember my last meal, and realized I'd eaten a bowl of Rice Krispies for breakfast fourteen hours ago.

If it was my last night of freedom, I figured I might as well have something good.

Ten minutes later, I pulled into the drive-through of In-N-Out Burger, ravenous.

In-N-Out—in case you're unfamiliar with the brand—is the finest fast-food chain in the world. Never-frozen beef. Hand-cut fries. Thick, creamy Neapolitan milk shakes. Though I heard the restaurants were located only in California, Nevada, and Arizona, the chain had recently opened this particular location, perhaps to take advantage of tourists who came to the area for alien-themed attractions. I had been to In-N-Out once before with my parents, and the experience had made a profound impact on me. I had never known fast food could be like this. From my truck, I could smell the finely chopped grilled onions and special sauce. For a brief moment, I forgot that my prom date was gone and I would most likely soon be going to jail for her murder. *That's* how intoxicating the scent was.

But there was an obstacle keeping me from those burgers.

Blocking the drive-through was the largest, weirdest bus I had ever seen. It reminded me of a metal platypus—pudgy around the middle, where the wheels were, and then tapering out to a beaklike protrusion in the front and a thick tail in the back, which appeared to be an external trunk. A sharp sail ran down its center like a Mohawk, and its windows were tinted a heavy purple, nearly black.

My stomach grumbled in anticipation of a meal, but the bus didn't seem to be going anywhere. It was parked in the drive-through, its engine was off, and a team of In-N-Out employees was handing *dozens* of bags of food from the delivery window to the driver inside.

The driver's hand was as big as a baseball glove.

"Let's *go*. I'm *hungry!*" I yelled, honking my horn, but I was sure that nobody on the bus could hear me. Percussive music was pouring out of the vehicle—*BoombabaBoombabaBoom*. The bus was rocking back and forth, seemingly in danger of tipping over.

The In-N-Out employees handed over the final orders to the driver, who handed back a thick roll of bills as payment. Finally, the bus rolled out of the driveway and parked in the lot, where it continued to vibrate from the music.

I took my truck out of park and was easing it toward the drive-through when—*thunk*—my engine died. My seat shuddered underneath me, and I felt something fall from my car to the ground. I turned the key again, but nothing happened.

It was over. My truck had loyally taken me to Roswell, and then it had perished. In asking it to drive over one hundred miles in one night, I had pushed it beyond its limits. This time, I knew there was no point in massaging its wheel and telling it I loved it. It was gone.

I got out of the car and kneeled on the ground, and underneath the chassis I witnessed a pile of rusted gears and corroded metal. My truck's guts had disgorged themselves onto the pavement. Well, at least when I was in jail, I wouldn't need a car anymore. From now on, I was going to be on foot until the cops picked me up. I needed a cheeseburger for energy.

The tired worker manning the drive-through window poked his head out and looked at me standing there.

"Sorry, man, no more food," he said. "We're closing up."

"What do you mean, no more food? It's In-N-Out."

"There's nothing left," said the worker. "No more burgers, no more buns, no more potatoes. That weird bus cleaned us out. They've been here for an hour. I'm surprised you waited in line—all the other cars got annoyed and left."

"Can't you go into your storage locker and get more?"

"We *did* go into the storage locker. These guys rolled up and spent *thirty grand.* I'm telling you, we're *out.*"

"I can't get *one* cheeseburger?"

"If you want a burger, you ask the guys on the party bus. They have a hundred *cows'* worth of them. They're eating a *barnyard.* We're *closed.*"

The worker slammed the drive-through window shut.

I watched the bus shake in the parking lot. Not only was it not leaving, it sounded like the travelers inside had turned the music *up.*

BOOMbabawahBOOMbabawah

Weird laughter—*rargh rargh rargh*—was followed by bowling-ball-sized wads of paper cups and hamburger wrappers being tossed out the windows. I had never seen such flagrant littering.

It seemed *impossible* that the people on the bus needed *all* the food in the In-N-Out, so I decided I was going to try to buy something off them. I had nothing to lose.

I walked over to the bus and knocked on the door. It made a sound unlike any metal I had ever heard before—hollow, but with a high-pitched clanging noise.

"Hey!" I yelled. *"Open up!"*

I heard footsteps. The door swung open, and suddenly I was face to face with the driver—or rather, I was face to face with the face the driver had decided to *wear*, because he was in disguise.

From a distance, you *might* have thought the driver was human—he had eyes, ears, a nose, he was about six feet tall and maybe three hundred pounds, so the proportions were right—but up close it was clear that his skin wasn't skin at all, but a rubbery peach-colored mask. His lumpy torso was jammed into a ripped T-shirt, and his legs were bursting from a pair of stonewashed jeans.

His figure resembled those of the messed-up Vikings who had taken Sophie, which gave me chills. Perhaps it hadn't been such a great idea trying to get her abductors to come back.

"Rargh garh ragh," he said, though his mouth didn't move because of the mask. *"Rargh grargh gargh."*

"I'm sorry . . . ," I said, suddenly very aware that I had made the Wrong Decision by coming to this bus. "I must have knocked on the wrong door."

"Ragh garf raghr," said the driver. *"Ragha arghag rafg."*

"I'm truly sorry. I'll leave you alone."

The driver shoved a bottle of wine into my hands.

"No thank you . . . ," I said. "I don't want any wine."

"Raghag fargh . . . wine *. . . ragh,"* the driver insisted, grabbing my shoulder and slamming the wine against my stomach. He spoke at least one word of English. *Wine.* I guess in some cultures, that's all you really need to get by.

"*Fine.* I'll have a sip, but then I'm going."

The wine tasted bitter and slightly nutty, but I gulped it down and handed back the bottle.

"*Thank you,*" said the driver, sounding remarkably civil, with a lilting, almost Scandinavian accent. He took off the mask, and underneath he looked *exactly* like the aliens who had abducted Sophie. I froze.

"You know, when somebody offers you a drink, it's bad form not to accept," he said. "*Now* we can talk like gentlemen. What brings you to our door?"

I was too stunned to speak.

"Do you still not understand? Let me try again, more slowly this time. Hello. Stranger. What brings you to our door?"

"I don't know. . . ."

"You must have had *some* reason. You were pounding hard. And at this time of night, that can be construed as rude. This may be a bus, but look at the size of it—it's our home away from home, and nobody likes unexpected evening callers to their home. It makes everybody assume the worst."

"I wanted a cheeseburger," I said. "And the guy at the window said you had bought them all."

A voice cut in from inside the bus: "Driver, what's going *on* with this open door? The temperature in here was *unbelievably pleasant,* and now you're letting in the dry desert air. Do you *know* what this heat does to my voice?"

"A gentleman up here wants to buy a cheeseburger off us," said the driver.

"Good Lord, the cheeseburgers are almost gone," said the voice. "Perhaps you should send him on his way, Driver. I can't bear to see disappointment on the faces of humans, though it seems like they wear such expressions *all* the time. Probably why nobody wants to visit this planet—no offense to you, Cad."

"None taken," said another voice from somewhere in the bus, this one with what seemed to be a New York or New Jersey accent. "I don't like visiting here either."

"I don't know if we should turn the stranger down—he looks *angry,*" said the driver, examining my face. I could tell he was messing with me. "I think he made a gesture like he's going to slit our throats unless he gets what he wants."

"A murderer darkening our doorway," said the first voice. "How wonderfully romantic."

"I didn't *make* any gesture," I said. "I'm just a high school student. I didn't mean to interrupt you. I'm sorry for coming over here. I'll leave. . . ."

"Wait wait, hold on, and *pause,*" said the first voice. "I'm reconsidering what I said about having no cheeseburgers for this wretched straggler, Driver. It's not in my *blood* to let a man go hungry. He can share my meal. We will sup as brothers, he and I."

The driver—who, from the way the people on the bus were referring to him, appeared to actually be named Driver—stepped out of the way and gestured to the stairs.

"The band is requesting your company," said Driver. "Lucky boy."

The band?

"Come on, come on," said Driver. "Let's go, up with you."

Driver put his meaty palm on the back of my neck and unhelpfully shoved me up the stairs. Suddenly I was standing in the middle of what appeared to be a seventeenth-century French brothel.

The interior of the bus had been hollowed out, giving it the appearance of a long studio apartment, and was covered in purple pillows. Every few feet there were tables holding decanters of a glowing, ominous red liquid and towering brass hookahs sprouting tentacles like burnished metal octopi, wisps of smoke wafting above them. A pyramid-shaped disco ball hung from the cabin's ceiling, and piles of what seemed to be male fashion magazines were stacked haphazardly all over the place.

I stared into the shadows of the dim room, but all I saw was silhouettes.

"Cad wasn't kidding when he said humans who lived in the desert were unattractive," said the first voice. "Look at how *thin* this one is. I can't say that I'm not a little threatened. Only *I* can have such an elegant waistline, so eat, intruder, eat. The fatter you get, the better I look."

A cheeseburger flew through the air and splattered against my shirt. Driver laughed behind me—*wah ha ha ha ha.*

"I suppose I'll now have to give him something from my personal wardrobe, though I'm not sure he has the *attitude* to pull it off. Bring him closer so I can take a look."

Driver gave me another heave in my back, prompting me toward the darkest corner of the bus. There I saw the dim outline of a lanky man, along with the flash of a glittery sleeve and the tip of a snow-white leather platform boot.

"Closer . . . closer . . . don't be scared, I don't bite, though I have been known to *stab*. Never can be too careful, and it's best to strike first, particularly when you have an advantageous reach like mine."

The figure leaned closer. "My goodness, your pores look terrible. If you used a skin-tightening mask at *least* once a week, it would help with those zits. I just want to grab your face and *pop* them. Or maybe pop your whole head. How hideous."

Driver nudged my shoulder, and I took another step forward.

"Apologies for sending mixed signals, but that's *quite* close enough for the moment," said the figure. He reached underneath the gold-tasseled shade of an antique parlor lamp, and I heard his bracelets jangling as he gracefully twisted his wrist.

The lamp snapped on, and light ricocheted off the heavily sequined jacket the man was wearing and up to the disco ball above. It was like having a cluster bomb going off around me. I recoiled.

"Oh, stop squinting and get used to it," he said. "If you're going to be spending any time at all around here, you'll learn to love cutting-edge fashion. I like to make sure I'm seen, which is the nature of my profession, as you might imagine."

I tried to look back at the man, holding my hands in front of my face to cut down on the glare.

"I told you to *stop* making such a *show* of how uncomfortable you are," said the man. "I can't stand theatrics unless they're my own. But for the sake of adjustment, here, let me help you out, if you're going to be such a demonstrative hobgoblin."

The figure pressed a button on his sleeve, and the sequins on his jacket flipped over and clipped into place, as if he was instantly changing clothes. A moment later, he was in a white jacket made of scaly leather.

For the first time, I looked into the face of the person who I would soon come to learn is the lead singer of the one billion sixteenth most popular musical group in the universe.

"Good evening," he said, bowing slightly, but without a trace of humility. "I'm Skark Zelirium. But I'm sure you knew that already."

He searched for recognition in my eyes, but found none. He frowned.

"Hmm. I understand. In dim light, it is sometimes difficult to recognize your heroes. But get on with it—introduce yourself, who are you?"

"I'm Bennett Bardo," I said.

"What a *dull name.* We'll have to fix that if you end up hanging around. I could see you being a Chester, but certainly not a Bennett. Though Chester isn't terribly provocative either. Hmm. I'll have to think about this a bit. Maybe something sexy like Zaza."

Skark didn't look like anyone I had ever seen, though the dimensions of his body were such that at night, from a distance, he might pass for an emaciated man with an overconfident sense of style. He was wearing a tight white jumpsuit under his jacket, and his boots came over his knees. His fingers had rings with stones that changed color mercurially, flickering from sapphire blue to a splendid opal to charcoal black.

But where Skark looked truly otherworldly was from the neck up. His chin was pointed, coming to a dimpled tip that jutted out an inch beyond the rest of his face. His top and bottom lips were the same thickness. He was clean-shaven—either that or he didn't grow facial hair at all. He was wearing makeup—orange blush on his cheeks and green shadow under his eyes, which were speckled like the shell of a sparrow's egg—and yellow curls sprouted from his scalp and cascaded over his face and shoulders. His complexion was a subtle off-pinkish color, which gave an overall effect of sickly paleness, like a patient in a pre-industrial tuberculosis ward.

He presented me with another cheeseburger, this time handing it to me instead of whipping it at my chest.

"You're lucky I only ate a couple hundred," he said. "I'm dieting, you see."

"A couple hundred?"

"My metabolism is extraordinary. One needs such a prodigious number of calories when one performs onstage at the level I do. But right now I'm trying to fit into a Gucci suit I picked up when we flew over Italy. It's a beautiful thing. Kingfisher-blue charmeuse. You'll *die* when you see it."

My body stiffened.

"Ah, my band's reputation precedes us, I see," said Skark. "I didn't mean you're *literally* going to die when you see it, though if you *did* die, I assure you, you would go with a smile on your face and you'd be in very good company. Look for yourself."

Skark gestured with a gold-tipped cane to a row of close-up photographs of alien smiles—some fanged, some drooling blue spittle, some double-tongued—which were hanging on the wall of the bus.

"Are those all pictures of creatures who died smiling in here?" I said.

"Some individuals can't keep up with the lifestyle, I'm afraid," said Skark.

"Are you going to keep talking down there, or are you going to introduce me?" said a voice above me.

I looked up. Dangling inches from my head was a guy in his late twenties or early thirties who was doing pull-ups on a bar bolted to an apparatus that looked a bit like an air conditioner. He was obviously human, and he was wearing a brown knit hat and a white tank top printed with the Statue of Liberty, which showed off his defined biceps. He looked like he hadn't shaved in a few days, and his cheeks were smeared with brown and black whiskers.

"Bennett, I give you the second member of my band and our only thoroughbred human . . . bassist Cad Charleston."

Cad dropped to the floor and shook my hand.

"Good to meet you," said Cad. "Sorry about how much of a pain it was to get a burger. We don't come here often, and you know how singers and drummers have appetites."

"Who's the drummer?" I said.

"*I* am the drummer," said Driver. "And the driver, and the band's manager, ever since we ran into financial—"

"I will *not* talk about money with new friends," said Skark. "It is the *pinnacle* of impoliteness. I'm sure such a young fan has questions he is burning to ask the band, so let us hear them."

Skark, Driver, and Cad looked at me.

"Well?" said Skark.

"What . . . band is this?" I said.

Skark's eyes went wide, and he lifted himself to his feet. He was easily eight feet tall, and he towered over me, which had become increasingly uncommon for anyone to be able to do in the wake of my growth spurt.

"*What band is it?* You *snuck* onto this bus, and now you're pretending you don't know the name of the band?"

"He came on the bus for a cheeseburger, not to ask the band questions," said Driver.

"I don't care *why* he got on, I'm insulted," said Skark. "Bennett—you are standing on the tour bus of one of the musical treasures of the universe. The band whose music forged peace between the Bluebranch Lantern Galaxy and the Mosaic Mauna Cluster. The band whose tight clothing caused a sexual revolution in Poochicana Nebula B-67. The band who with *one slow jam* created the building blocks of *life* on the barren Spindlefan Asteroid. We are the Perfectly Reasonable."

I chuckled.

"I'm so tired of people laughing whenever they hear the name of our band . . . ," said Driver.

"The Perfectly Reasonable is a *wonderful* name," said Skark. "It captures our good looks and our judicious minds in three small words."

"*Reasonable* isn't that small a word," said Driver.

"We're *not* one of the musical treasures of the universe," said Cad. "*Universal Beat* magazine just ranked us out of the top *billion*."

"We're one billion sixteenth," said Skark. "Let's not blow it out of proportion. Nobody reads past the first fifty or so anyway."

"We used to have our own space station, with *swimming pools,*" said Cad.

"I miss our private chef," said Driver.

"I miss our menagerie of exotic animals," said Cad.

"Would you please *stop* bitching," said Skark. "We are playing the Dondoozle Festival in less than a week, and when we do, our comeback will be complete."

Skark turned to me.

"Forgive me if it sounds like we're speaking in code here," he said. "Dondoozle is a bit like Lollapalooza or Coachella that you have here on Earth. I don't know why these festivals always seem to end in vowels. There's one in the Nardo Cluster that's just called Auooooaouuuo. It's almost impossible to order tickets for."

Skark turned back to the band.

"One performance and we'll once more be on top," he said. "Plus, those rankings aren't scientifically accurate—they're used more to provoke discussions among critics, who aren't our core audience now."

"Who is our core audience now?" said Cad.

"Fans who remember when we were *good*," said Driver.

"We are a *brilliant* three-piece," said Skark. "We are fiery coral in an ocean of mediocrity. We are an amplified earthquake in the fault line of recycled melody. We are—"

WHOOP

A police siren exploded behind the bus.

"Cops!" yelled Driver, running toward the front seat.

"Hide everything," said Cad.

"Relax, *please*," said Skark. "The more you panic, the more suspicious you look. This is a moment that calls for calmness and clarity of thought, as all moments of great seriousness do."

Skark opened the ottoman and hid several bottles of wine inside. From the way the band members were scooping up bottles and powders and pills and hiding them in the nooks and crannies of the bus, it was obvious they were carrying a significant amount of illegal contraband on board.

WHOOP WHOOP

The voice of Officer Welker erupted through a megaphone.

"I told you to go home, *kid. I told you I didn't want to see you again tonight. If you're not in your truck, I know* you're on that bus. It's the only other vehicle in the lot."

Through the window, I saw Officer Welker get out of his cruiser and walk over to my truck with a pad in his hand, writing me a ticket.

"If he's telling us to go, I suggest we listen," said Cad. "It's a bad idea to mess with bored cops who live in the wastelands."

"I think he's talking to me . . . ," I said, but nobody was listening.

"I'm getting us out of here right now," said Driver, whacking a rainbow of buttons on the dashboard. Without his disguise, it was clear he was definitely of the same tweaked Viking pedigree as the individuals who had abducted Sophie.

Driver pushed a long, flat lever with his foot, and the bus began trembling violently, rivers of electricity running over its outer shell.

"Good Lord, man, shut that *window,*" said Cad, running over and closing the window where I'd been looking at the cop. "If you leave one open, we'll be sucked outside. In space you have to pay attention to these sorts of details."

"Space?"

"You're coming with us, right? I assumed you were because you're wearing a trucker hat and I noticed the crutches in your car. You must have wanted *somebody* to abduct you."

I felt the bus lift off the ground. The back end pitched upward first, nearly sending me somersaulting into Driver's flabby chest, before its front finally lurched upward as the vehicle balanced itself out.

"I'd *normally* suggest you buckle up!" yelled Cad over the

sound of the engine. "But Driver ate the seat belts last week when we got stuck in an asteroid field and couldn't get to a decent restaurant before closing."

"I mistook them for fruit leather at the time," said Driver. "I was buzzed."

"You were drunk out of your *mind,*" said Cad.

"I don't think anybody here can pass judgment on me for that," said Driver.

"When I drink, at least I don't destroy the *bus,*" said Cad.

"Just marriages," said Driver.

"*Please* shut up," said Skark. "Everybody in this band drinks, everybody has been with each other's lovers, there's no sense yapping at each other about it."

Skark turned to me. "Hold on and try not to get any blood on the couch. There are no decent upholsterers where we're going, which is an unending source of irritation for me. I can't even *think* about how I would redo the interior design of the bus without feeling woozy and overwhelmed."

For the briefest moment, the bus became still, hanging in the air above the In-N-Out drive-through, and I heard Officer Welker one more time: "*Put that* bus *back on the* ground. License *and* registration. *Where are those license plates from? The Yarkson Cloud? What is that? Is that a state I don't know about? Some East Coast place?*"

The engines roared and the bus shook like it was about to come apart at its joints.

"There's still time to get off if you want," said Cad. "Space is no easy place to visit."

"It's fine," I said. "I'm looking for someone up there."

"Always good to have a goal," he said. "You're stuck with us now, young Bennett."

The front of the bus jerked sharply upward, as if doing a wheelie. Through the window, I could see currents of power running over the bus and changing color from blue to green. On the other side of the windshield, stars blinked like ocean phosphorescence.

"Welcome to the tour," said Cad.

And with that, we shot into space. . . .

BANG!

MONDAY

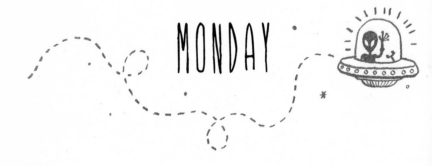

In the hours following my departure from Earth, I learned that the Perfectly Reasonable, the one billion sixteenth greatest band in the universe, had been in America because they were looking for a record deal anywhere they could get one.

"We drove this bus to every record company in Los Angeles and dropped off old demos," said Skark, filing one of his fourteen fingernails into a sharp point. "Nobody responded, no doubt because they found our sound confusing. You see, we can do anything—a cappella, dream pop, reggae fusion, Tropicália. It's the natural instinct of humans to want to categorize *everything,* but that is quite impossible when it comes to my band, and I refuse to be categorized by something as asinine as just *rock.* The goal should always be to move an art form forward."

Skark used his fingertip to extract the cork of a wine bottle, removing it with a twist and flicking it aside.

"But we're broke, so we need any record deal we can get," said Cad.

"It's not my fault that the cost of travel has gone up. Inflation is bad everywhere," said Skark.

"It *is* your fault all our other labels dropped us," said Cad.

"I admit no such thing. Foreign businessmen have no patience when it comes to nurturing genius."

"I think it's more that they have no patience when one of their artists has stopped writing songs and is spending all his money on Spine Wine," said Cad.

"Oh, shut up," said Skark.

"Is that what the wine is called?" I said, pointing to the bottle Skark was holding. "Spine Wine?"

"Ah, sweet siren Spine Wine," said Skark, wistfully looking over the bottle. "Friend, lover, inspiration, companion. That is its name."

Skark explained that Spine Wine got its name from the tingle felt at the base of the neck upon drinking a great deal of it—provided the imbiber had a neck, which was by no means common among all alien races. Made from the triangular grapes of the Blado Constellation, Spine Wine was expensive because it was meant to be an after-dinner drink—a small glass helped with digestion following a large meal—though apparently there were also cheaper blends, the existence of which Skark dismissed with a wave of his hand.

Spine Wine was also what Driver had made me drink when I got on the bus, but I hadn't consumed quite enough to get the treasured tingle.

"If you drink several glasses, the world *brightens* and the ego disappears—or so I've heard, I'm afraid my ego is a bit too large to ever be fully displaced—and the mind begins operating independently from the rest of the body," said Skark. "It's a marvelous liquid, and fully non-habit-forming, which is its finest quality."

"But you're all drinking it constantly," I said.

The band reacted like I had sprung a licensed interventionist on them.

"*Easy* there," said Cad.

"Whoa now, *addiction* is a strong word," said Driver.

"I didn't say *addiction*," I said.

"I've met addicts," said Skark. "And we are *not* addicts."

"*All right,* I'm sorry," I said. "You're right, I'm an outside observer, I don't know anything about the dynamics of your band. And as much as I appreciate hearing about the *difficulties* of securing a record contract in the modern universe, I'm not here to go out on tour. I'm here because I'm looking for someone, and I need your help navigating *that*."

I pointed out the window of the bus at the universe.

I'd always imagined outer space would look a lot like it did through the telescope in my backyard—thousands of pinpoints of white light, with the occasional comet whizzing past—but the endless horizon here was glowing with clouds of electric blue gas and newborn galaxies shaped like seashells and red-

and-purple nebulae that made me feel like I was staring into the eye of a god-sized feline. The universe was on fire with color.

"Here's my situation: On Friday, I'm supposed to go to prom with a girl I have wanted my entire life. She's beautiful. She's unique. She's got the cutest laugh I've ever heard. She is cooler than me, and I still have *no idea* how she ended up agreeing to be my date. Everything was going *perfect* for once in my stupid life—and then she was abducted by aliens."

The members of the Perfectly Reasonable nodded their heads, seemingly unsurprised to hear Sophie's fate.

"What did the guys who grabbed her look like?" said Cad.

"A lot like Driver, to be honest. No offense, Driver."

"None taken. People always think I look like someone they know. I have one of those faces."

"They had a van, and they tossed this stuff at her that looked like confetti and caused her to roll around on the ground."

"Brainsnuff," said Driver. "It grows naturally on Jyfon, and incapacitates any creature with an IQ of less than two hundred."

"Jyfon?"

"The planet where he's from," said Cad. "He's a Jyfo."

"I hate to say this, but if your girl got kidnapped by the Jyfos, kiss her goodbye," said Skark. "Or I suppose you should *imagine* yourself kissing her goodbye, because you're not going to see her again."

"Knock it off, Skark," said Cad. "The kid's emotional."

"I don't think the reality of the situation needs to be *disguised* from him," said Skark.

"What are you talking about?"

With that, Skark explained that the Jyfos were a well-intentioned yet inept race—always trying to *save* and *preserve* species but accidentally destroying them in the process.

To illuminate his point, he told a story about how, years before, the Newman Solar System had been suffering from mild solar warming. All the planets in the system had seen their surface temperatures tick up a couple of degrees, which concerned the Jyfos greatly, so to fix the problem, they simply blew up the solar system's sun. This stopped the solar warming—and by definition also stopped the solar system from being a *solar* system—but rendered the thirteen planets in the system lifeless granite spheres floating forever in limbo, sailing silently across the heavens.

"What does that have to do with Sophie?" I said.

"Pretty name," said Cad.

"If I had to guess, I'd say she's been taken by the Ecological Center for the Preservation of Lesser Species," said Skark.

According to Skark, the Ecological Center for the Preservation of Lesser Species was Jyfon's primary charitable cause—or at least he assumed it was based on the amount of *mail* they sent him asking for money. The Ecological Center for the Preservation of Lesser Species was a rescue operation for species the Jyfos viewed as close to extinction, in which they tried to make the species feel like they were at home.

The problem was, in researching what kind of environment might be best for humans, the Jyfos looked at the wars that were constantly taking place all over Earth, they watched movies depicting people getting blown to shreds for the audience's entertainment, they read books about games of death and unsolved murders, and from all that information they gleaned that what humans really enjoyed was violence (and plentiful access to low-quality foods, which was another issue, separate from what we were talking about).

Furthermore, Skark explained, the *reason* the members of the Perfectly Reasonable were so knowledgeable about the Jyfos and their misguided conservation efforts was that the Ecological Center for the Preservation of Lesser Species had its own in-house documentary team broadcasting the various creature environments the Jyfos had created, day and night. The Jyfos' public relations rationale behind these broadcasts was that allowing the universal population to see their efforts helped with fund-raising—but, Skark said, in reality they were simply gluttons for credit who wanted to show everyone how morally superior they were because they "cared" about the miserable animals everybody else ignored.

"So wait . . . if it's a conservation society, that means she's safe, right?"

The band looked at each other. There was something they didn't want to tell me.

"What?" I said.

Cad went back to the idea of violence. Though the Jyfos generally liked to keep a well-managed, docile herd of humans at the Ecological Center for the Preservation of Lesser Species—having people sedentary made it easier for the documentary crews to record their behavior—every now and then, to spice up their programming, they would drop someone who didn't look like the other residents—a pretty girl, a weight lifter, a couple of twins—into the compound and tell the rest of the inhabitants to hunt the newcomer down. Cad told me to think of it like a *National Geographic* special that showed predators stalking an animal that the audience wasn't used to seeing flee for its life—for instance, a group of leopards going after a sick lion—with the exception in this case being that the predators here moved *slowly.* However, there were so many of them, they were impossible to avoid forever.

"So you're saying she's bait," I said.

"Most likely," said Cad. "Next time we're around a TV, I'll show you what I mean."

I felt sick, but there was one thing I didn't understand. If the humans at the Ecological Center for the Preservation of Lesser Species had all the food and clothing and cigarettes they could ever want, why would they even *care* if the Jyfos brought somebody new into their environment?

"Is there a *prize* or something?" I said.

"Yeah," said Cad. "The Jyfos tell them that whoever hunts down the new blood gets to go home."

"Oh God."

It was even worse than I had allowed myself to think it might be. Sophie wasn't just having to deal with her abductors—she had been dropped into a *population* of individuals who were after her. I felt desperate.

"This is *insane*," I said. "We need to go get her *now*."

"We won't be anywhere near Jyfon until next week," said Skark, finishing off his bottle of Spine Wine. "We've got two gigs to play before Dondoozle, and we can't afford any distractions."

Skark pointed at a schedule hanging on the wall above my head:

MONDAY	Berdan Major Arena
TUESDAY	Dark Matter Foloptopus
WEDNESDAY	Travel Day
THURSDAY	Leisure Day
FRIDAY	Dondoozle Festival (Opening)

"I still can't believe we have to play the opening slot," said Skark. "We used to *close* festivals, and now we're playing first."

"It was the only slot offered," said Driver. "We're lucky they're letting us play at all."

"Tour aside, Bennett needs our help, Skark," said Cad.

"If he requires help, it will be provided *after* the Dondoozle Festival. I didn't *know* he had ulterior motives when he got on this bus, I think I've been very accommodating in welcoming him, and for now, this discussion is *over*. If you need me, I'll be chatting with the ram. I must get my head straight before my performance."

Skark pivoted on his heel, opened a door, and disappeared into what looked like a walk-in closet, where he was greeted by a long *baaaaa,* followed by a sarcastic "Hello, Skark. Really good to see you."

"There's a goat in the closet?" I said.

"An adult ram," said Cad. "That's Walter. Skark kidnapped him from the Nevada desert a few years back. He thinks Walter's his spirit guide, but he's clearly only a ram. It's a side effect of Skark constantly battering his brain with wine."

It seemed strange that Cad kept bringing up Skark's drinking, considering he himself had also been steadily sipping wine for the past few hours.

"I'm going to help you figure this out," said Cad. "Nothing is going to happen to your girl. Let's go to the bar in back and talk. I'm sure you have a bunch of questions."

"Yeah, the first is, how do I help Sophie?"

"You *can't* help her right now. That's what I'm trying to tell you. We will come up with a solution, but right now you need to relax. You drink?"

"As of a few hours ago, apparently."

"Good. It looks like you could use something to steady your nerves. The weirder you allow yourself to get up here, the better you'll fit in."

In an attempt to keep my mind off Sophie, Cad told me about the Perfectly Reasonable's bus, which the band had named the Interstellar Libertine.

During the 1970s, the bus had been owned by Led Zeppelin, which was how Skark had become interested in it, his rationale being that if it was able to stand up to the hardest-partying band in Earth's history—hence the "Libertine" moniker—it would most likely be able to endure the difficulties of touring deep space.

After purchasing the bus at an auction house in London, Skark had had its exterior retrofitted with compound silica-fiber ceramic tiles and the floor redone with a gravity-producing surface. Air was produced by something called a True-Atmosphere Atmosphering Apparatus—I don't know why the name was so redundant, maybe the manufacturers were trying to distinguish it from a rival product—which was the box to which Cad had attached his pull-up bar. Skark had installed the unit so musicians from a variety of alien species could ride along.

Cad explained that the True-Atmosphere Atmosphering Apparatus had been designed by a superior race—boringly called the Millers—to produce air that all carbon-based life-forms could breathe, though the air it created was deeply poisonous to silicon-based life-forms. That was fine with Skark, who considered most silicon-based life-forms to be both tone-deaf and poor technical musicians and therefore made a point of never having them in his band.

The functions of the True-Atmosphere Atmosphering Apparatus were easier for Cad to explain than the mechanics of the bus's engine and the means by which we were speeding through space. When the bus was really *moving,* it looked like space was simply folding around us as we traveled, one astonishing vista of distant stars or brushstrokes of color giving way to the next, almost like flipping through a book of photographs from the Hubble Space Telescope. Each time my eyes would focus on a cluster of periwinkle planets blanketed with neon green clouds or a supernova throwing out pulses of nuclear white light, the image would swiftly melt out of existence and be replaced by an equally incomprehensible panorama. It was a little jarring, never quite knowing where you were or what you were going to see next, the only guarantee being that it would be something spectacular.

Cad—doing his best to explain concepts clearly beyond him—likened the way the bus moved to passing through a series of little doors, one after the other, which is why it felt like we were jumping from place to place. The leaping required great speed, and while more technologically up-to-date engines allowed ships, buses, sedans, and whatever else aliens were driving to simply leap from one place to their exact destinations, the Interstellar Libertine was old and hadn't been built for this purpose in the first place and could only make its journey in lurching increments. In a final effort, Cad told me to picture it as a smaller, crappier starship *Enterprise* that had to keep taking breaks as it stumbled its way through space.

"It's why it takes us forever to get anywhere," said Cad. "If we had money, we'd be able to get a new engine, but the band has barely paid this one off."

"How did you end up in the band?" I asked.

"Have you ever been to Atlantic City?" he said.

"Before today, I'd barely been out of southeastern New Mexico."

Cad told me his story. After high school, he had managed to get a job playing bass in a lounge band at the Tropicana Casino in Atlantic City, backing an awful lead singer—bouffant hair, cheap suit, heavy cologne—on cheesy soft-rock ballads from the seventies and eighties: "Mandy" by Barry Manilow, "I Want to Know What Love Is" by Foreigner.

The lounge act had been between sets when Cad first saw Skark. Cad was eating some peanuts when all of a sudden he heard a roar from the craps table in the high-roller section of the casino. He peeked his head out of the lounge, and there was Skark, standing at a table surrounded by a huge crowd of gamblers, with the tallest pile of chips Cad had ever seen in front of him. The fact that Skark was an alien drew little attention—he looked human *enough* to pass as a giant with odd bone structure who was at the tail end of a bender. Atlantic City was used to eccentrics, and as long as he had money to bet, no casino would ever kick him out.

Skark jerked his arm back and threw the dice. The dealer yelled "Seven!" and there was a cheer, followed by the dealer pushing another stack of chips in front of Skark. Cad had never seen so much money in his life. And that's when Skark looked at him across the room.

"You with the bass guitar," said Skark. *"You need a job? My bassist is in jail for getting high and trying to ride the roulette wheel, so I need a new one. You have six seconds to decide."*

Skark started counting down: *"Six ... five ... four ... three ..."* At that point, Cad figured that *whatever* Skark was doing to have that much money was better than what he was doing, so he joined. Ten years later, he was still in the band.

"Are you happy about that decision?" I said.

"I'd be happier if I got to play one of my own songs one of these days," said Cad. "But Skark won't allow it. He says he writes all the songs ... even though he hasn't actually written a song in years."

"Do you ever see your family back home?"

"I don't have a family back home," said Cad. "My mom passed away when I was young, and my dad has been living with a wife and kid he cares about much more than me for as long as I can remember."

"I'm sorry."

"I've had a long time to get over it," said Cad. "For better or worse, this band has *been* my family for a decade. It's just dysfunctional as all get-out."

"Attention, ingrates," said Driver over the bus intercom. "It's showtime. Remember: we're playing Berdan Major Arena tonight. Write the name on your hand so you don't forget. Audiences don't appreciate it when they realize you don't know what planet you're on."

Cad picked up a pen and wrote *Berdan Major Arena* on his palm.

"I have to get ready," said Cad. "If you have more questions, I'll answer them after the gig."

"One more and I'll leave you alone," I said. "How am I able

to understand what everybody is saying if I only speak English and the band is from all over the universe?"

"It's because of the Spine Wine. You know how when you're buzzed, you feel like you can completely understand everything people are saying because you're on the same cosmic level?"

"I guess. I'm pretty new to it."

"Drinking the wine follows a principle similar to sitting around with your friends on a Friday night—sip a little bit of that stuff and you get *just* mellow enough to understand what any creature, animal, or inanimate object in the universe is saying. You just *understand.*"

"So I was drugged, is what you're saying."

"Technically, you were drugged, but I wouldn't worry about it. On tour you could get dosed at any time."

"Does that mean I have to keep drinking it to know what everybody is saying?"

"Nah, it stays in the body for years," said Cad. "It's like LSD in the way it changes the brain so you can never *totally* go back, but at some point your translation skills will start to fade. Now I have to get ready. I suggest checking out the view. Just don't bother Skark—he's a nightmare to deal with before gigs."

I didn't care that there was an embargo on talking to Skark before shows, or that the band had an engagement, or that if they were to kick me off the bus, I would be in a *deep* amount of trouble. I needed to help Sophie, *now.*

I found Skark standing in front of the bathroom mirror,

painting a blue rectangle over his eyes with granular makeup. He was naked except for a pair of white leather jeans, and he was so thin I could see his ribs under the skin of his torso, which he had powdered to match his pants.

I lingered near him for a moment. He sighed, then spoke before I even had a chance to start the conversation.

"Good God, man, I hope you're not going to ask me again about stopping the tour for your girl," he said, pressing his eyelashes with a delicate metal curler. "If I'd known you had selfish reasons for joining us, I would have never invited you on board."

"I'm not asking for you to stop the tour. I'm asking if we can get her before something *bad* happens. I know it's a pain in the—"

"Truer words have never been spoken. Whatever part of the anatomy you were about to reference, it is a pain in that particular place. Let me ask—did I or either of my bandmates kidnap your prom date?"

"No."

"So you agree that we are not *responsible* for the kidnapping of your prom date, yes? Please say that for me if it's true."

"You're not responsible for her kidnapping."

"And did we bring you aboard with the *promise* that we would help you in this heroic quest? That I would interrupt our tour for a lovesick member of a doomed race who happened to stumble onto my bus because he was too dumb to locate a cheeseburger on his own, and chose to beg for scraps like an underfed animal?"

"I'm not sure if insults are called for," I said. "I'd think you could maybe try to be sympathetic to my position here."

"After the Dondoozle Festival we will either reevaluate your situation or safely return you to your planet, but until then you will mind yourself and you will stay out of my way and you *will not* ask me to help you again, do you understand that? Now *go.*"

Skark slammed the bathroom door in my face.

"Don't worry about him," grumbled Driver, looking back at me over his shoulder. "These days he's always irritable before shows, because the crowds aren't as big as they used to be."

"Considering there are trillions of planets in the universe, being the billionth biggest band still seems like it could be lucrative," I said.

"We're one billion sixteenth," said Driver. "But people only want the top bands, so I guess we're lucky to still be playing at all. I don't know. Sometimes I think I should have stuck with fashion."

"You were a fashion designer?"

"Aspiring designer," said Driver. "When I was younger, it was always difficult to find clothes that fit, so I started making my own."

I glanced at Driver's stained shirt and stonewashed jeans. He caught me looking.

"I've put those dreams on hold," he said. "I don't know. Maybe someday I'll make an outfit I'm proud of, and the creative spark will return. I'm in a little bit of a personal and professional lull at the moment."

"Is Driver your real name?"

"Of course not. But everybody has a tough time remembering Queckburt Hodabink, so I make it easy for them."

"That is tough."

"In my language, it means 'energy-efficient heater,'" sighed Driver. "I'm not sure if my parents ever loved me. But enough about the past. Come look at this—it might take your mind off your girl for a moment."

I joined Driver at the wheel, and what I saw seemed impossible. In front of the bus was a stadium hollowed out of an entire *planet,* and it was on *fire.* There were thousands of seats. As we got closer, I saw a scoreboard the size of a *continent* blaring a message:

BERDAN MAJOR ARENA WELCOMES THE PERFECTLY REASONABLE

"I've never seen anything like it," I said.

"It's not even one of the good stadiums," said Driver. "This is the musical boondocks, whether or not Skark wants to admit it. To be honest, we didn't sell enough tickets to even justify being here."

"There are better places than this?"

"Wait until you see the Dondoozle Festival," said Driver. "I swear, it's like heaven without the halos."

Driver thought about this.

"Actually, that's not true," he said. "Last time I was there, I saw a creature who *was* a halo. Just this golden disk, floating through the air, minding its business. I followed it for hours, trying to find a way to put it on my head, thinking it would give me some divine powers or something. I was pretty blasted at the time."

"Did you get it?"

"No, it ended up biting me," said Driver. "Wouldn't have even thought it had jaws."

Driver looked at a C-shaped scar on his arm. He rubbed it with his thick fingers, recalling the pain.

"I realize that's not a great representation of the festival," he said. "Trust me, Dondoozle is better than I'm making it sound."

"All I care about is getting to Sophie."

"Patience," said Driver. "Cad and I have your back. But Skark calls the shots, which means that for the moment he's got every other part of you."

I was terrified to eat the snacks backstage at Berdan Major Arena. The tables were packed with finger sandwiches stuffed with slices of strange glowing meats, fist-sized snails hanging limply from their spiky shells, and edible flower buds that blossomed when you picked them up.

One of the band's roadies—an anthropoid in a black T-shirt who resembled a lowland gorilla and had the musky scent of a bag of decaying leaves—lumbered up next to me and surveyed the food.

"Decent spread," he said. "Better than the reheated crud

they've been serving us lately. I've lost three hundred pounds since the start of this awful tour, if you can believe it."

"I'm overwhelmed," I said. "I've never seen a buffet like this."

"You should have seen the food at the places we used to play. I've seen eyeballs pop out of roadies' heads while they were looking over the selections. Then I've seen *other* crew members accidentally eat those eyeballs because they thought they were exotic delicacies. You ever eat an eyeball?"

"No."

"Fatty, but delicious. After you've had a couple, you want to hit the gym to work off the guilt."

"If the band is out of money, how do they afford roadies?" I said.

"They have no choice," said the roadie. "Without us, there's no show. You think these clowns could set up their own equipment? Skark couldn't figure out how to plug in a blender these days. He's a washed-up drunk."

I had learned from Cad that the Perfectly Reasonable's roadies traveled in a brigade of trucks separate from the Interstellar Libertine because Skark found them slovenly in appearance and crass in behavior. He refused to even *see* the roadies until the day of a show, which meant the equipment caravan was forced to travel different routes to the band's gigs, often through dangerous space. As a result, Skark was not popular among his crew.

"By the way, since you're human, I'd stay away from the

crayborps," said the roadie. "Your species can't digest them. They'll crawl up your backbone and eat your brain."

"Good to know."

"Enjoy the show—if Skark can get through it without passing out or storming off. These gigs have been touch and go recently."

The roadie grabbed a Coca-Cola—which seemed to be as common in the rest of the universe as it was on Earth—and trotted off toward the stage to help with the setup.

I went exploring backstage.

Skark, Driver, and Cad each had their own dressing rooms, which I knew was a bad sign. Throughout high school, I had spent countless weekends in my room watching music documentaries, and from those docs I had learned that whenever the band members stopped preparing for gigs together in the same room, it meant that there wasn't much time left before a breakup.

Cad popped out of his dressing room. "Bennett, come here," he said, waving me over. I had been trying to avoid getting in his way prior to the gig, but now he was lifting the embargo. "I want to show you something."

I walked into his dressing room, which was a bit like what I imagined the presidential suite at a high-end boutique hotel would look like. Chandelier. Canopied bed. Beer bottles chilling in champagne buckets. A pair of vaguely human-looking girls were lounging on a red suede couch, bored.

The band might be broke, but they seemed to still have excellent backstage perks.

"Stenya, Delya, this is Bennett," said Cad, introducing me to the girls. "He and I are from the same planet, but he's a little young to handle the two of you, so I'm going to need you to leave him alone."

The girls pouted.

"Aww," said the one I guessed was Stenya. "But he is so *cute.*"

"And we are *bored,*" said Delya.

"Where are they from?" I whispered.

"I have absolutely no idea," said Cad. "They were here when I showed up, which happens sometimes. Such is the life of even a fading star. But they're not what I wanted to show you."

Cad pressed a button on a remote control, and an entire wall lit up with images. As he began flipping through the channels, he explained that television was intense in the rest of the universe because there was no censorship. What was fine on one planet—for instance, a cooking show featuring a chef preparing clams—might be offensive to a culture that regarded clams as gods. Since the universe had a near-infinite number of worlds, it meant that *everything* would be offensive to somebody, so nobody knew *what* to censor. As a result, the networks would put absolutely anything on the air, and they just let different cultures react how they saw fit. Occasionally this policy led to wars or to different species exterminating each other entirely, but from the networks' perspective, there was no other way to deal with such a vast audience. Ratings were ratings.

As Cad flipped through the stations, I caught glimpses of

some of these alien programs—a show devoted to gelatinous blobs wrestling above a pit of salt, a program featuring clouds striking each other with lightning, a half dozen channels playing music videos starring familiar-looking female pop stars dressed in scanty neon outfits.

"Wherever you go in the universe, pop stars are exactly the same," said Cad. "Here, this is what I was looking for . . . the All-Universe Nature Channel."

But what Cad showed me didn't seem nature-ish at all. Instead, it resembled the inside of a mall. There was an Adidas. There was an Orange Julius. There was a Starbucks across an atrium from another Starbucks, with a third Starbucks just down a corridor and a fourth Starbucks being remodeled nearby.

"How is that nature?" I said.

"That's what the Jyfos think Earth looks like," said Cad. "Correction—it's what they think America looks like, because America is where they get most of their specimens."

"Why?"

"It's a nation of slow-moving people, filled with wide-open spaces where the Jyfos can land without attracting attention. Seems like a no-brainer to me."

The camera panned over the mall, and for the first time I saw that it was *packed* with agitated-looking men and women. They were sitting on benches drinking Big Gulps, smearing sauerkraut on hot dogs at food kiosks, trying on cheap pants at Old Navy, all constantly sizing each other up with their tiny eyes. The residents of the enclosure seemed to be the type of individuals you always heard about aliens abducting—obese truck drivers, flannel-wearing lumberjacks, dead-eyed mental patients shuffling around muttering to themselves.

The Internet was right—alien abductors definitely had a specific type they targeted.

Some of the residents of the enclosure were holding baseball bats and wearing protective sporting gear—catchers' chest protectors, Rollerblading kneepads, bicycle helmets—while others were outfitted in camouflage cargo pants and heavy boots. Some were traveling in groups, some were walking alone, some were limping, some had visible wounds on their arms or legs. Nobody seemed relaxed, except for those individuals who were sucking back Spine Wine. The hooch didn't seem to be as high quality as Skark's beverage of choice—instead of Skark's small-batch, individually labeled bottles of the liquor, the residents of the enclosure were guzzling generically packaged boxes of the stuff straight from the spout, snapping at each other when fellow drinkers hogged them for too long.

If it was just humans here, I didn't know *why* they would need the Spine Wine, unless it was to facilitate discussion between residents who were abducted from different countries—though from my cursory analysis of the inhabitants, it didn't seem like a whole lot of intellectual discussion was probably taking place.

The camera pushed in on the window of a Starbucks.

"What's happening?" I said.

"The documentary crew always does that zoom thing when

they see something interesting," said Cad. "The cinematography is incredibly predictable, which is one of my problems with the show."

Through the windows of the Starbucks, I could discern the faint outline of a girl. The image was blurry, so at first I couldn't be sure it was Sophie. She had her hands cupped around her eyes and was looking outside, sweaty bangs hanging down over her fingers.

Then the girl took a step back and in one definitive motion pressed her middle finger against the glass, flipping off whoever was looking at her from outside the coffee shop.

Yep, it was definitely Sophie.

Seeing that she was still alive—not necessarily *safe,* but living—caused relief to ripple through my body. I pushed as close to the television as I could without the high-resolution image burning my eyes, straining to see whether or not she was injured. All I wanted was to know that she was okay.

Sophie moved to the front entrance of the Starbucks. She had barricaded herself inside the coffee shop with tables, chairs, and other pieces of furniture, which she started rapidly moving away from the door one piece at a time.

"So she really is bait," I said.

"Is that her?" said Cad.

"That's her."

The camera panned over the mall, revealing hordes of weirdos—drooling women, limping men—all lumbering toward the Starbucks, alerted by the sound of Sophie moving inside. The camera zoomed in for another close-up through the glass, focusing on Sophie's eyes as she looked back and forth.

"So that's really her?" said Cad.

"That's her," I said.

"She's hot," said Cad. "In a crazed kind of way, you know."

Sophie dragged the final chair out of the way and flung open the door. Her hair was matted to her forehead and her clothes were sticking to her skin. She chucked an espresso machine at the pack of goons approaching her, which was the wrong move. Seeing that she was now unarmed, the mob pushed forward, and Sophie took off running.

The throng chased her, but none of them could get within a hundred yards. She zipped past a Hugo Boss, accelerated down the tile floor in front of a See's Candies, and was gone from the camera's view.

"Poor girl . . . ," said Cad. "She's fast, but she's not going to be able to run from that mob forever."

"We need to *help* her."

"I know we do. But unfortunately, we also need to play a show, and at least it looks like your girl has a head start on those idiots. She's pretty nimble."

"She does mud runs."

"That makes sense. We'll figure this out after the gig."

Driver pounded on the dressing room door.

"Get ready, we're on in two minutes," he said.

I heard the voice of the stadium announcer through

the walls of the dressing room: *"Ladies and gentlemen and lady-gentlemen, please stand on your hands and clap your feet for one of the Greatest Bands You Will Ever See—as long as you don't see one of the billion or so bands generally considered to be better than them. . . ."*

"I *hate* it when the announcers mention we're ranked out of the top billion," I heard Skark complain as he stood outside his dressing room. "It needs to *stop.* Next show, I want that specifically written in the concert rider."

Cad walked out into the hall, holding his bass. There were no smiles between him and the rest of the Perfectly Reasonable, no nods hello, no joy. Playing this gig was business, and that's all. They walked onstage.

"So please give a head-shattering welcome to your gods made flesh . . . the three . . . the only . . . THE PERFECTLY REA-SONABLE."

Skark strummed a guitar chord—*BARRUMPH*—and I saw blood trickle from the left ear of the roadie I had been speaking with earlier. He noticed me staring.

"My eardrum explodes a couple times a week," said the roadie. "I'd get it fixed, but the band can't afford to pay the crew's health insurance anymore."

"They're that poor?"

"Unless something happens to put them back in the spotlight, soon they'll be playing weddings, though even that career would probably last about ten minutes."

"Why?"

"No man in his right mind would trust Cad around his bride. The man is a *fiend.* You know bassists."

"What about them?"

"Chicks love a man with good hands. Do yourself a favor. Never bring a woman around Cad."

Every time Driver hit his snare drum, he wrenched my spine out of place; every time he hit a cymbal, he split my skull.

On bass, Cad could do anything—bossa nova, Philadelphia soul, gypsy rumba—his hands moving so quickly they gave the visual effect of being at rest, draped over the fret board, shuddering every now and then before snapping back to their home position.

And soaring above the fray were the sounds of both Skark's guitar and his *voice,* which left no doubt in my mind that he was more alien than human.

His range was stunning—one moment his voice was a crisp, pitch-perfect tenor, and the next it would rise to hit notes so high I couldn't hear them at all, climbing upward and then disappearing from my auditory range altogether, even though I could see that his mouth was still open. If he fell silent, the audience did the same, waiting for him to speak. If he motioned for them to clap, they continued unprompted until he cut them off with a slash across his throat with the neck of his guitar. If he put his hand to the side of his temple to hear them sing his lyrics, they did so at full throat, or whatever parts of their bodies they used to make noise. When he asked if they wanted to go home with him, their affirmative response echoed through the stadium.

The crowd was surprisingly noisy, considering there was barely anybody present. The stadium itself was massive—if you told me a hundred thousand people could have sat comfortably, I wouldn't have been surprised—but it looked like there were only a couple hundred fans in attendance, most of whom had crammed themselves into the first five rows. The rest of the arena was a ghost town, with the fans in the back having entire sections of bleachers all to themselves. I saw wisps of smoke rising above these nomads, who were altering their consciousness for the show, no doubt.

It was a depressing scene, though the fans who were there were quite loyal—wearing T-shirts bearing Skark's face, singing along with every lyric, shouting out song requests.

But halfway through the show, something went wrong.

The incident occurred while Skark was finishing a song called "You Can't Hide," a hard-driving dance number about visiting different planets in search of the perfect girl, which Driver had told me was one of the band's biggest hits.

For most of the song, the fans were rapturous—dancing wildly, singing along, using face tentacles to make out with each other. But as the song was ending, somebody shouted at the stage.

"Play something new *for once!"* said the heckler. *"This is the same set you did five years ago. You think I don't remember?"*

"Who said that?" said Skark, putting his hand over his eyes to block the lights.

"I *said it,*" said the heckler. *"And you know it's true."*

"I can't *see* you."

"Then apparently the song you just sang is wrong," said the heckler. *"I guess I can hide."*

"*Coward,*" said Skark. "Insulting me and then refusing to show yourself. Where *are* you?"

No response.

"It *better not* be Ferguson out there harassing this band," said Skark. "Is it Ferguson? I know it's Ferguson."

Ferguson?

"It's not Ferguson," said the voice. *"But the band was better when Ferguson was in it, if you ask me."*

"*Cower* in the crowd all you want, poltroon," said Skark. "But this Friday afternoon we're playing the Dondoozle Festival, and we'll have a whole new *set* of material."

Cad and Driver looked at each other. The idea of having a new set of material by Friday seemed to be news to them.

"Who the hell plays the opening slot?" said the voice. *"Didn't you used to* close *festivals?"*

Skark climbed an amplifier at the front of the stage, holding the mike at his side and staring into the crowd, searching for his accuser.

"*Somebody* has to open the festival," he said. "It's an *honor.*"

"Nobody cares about the opening act," said the voice. "*You guys* suck."

"Tonight is a warm-up for our *true glory,*" said Skark. "A warm-up you don't deserve, based on these outbursts."

The crowd grumbled.

Cad leaned into his microphone and tried to do damage control.

"You actually do deserve it," said Cad. "We love you. Sorry about Skark. Let's move forward and give you a good sho—"

"Don't you *dare* apologize for me," said Skark. "If you want to continue the show on your own, you're more than welcome to, but I'm done. *Good night.*"

Skark kicked down his mike and stormed away from the stage, grabbing his Spine Wine off an amplifier as he disappeared into the wings, the audience booing him in his wake. Food and beverage containers rained down on the stage. Cad watched Skark go, then turned back to his microphone and spoke again, dodging cans and tubes of meat.

"I'm *sorry,*" he said. "I'm as angry as you are. Full refunds will be offered at the door. . . ."

Driver shook his head at Cad. *We can't do that.*

"Full refunds will be offered *eventually,*" said Cad. "We're running a little tight at the moment."

I saw audience members working in teams to rip seats from the floor, pushing and pulling until the chairs broke free. They lifted them above their heads, and furniture poured onto the stage as Cad and Driver bolted for the wings. If ever there was a band that needed to break up, it was this one. I just hoped it didn't happen until I found Sophie.

Getting probed would have been better than dealing with these guys.

✩ ✩ ✩

Backstage, Skark and Cad were screaming at each other as the roadies and Driver stood around bored, having seen this display many times before. I lingered off to the side, munching on an appetizer that tasted like a crab cake but looked a bit like a marshmallow Peep. I was annoyed with myself for not possessing any culinary talent—if I had kitchen skills, maybe I would have been able to reverse engineer some of this food and open an artisanal small-plate restaurant if I ever got back home. Another employment opportunity if and when I didn't get into college.

I licked the crumbs off my fingers and waited for the drama to settle so I could get back to the business of finding Sophie.

"You *cannot* keep stopping our shows to yell at hecklers," said Cad. "Especially one who is telling the *truth*. The last time we were here, we *did* play the same set list, and the crowd *knew* that fact because these are the only fans we have *left*. And what about telling the crowd we'll have an entire new *set* of material at Dondoozle? You haven't written a new song in *five years*."

"It's not my fault if I'm still waiting for inspiration's gentle touch," said Skark. "It will come, it always does. I wrote my first album in a weekend."

"Yeah, but you were *good* then," said Cad. "Your head was clear. And what was that crap about Ferguson?"

"Ferguson sent me a letter threatening to sabotage our

shows," said Skark. "Don't pretend like I'm being unreasonable with my security concerns."

"Ferguson hasn't been in the band in *nine years,* and he's been sending us threatening letters the *entire time,*" said Cad. "He never does *anything.*" Cad pointed to the open bottle of Spine Wine in Skark's hand. "Your *habits* are making you paranoid, man."

Skark grabbed Cad by the neck. Cad might have been in excellent physical condition, but Skark was far taller and built like a powerful, wine-fueled insect. He squeezed Cad's throat.

"After all this time together, it *appears* you still think this band is a democracy," he said. "If I say we will have a new set of material by Friday, we will *have it.* Until then, keep your mouth shut and play your bass."

Skark released his grip and Cad fell to the ground, gasping for air. A roadie tried to help him up, but Cad waved him off.

"If I wanted to play with a washed-up singer, I would have stayed in Atlantic City," said Cad, wiping spittle away from his mouth with his arm.

"I *hate* to interrupt you while you're re-creating your normal scene," said Driver. "But the bus needs to leave *now* or we're going to be late for our next gig, so if you have more fists to throw, I suggest you get it out of your system. . . ."

"Leave without me, I don't care, I'm out," said Cad, climbing to his feet and walking away.

"Good Lord, you quit the band every week," said Skark.

"*And why* do you think that is?" said Cad. "Maybe it has

something to do with me wanting to *leave the band.* Imagine that."

Driver sighed and shrugged and headed back in the direction of the bus, while the roadies put their heads down and tried not to make eye contact with Skark as they packed up gear, placed instruments in cases, and loaded amplifiers onto their trucks.

When Driver's drum set rolled past, Skark grabbed a polished cymbal and held it up to his face like a mirror. He took a handkerchief out of his pocket and dabbed at his makeup, which was smeared from the confrontation. He looked at me.

"Would you *please* stop staring?" said Skark. "You're like a pestiferous canine looking for a handout."

"I saw my prom date on the All-Universe Nature Channel," I said. "She's at the Ecological Center for the Preservation of Lesser Species, and everyone there is chasing her. If I don't get to her before they do . . ."

"Let me *once again* make this clear, because you're having trouble understanding," said Skark, placing the handkerchief back in his pocket and staring at me. "Even if Jyfon was *on the way* to our next gig, we wouldn't stop this tour to get your prom date. What we are doing now is *calculated preparation* for the Dondoozle Festival. We can't afford distractions."

"You sure seemed distracted out there tonight," I said.

Skark poked his fingernail into my chest and pushed. He could have broken the skin if he wanted.

"Mind your mouth or I'll make sure you find yourself burning up in some distant atmosphere," he said. "You wouldn't be the first stowaway I've had to dispose of when he became too conspicuous a presence. I should have seen through your cheeseburger scheme, using me for cheap transportation and a way to the stars."

Skark walked back toward the bus, crushing a soda can under his foot and booting it a hundred feet with a frustrated kick.

I didn't want to follow him. I asked a roadie where Cad had gone, and the roadie responded with a plump finger pointed outside. After a short walk, I was in the stadium parking lot, which was packed with equipment trucks and other grunts finishing up disassembling pieces of the set.

It felt odd to be strolling normally in such a strange world. Comets zipped through the atmosphere above me, beyond which I saw green spiral galaxies and hot pink nebulae that looked like they'd been poured from a paint can into the sky. I followed a copper-colored river that ran along the perimeter of the parking lot until I reached a clearing, where Cad was sitting on a bench with a half-consumed bottle of Spine Wine. I sat next to him and waited for him to finish downing a long gulp.

"I'm sorry you had to see the fight back there," he said, wiping the liquid from his lips. "I don't like arguing in front of guests, but if you haven't already figured it out—this band is breaking apart in a real way."

"Did you mean what you said about quitting?"

"I mean it every time I say it," he said. "Not that it matters.

We haven't gotten along with each other in forever. Nobody takes anybody seriously anymore."

"Have other members left?" I said. "I don't know much about the history of the band."

"Everybody leaves, eventually."

Cad took me through the litany of musicians whom Skark had fired since he started the band—a pair of bassoonists back in the eighties, a beatboxer in the early nineties during Skark's brief hip-hop phase, a pan flutist who might have actually been the god Pan, along with dozens of bassists and keyboardists whom Skark had used for a moment and then summarily dismissed.

In fact, at this point, Skark and Driver were the only original members of the group, having met each other while incarcerated in a juvenile prison, which Skark was in for multiple counts of shoplifting—starting with lip gloss and skinny jeans, but eventually moving up to microphones and guitars. Driver was constantly in trouble for putting his fists through walls or pounding on school desks until they broke. That one of them would become a singer and the other a drummer was a natural progression.

Cad explained that the original lineup had also included an arsonist from the detention center, who was kicked out after three years for using a suitcase bomb to light his bass on fire at the end of a gig, necessitating the evacuation of a large city. He was followed by a never-ending rotation of bongo drummers and clarinetists and whip dancers, with Skark constantly trying to assemble the correct lineup to replicate the music in his head. Now they were just a trio. As long as his voice and his guitar were part of the sound, the audience didn't care who was backing him.

Having lasted more than a decade, Cad was now the longest-serving member the band had ever employed, during which time he'd seen endless musicians come and go.

"But the worst was getting rid of Ferguson," said Cad.

"Who's Ferguson?"

"Ferguson is who Skark was howling about out there tonight," said Cad. "Ever since we kicked him out, he's been in Skark's head."

"What did he play?" I said.

"Triangle."

"You had someone in the band just to play the *triangle*?"

Ferguson had already been in the band when Cad joined, because Skark had thought some of his songs could use a little *ding* from time to time. Skark was a madman, but to his credit, he was against bringing in session musicians to lay down a track or two, instead reasoning that if he made music with somebody, that person was his *brother*, at least until Skark let him go. (Or his sister, as it turned out. Skark had had a handful of talented female artists join the band over the years, all of whom were too smart to put up with his crap for more than a few days.)

When Cad was hired, the band's popularity had been growing steadily over the previous decade. With the fame, Ferguson's ego ballooned, which made touring miserable for a band already dominated by Skark's life-guzzling personality. Ferguson started fighting Skark for the microphone, missing his cues, insisting he be in the foreground of band photographs even though he was, as Cad described him, a scoliosis-ridden troll.

"We were riding high back then, and the lifestyle had gone to Ferguson's head," said Cad. "All he had to do was hit a triangle with a stick, and he was too screwed up to even do that. Eventually we just left a bus ticket at the brothel where he was staying, with a note that he wasn't in the band anymore. That was nine years ago."

"Did you ever see him again?"

"Skark claims to see him all the time, but I never have. He thinks Ferguson has been trying to kidnap him and get some sort of revenge. He's written us mail for years—in one sentence he talks about how much he hates us, and then he begs to get back in the band in the next."

"Is he actually a threat?"

"He hasn't been yet, as far as I can tell."

A burst of air nearly knocked Cad and me off the bench. We looked up and saw the Interstellar Libertine hovering over our heads, Driver hanging out the window and looking down.

"If you're not on this bus in the next *eight seconds,* we're leaving you behind," said Driver. "We're already late to our next gig because of you malcontents."

"Does this mean Skark still needs a bassist?" said Cad.

Skark lowered a window and looked outside.

"All it means is that I've decided to temporarily forgive you for your insubordination," he said.

"I never said I was sorry," said Cad, looking at Skark. He turned back to Driver. "Did we get the Chinese food order?"

"I'm holding your pork fried rice as we speak," said Driver.

Cad turned to me. "One of the advantages of playing out here is that Berdan Major has terrific Chinese."

"How is it possible there is Chinese food in space?"

"Everybody loves Chinese food," said Cad. "Why wouldn't there be Chinese food out here?"

Driver opened the door, and metal steps lowered from the bus, accompanied by an ear-rupturing *creeeeaaak*. The smell of lo mein was overpowering.

"Does this mean you and Skark are cool?" I asked.

"Only until the next gig," said Cad. "Which—I forgot to mention—is inside the belly of a Dark Matter Foloptopus, one of the largest and most unpredictable animals in the universe. Not to freak you out."

"That *absolutely* freaks me out," I said. "Why would you play a gig in a place like that?"

"Skark is trying to toughen up our image," said Cad, stepping up the stairs. "This is what we have to do now to get attention, because he's forgotten how to write new material."

"Because your negative attitude sucks me *dry*," said Skark, shouting from inside the bus.

"You can't be sucked dry if you have nothing left creatively."

"You're a parasite."

"You're a wax figure of your former self."

"Churl."

"Reptile."

"The wontons are getting cold," said Driver.

TUESDAY

Cad had been right about the Chinese food being good—a little salty, but considering we were hundreds of light-years from Earth, it was nice to have a taste of home. I gobbled it down and looked around to see if anyone in the band had leftovers, but they didn't. Our stomachs full, everyone headed off in different directions to go to sleep.

Though I'd been up close to fifty straight hours, I couldn't inch my way over the threshold of exhaustion into unconsciousness. The band had climbed into their beds and passed out instantly—Cad in a hammock hanging from the ceiling, Skark in a cryogenic pod at the back of the bus designed to keep him young, Driver in an oversized bassinet, where he was snoring like a terrarium toad—but I was on the couch, which was covered in crusty stains and pungent smells that lingered no matter how many times I scraped at a crumbly spot or flipped a cushion. It was a couch that had clearly been sat on and spilled on and God knows what else, and now I was paying the price for all the idling and snacking and gas passing that it had experienced.

Skark had conveniently left a bottle of Spine Wine at the base of the couch, so I swigged a mouthful in the hope that it would help me sleep. The liquid burned my throat, but I gagged it down before my body forced me to spit it out. My sleepiness turned to queasiness. Instead of thinking about how I couldn't pass out, now I was focused on the astringent aftertaste and my bubbling stomach.

That's when the closet spoke to me: "I really don't blame you for drinking alone."

"Hello?" I said.

"In the closet," said the voice. "I can see you through the crack at the bottom of the door. Do me a favor and open it. I need some air. Everybody is asleep."

I double-checked the bus to make sure everybody was indeed unconscious, and then turned the handle to open the door.

The ram was staring at me. The sides of his face were brown, and a thick white stripe ran down the middle of his nose. He had two spiraling gray horns, and an uncombed white beard hung from his bottom lip.

I hadn't been face to face with an animal other than a dog or a cat since I had reached up to touch a petting zoo pony when I was five years old. I found the ram's stare unsettling—he seemed to be pleading to me with his eyes, but I didn't know what he wanted.

Then he spoke and told me exactly what he wanted.

"My name is Walter. You're from Earth, right?"

"Right."

"*You need* to take me back there. I have a job. I have friends. I have responsibilities. Skark has *destroyed my life* by keeping me on this bus."

"I'm so sorry."

"*Sorry* doesn't help get me out of here. This band is about to break up, and when the last gig happens, I don't want to be stuck in some wasteland millions of miles from home. I've been on this bus for *four years,* and I already had a touch of claustro-phobia before I even got here. I'm going to need twenty years of psychiatric analysis to unwind all the issues I've developed because of this."

"Four years?"

"Skark picked me up in northern Nevada and said I was his spirit guide, which I am *not.* I'm not even religious. I thought he might let me go, or at least let me see my *wife,* when the band made that pit stop at the In-N-Out where we got you, but nope—he didn't even think about me. Which is typical. That guy *only* acts in his self-interest."

"As I'm learning."

"Right right right, how could I be so insensitive?" said Walter. "I'm sorry about your prom date. I have fond memories from my own prom. I went with this plump little golden-furred girl. You should have seen the thigh hair on her."

At the back of the bus, Skark's sleeping pod popped open.

"*Quick,* close my door," said Walter. "We'll talk more later. Pretend like you're asleep. If you think he's moody before a show, you have no idea what he's like when he can't sleep."

I shut Walter's closet, flopped back down on the couch, and kept my eyes shut. I heard Skark stumble down the center of the bus and grab the bottle from my side.

"Freeloading human," I heard him mutter. "Find your own wine and leave mine alone."

Once he had the bottle, Skark shuffled his way to the kitchen. I heard a chair scrape the ground and the refrigerator open and shut. I heard the wine hit the bottom of a glass and Skark take a long gulp. Then I heard nothing at all, so I peeked.

Skark was sitting at the small, round kitchen table, without any makeup on, donning none of his typical tight, fancy clothing. He was shirtless, revealing his bony frame, and he was wearing a pair of beaten yellow track shorts. His hair was uncombed and hanging loosely down his back, and his limbs were cadaverous.

He pulled a pad of paper out of a stack of fashion magazines and picked up a pen. He licked the tip of the pen, took another gulp of wine, and then . . . nothing.

"Come *on,*" I heard him mutter. "Dondoozle is *Friday.*"

He was trying to write a song.

"Useless petrified lump of a brain," he said.

It was an odd feeling, but in that moment I felt myself iden-

tifying with Skark for the first time. He had a few more ver-
tebrae and ribs than I did, but underneath his makeup and
flashy reversible gemstone jackets, he was simply an awkward
guy, same as any other musician who started out playing songs
by himself in a bedroom. Even the way he was *sitting* seemed
familiar—slumped over a table, holding a pen, staring help-
lessly at a pad of paper, disbelieving that anything was achiev-
able. I heard him hum a few notes, scribble a few lines, stare at
what he had written, and then cross it out, frustrated.

"Dammit," he said. "Come on, come on . . ."

I watched him repeat the pattern for as long as I could stay
awake—scribble, cross out, scribble, cross out—but soon a
combination of exhaustion and momentary distraction from my
nausea overtook me, and I closed my eyes.

Walter the ram whispered to me before I passed out.

"If I were you, I'd get myself home as soon as possible too,"
he said. "And if you could find me some fresh grass, that would
be great. I'm *so tired* of Chinese. I used to be gluten-free."

I awoke to find Driver yanking a skintight yellow latex jumpsuit
over my half-naked body, putting his scabrous foot on my chest
to give himself extra leverage for the pulling.

"I've never seen anybody with a body as *weird* as this kid's,"
said Driver. "He's tall, and he's thin, so you'd think that a
jumpsuit would be fine, but his calves are disproportional to
the rest of him, so the pants are too tight."

"The pants are *supposed* to be tight," said Skark, himself

wearing bright orange lipstick and a mirrored unitard. "Remember—it's a jumpsuit. It's supposed to highlight one's figure, and the best way to do that is by making it as formfitting as possible."

"Get your foot *off* of me," I said. "I was *sleeping.*"

"Ah, *now* you've woken him up and he's cranky," said Skark. "At least we got it on him before the theatrics began."

"Now. Foot. Off."

"Let him go, let him go," said Skark. "I can't handle hearing humans complain. They always skip reasonable discussion and go straight to melodrama."

Driver took his heavy foot off my body, lifted me up, and sat me down on the couch.

"Don't act like it was an assault on your modesty or some such stupid thing," said Skark. "I couldn't bear looking at your awful clothing anymore, so—though you have been a *profound* nuisance during your time on this bus—I magnanimously decided to give you a jumpsuit from my personal collection. An archival-quality item, I've been told by the curators of various museums' fashion collections. Driver did the alterations to make sure it would fit. He's a wizard with a needle and thread."

"To tell you the truth, I've always wanted to start a menswear line," said Driver. "Suits, ties, but my own haute couture version of—"

"Enough, Driver. On this bus, only my dreams are worth discussing," said Skark.

"You could have waited until I woke up instead of manhandling me," I said. "Or even better—you could have *asked* me if I wanted to wear something new and given me the chance to say no."

"Why waste the time trying to convince you to put it on if I was going to make you wear it anyway? My bus, my rules. Now stop complaining and look at yourself. You're *marvelous.*"

I looked in the mirror. Banana-yellow latex hugged every bump and ridge of my skinny body. The jumpsuit had sequined cuffs, and its neckline was cut into a sweeping V that extended to its lightning-bolt-embroidered belt, placing maximum attention on my understuffed groinal region.

"That jumpsuit is a collector's item from our 2005 tour of the Pindino Nebula," said Skark fondly. "You wouldn't *believe* how much sweat I shed in that outfit. It was murder to find a dry cleaner who could get out the stains, but it was worth it to restore it to its former majesty. Though the ensemble does seem to be missing something. Driver, are you *sure* there isn't an accessory you forgot to put on him? Some sort of bauble? I seem to remember there was more to it than just the belt with the lightning bolts."

Driver searched his pockets and pulled out a yellow headband.

"You're right, I forgot to give him this," he said.

"I *knew* there was something else," said Skark. "Wonderful."

Driver grabbed the top of my head to keep me still and pulled the headband over my ears.

"Oh God yes, *now* it's perfect," said Skark. "Details are so *important* to an outfit, don't you think? Now don't let me catch you trying to take that jumpsuit off, Bennett. That's a *personal gift* and I would be insulted. This is my peace offering for our arguments, by the way. Outsiders should never be exposed to a band's internal drama."

Skark marched to the back of the bus. Driver returned to the wheel.

I stared at myself. The jumpsuit's V-neck exposed my hairless, nonmuscular chest, while the latex made my elbows seem bonier and my legs look positively giraffelike. Hideous.

Then: *BOOM!*

The bus was walloped by a blow that flipped it on its side, followed by a second impact on the ceiling. I was hurled end over end toward Cad's pull-up bar, which I grabbed the moment before it beheaded me. One of Skark's decorative canes whizzed past me and burst open the True-Atmosphere Atmosphering Apparatus like a piñata, scattering purple powder through the room. Skark apparently had a taste for harder intoxicants than mere Spine Wine.

"Looks like we found the Dark Matter Foloptopus," said Driver. "Hold on, I'm going to try and take us in without making it mad. . . ."

"You could have *warned* us you'd come upon the Foloptopus *before* it started trying to kill us," said Skark.

"You asked me to help you with Bennett's jumpsuit. . . ."

"I would have *waited* had I known we were in a dangerous area. . . ."

BOOM BOOM BOOM

A mass blotted out the windows on the left side of the bus, and I realized it was just the *pupil* of the Foloptopus's eye. I felt like a goldfish in a pet store aquarium being scrutinized by a customer who was *really* eager to tap on the glass.

BOOM BOOM BOOM

"Driver, while this dance with death is lovely," said Skark, bracing himself against his sleeping pod, "do you *think* you could *possibly* get us into the stomach of this Foloptopus *without* letting it crack the bus open?"

I saw three sucker-covered tentacles shoot toward the windshield, and Driver jerked the wheel to avoid them. In front of us, I could see the Foloptopus's beak, and the metal slivers of other ill-fated spaceships caught in the corners of its mouth.

"Here goes, hold on," said Driver, slapping a square button at the base of the dashboard.

Cad threw open the bathroom door, holding an electric razor.

"What the *hell* is going on out here?" he said.

"I'd get out of the restroom if I were you," said Driver. "You don't want any splash back."

The bus surged forward and I lost my grip on the pull-up bar. I tumbled through the air and smacked the wall. I heard Walter *baaaaa*ing as his body thudded against the walls of the closet, and I saw Skark soar across the room and whack into Driver's bassinet, snapping it with his body, spraying splinters into my face.

Outside, there was a tremendous *squish* sound, and the bus came to an abrupt, merciful stop. Everybody was alive, barely.

Somehow, Driver, Cad, and I were piled on top of each other in the back corner of the bus, with Cad at the bottom of the tangle of bodies, his face wedged in Driver's buttocks.

"This . . . is . . . horrible . . . ," said Cad, muffled.

Skark came to the rescue, grabbing Driver and Cad and pulling them to their feet, allowing me to roll to freedom.

The bus started rocking, and from outside came a chorus of voices and *whoooooo*s:

"*Skaaaaaaaarrrrrk.*"

"*You've been my hero since I was two hundred years old, man.*"

"*I've loved your music since I was a toddler in the pouch.*"

"*Skark. I think you're my dad. I'm not even kidding. My mom has pictures of the two of you at a motel. . . .*"

I peeked out the window and saw that fans wearing Perfectly Reasonable T-shirts were surrounding the bus.

A chest-high android pushed its way through the fans. It looked like it had been constructed from hardened gelatin, its partially translucent skin revealing an inner metallic structure, while its head contained two asymmetrical eyes stacked on top of each other, giving it the appearance of an old stereo speaker. It started slapping the side of the bus with its semitransparent palm.

"You're *late*," said the android. "You're supposed to be

onstage *now.* Your crew set up hours ago, where were you? Get ready and get *out there.*"

"You were supposed to *sedate* the Foloptopus before we arrived," said Driver. "It's in our *contract.* Do you know the damage you've caused to this bus?"

"Not as much damage as I'm going to do to you unless you start playing *now.* You think it's cheap to lease space inside a Dark Matter Foloptopus? No *wonder* your band has a reputation for being unreliable."

"We're *here,* aren't we?" said Driver.

"Maybe, but if you're not out there in ten minutes, you're not getting paid. I already contacted your lawyer, so you better *hustle.*"

That struck me as interesting—the android had contacted the band's *lawyer.* Assuming the lawyer didn't have his office *inside* the Dark Matter Foloptopus, which seemed like an unlikely place for a firm, it meant that the robot had somehow reached out to another planet.

I whispered to Cad under my breath: "How, exactly, did he contact your lawyer?"

Cad looked at me like I'd suffered a head injury. "Do I have to explain the concept of a phone to you? I know you're from a hick part of New Mexico, but come on."

"There are phones that can make calls between planets?"

"You're on a *bus* with the technology to bounce between *solar systems* in a few hours," said Cad. "You don't think these aliens have figured out a way to make long-distance calls?"

At the front of the bus, Driver was reading a voluminous contract while the android stood next to him, pointing at provisions buried deep in the back.

Driver frowned. He checked his watch and turned to the rest of the band.

"The promoter is right. If we're not onstage in ten minutes, we default on our fee, which means we won't have enough money to get to the next gig."

"You're that broke?" said the android, genuinely surprised. "I thought the stories about your finances were just rumors. How could you possibly lose all the money you've earned over the years?"

"It would take me a hundred lifetimes to spend my savings," said Skark. "Now show me to the stage and let's see if we can make this Foloptopus explode from the vibrations."

"It says in the contract that if we kill the Foloptopus, we also don't get paid," said Driver.

"Then we'll stun it a bit," said Skark. "It'll be dramatic."

"If you hurt it in any way, you only get half your fee," said the android. "You can imagine the veterinary costs for providing medical care to a creature like this. Nobody wants to lose this venue."

"Fine. As an animal lover, I will do my diligence to make sure this noble creature emerges unscathed. Now please, show me to the stage. I burn for my fans."

I was upset with myself for not even *considering* using something as basic as a phone to contact Sophie, but back on Earth I wasn't accustomed to looking at stars as places that could be contacted on a whim. I needed to erase the demarcation line I had drawn in my mind between our planet and space and assume anything that had been figured out in our solar system had been figured out somewhere in the rest of creation a *long* time ago.

My plan was to call the Ecological Center for the Preservation of Lesser Species and simply explain that the Jyfos took the wrong girl and that I needed her back to go to prom and that they should keep her away from the multitudes trying to kill her in the forced Darwinism of their misguided nature game.

However, there was a problem with my mission to find a phone—even though I now knew that there had to be at least one *somewhere* in the Foloptopus, since the android had made a call, I couldn't find it. Cad hadn't been kidding when he said Skark was trying to make the Perfectly Reasonable seem tougher by booking the band to play inside the Dark Matter Foloptopus. Compared to Berdan Major Arena and its luxurious spread of backstage food, the conditions here were primitive.

The lining of the Foloptopus's gut was peppered with half-digested chunks of a charcoal-like substance—the dark matter from which the Foloptopus derived its name, I guessed, perhaps reacting with its digestive enzymes—and every few hundred feet I found myself stepping over a skeleton wearing a tattered rock T-shirt or holding a flask embossed with the logo of some alien metal group.

Clearly, only a certain hyperintense kind of band played gigs inside the Foloptopus. It seemed like the Perfectly Reasonable was out of their comfort zone, from what I had seen at the first show. While the band members were talented, I wouldn't have described them as *tough*.

The stage on which the Perfectly Reasonable was performing was in the back of the creature's stomach, and in front of it was an audience that seemed surprisingly large, considering the difficulty in reaching the venue. If I'd had to guess, I would have put the crowd size at two or three thousand fans—enough to make the belly of the Foloptopus look full. In order to create space for the crowd, workers had constructed a wall to hold back the Foloptopus's stomach acid. Green and yellow bile was lapping against the top of the wall, which looked like it needed to be ten feet higher, in my unprofessional opinion. When the Perfectly Reasonable started their show, I could see the wall shaking every time Driver hit the drums.

I was getting a bad vibe from the Foloptopus. All I wanted to do was locate a phone, make my call, climb back onto the bus, and wait out the gig until we could get the hell out of this place.

I was hustling through the Foloptopus, looking for anything that might resemble a communications center, when I saw what appeared to be a fat-necked ostrich sitting on the same kind of cinder block that had been used to construct the wall, drinking a bottle of brown, brandylike liquid. He was wearing a tool belt and his feathers were soiled. There were burn marks on his thin legs, which I guessed might be from the stomach bile. I walked over to him.

"Excuse me," I said. "Do you work here?"

"I *do* work here, as a matter of fact," he said, shaking his head in disgust and taking another swig from the bottle. "Can you believe this is my *job*? Humping construction in the gut of an animal like this? I screwed up my life somewhere along the way, man."

"Don't say that," I said, mostly because I didn't want to listen to a drunk complain about his life when I had something important to do.

"Why wouldn't I say it?" he said. "Everybody else does—my parents, my friends—so why shouldn't I? I'm saving up to use one of the time machines in Galaxy MC5-39133, so maybe I'll be able to solve my problems then, if I can ever manage to get an appointment. It seems like *everybody* in *creation* is trying to fix bad decisions they've made. I'm Thighbone, by the way. That's my nickname, because I've got these ugly legs. But you don't care. I don't see why you would, we just met."

"I'm sorry about the state of your life, Thighbone," I said. "We can talk about it more later if you want, but I need to find a phone to make an important call, and there doesn't seem to be one around."

"You can use mine if you need it," said Thighbone. "I bought an unlimited plan so I could talk to my girlfriend every night, but she broke up with me for molting in her apartment.

It was just *normal shedding,* but she thought I was going bald, and it turned her off. Romantically, you know. If that's a deal breaker for a girl, it's a deal breaker."

"Deal breaker. Sure."

"It's these stupid superficial problems that you never see coming. We'd always had intimacy issues, but does it look to you like I'm going bald? I don't see it."

Thighbone leaned forward so I could look at his scalp. His girlfriend was right, no question about it—a circle of missing feathers on the crest of his head revealed the bare pink skin underneath. He had to have been in heavy denial not to acknowledge it, but if I wanted to use his phone, I didn't see the advantage in telling him the truth.

"I'm not noticing any baldness," I said.

"That's what I'm *saying.* I don't *get* it. Sometimes I think that she wanted out of the relationship and made up an excuse. But I'm glad we broke up. No, I love her. No, I'm glad we broke up. I don't know. I'm a mess. I'm sorry, I'm distracted. Who are you trying to call?"

"The Ecological Center for the Preservation of Lesser Species."

"Ah, let me tell you—I've been down *that* road before. I hope you're not trying to buy a human as a pet, because I gave it a shot when I was attempting to win my girl back. They won't sell."

"I'm not trying to buy a human as a pet. I *am* a human, so that would be a little perverse."

"That's what I was thinking, but hey, to each his own. Everybody has weird things that they're into."

"They accidentally picked up my prom date and I need her back."

"Accidentally? No no. The Jyfos don't pick up anybody accidentally. Did they pass you over or something?"

"They did, as a matter of fact."

"I wouldn't take it personally. They probably just found something in your genes that they found alarming. *Something* in your DNA must be mutated to form that strange body. Do you have a Certified Receipt for the girl?"

"Certified Receipt?"

Thighbone cocked his head at me.

"Oh man, you don't think you're going to walk into the Ecological Center for the Preservation of Lesser Species and ask for one of their specimens without proof of ownership, do you? You need a Certified Receipt for your date if you're going to get her back."

"But she's not *mine,*" I said. "It doesn't work that way where I'm from."

"You better *pretend* she's yours, if you don't have a Certified Receipt. I'm telling you right now, it's going to be almost impossible to bluff your way through this. I've tried."

Thighbone unclipped a phone from his belt. It was a huge piece of equipment, like one of those enormous hand-cranked field telephones soldiers had hauled around in the Vietnam War. I had noticed it already, but I'd assumed it was used for carrying tools.

"You'd think they'd have streamlined this technology by now, but interplanet calls need a lot of juice," said Thighbone, dialing a number and handing me the receiver, which was even heavier than it looked. "But I know I need to upgrade. The idea of going back out on the dating scene carrying this phone is embarrassing."

The ringtone wasn't like the *bring bring bring* of Earth—instead, it sounded a bit like rain on a tin roof, which I found soothing. A brief respite from the oddness of my environment.

Somebody picked up.

"The Ecological Center for the Preservation of Lesser Species," said the Jyfo on the other end, in a singsong female voice.

"Hi. Yes. Great. Listen—I think you have a girl in your park who doesn't belong there. She's actually . . . with me."

"Wait—the new girl who runs all over the place is with you?" said the voice on the other end. *"What does that mean?"*

"She's my . . . date."

"Oh jeez. That is terrible news for us. Our ratings have gone through the roof in the last couple of days because of her, and the other members of the enclosure are finally managing to close in. Do you have a Certified Receipt for her?"

"Of course I have a Certified Receipt. I never throw away my Certified Receipts."

"At least that makes the paperwork easier. You wouldn't believe how many people call here telling us that we picked up one of their humans, only to have it turn out that they don't have Certified Receipts. Especially for this girl—the television audience has fallen in love. Everyone wants humans as exotic pets because they don't bite much and they taste great if you decide you'd rather eat them than have them in your home."

"None of that is comforting to me."

"I'll transfer you to the Ranger, but just to warn you—he's not going to be happy about this. The new girl has been great for our advertising rates. I almost wish she'd just stay alive forever."

"Me too."

I heard the *beep*s and *boop*s of different buttons being pressed, followed by hold music that was—coincidentally—an old ballad by the Perfectly Reasonable. The song seemed to be Skark singing to himself in the mirror. His voice had a lovely, innocent texture to it, different from the way he sounded now.

I'd already learned what being drunk all the time had done to his mind, but this was the first time I'd realized what it had done to his body. He was still terrifically talented, but the song on the phone was something almost *mystical*. He needed to stop it with the wine.

The phone clicked back on.

"The Ranger here," said a deeply annoyed voice. *"I hear you have a Certified Receipt for the new girl, but I hope it isn't true."*

"I do, and I want her back immediately."

"Not to criticize your decision-making skills, but maybe you should have kept an eye on her instead of letting her run around the New Mexico desert. Everybody knows that's where we get most of our humans. It's not like we try to hide it."

"She can go wherever she feels like going. I want her *back*."

"She's tired from running, and everybody wants to see the end of the hunt. You understand. All we're doing is applying your theory of survival of the fittest here."

"Put her on the *phone*," I said, losing it. "I have a right to talk to her. I want to make sure she's okay."

The Ranger grumbled. *"Let me see if I can put you through. We just started filming her for tonight's episode of her show, so keep the conversation short. Our viewers hate when humans talk on camera. Whiny voices."*

I was put on hold again.

"Is there a television around here?" I asked Thighbone, who was trying to examine his bald spot in the reflection of his brandy bottle.

"I think there's a TV in the opening band's trailer," he said, pointing at a tin shed with antennas poking out of it. "But I'm not sure they'll want you storming in. Most artists like to unwind after a show."

Hauling the heavy phone, I sprinted to the shed and barged through the door without knocking.

Inside, three skinny figures wearing suits were on the couch watching television, though I mean that loosely. Their faces were blank—no eyes, no mouths, no eyes as far as I could tell. They were probably terrible. I can't stand watching instrumental performances, even though I know I should develop an appreciation for jazz and classical compositions. I always need some vocals.

"Would you mind turning on the All-Universe Nature Channel?" I said. "I'm sorry I didn't knock, but it's important. My prom date is on and I need to make sure she's okay."

The faceless guys pointed at the screen—it seemed they were

already watching the All-Universe Nature Channel. Sophie's show was a hit.

The camera was focused on Sophie as she sat on a staircase inside the glass-ceilinged atrium of the mall. Her hair was sweatily matted to her, and her clothing was torn. She only had one shoe, but she seemed composed—no tears, no panic.

Brinnnnngggg

A phone began ringing inside the mall. The sound of it was barely audible through the television's speakers—this wasn't a full-wall set like the one I'd seen in Cad's dressing room at Berdan Major, just a normal flat screen hanging on a metal hook—but the ringing was there, echoing a moment after the rings I heard on my phone.

Brinnnnngggg

It was my call.

"Is someone there?" said Sophie, looking around the atrium. It was strange to hear her voice again. She sounded exhausted.

"Hello?" she said.

The camera tracked her as she made her way through the mall, looking over her shoulder to make sure nobody was following. She walked through a food court—passing Cinnabon, Pizza Hut, Orange Julius—the ringing of the phone increasing in volume with each step.

Sophie stopped in the doorway of a J.Crew and peeked inside. I didn't blame her for not wanting to enter. Even though the open corridors of the mall left her exposed, I could see how they seemed safer than a store, where anyone could jump out at her from under a table or behind a display case and prevent her from getting away. At least in a corridor she had room to run.

The phone continued to ring until Sophie finally dashed inside the empty store, darting around racks of cardigans and tables of jeans, and grabbed the receiver next to the register.

There was a *click* and suddenly I heard her on the other end. *"Hello? Hello hello?"*

"Sophie. It's *you.* Holy *crap.* It's Bennett Bardo."

"Bennett. Oh my God. You need to help me. I'm trapped in this mall with all these sketchy people who are after me. Where am I? What's going on? Are you here?"

"I'm not there, but I'm watching you on TV right now. Somebody is following you with a camera. . . ."

"I think I've seen the guys with cameras, but anytime I try to look at them, they hide themselves. Where am I?"

"You're in the Ecological Center for the Preserv— Never mind where you are, it's difficult to explain. You were abducted by Jyfos when we were in the desert, and now you're being hunted—but don't freak out."

"Jyfos? Being hunted? Don't freak out?"

"I'm going to find a way to get to you."

"Why haven't you come yet?"

I knew what I was about to say next wouldn't sound good.

"I'm kinda on tour with a band. . . ."

"You're on tour with a band and I'm running for my life? What's wrong with you?"

"I know it sounds bad, but it was the only way I could get into space. I'm figuring out how to get them to come for you, it's just been a little difficult. You need to trust me."

The camera rotated to reveal a group of bearded truckers and thick-armed lunch ladies lumbering into the J.Crew like catatonics. Sophie ducked behind the checkout counter.

"When will you come?"

"As soon as I can, I promise."

By this point, the band members who were sitting in the room with me appeared to be getting excited that I was *actually talking* to the subject on the screen, though it was hard to tell for sure due to their lack of faces. They were perched on the end of the couch, shaking a little, looking at the phone and back at the television screen every time Sophie and I said something to each other. I turned my back to them in some sort of attempt at privacy.

"Help me," Sophie whispered. *"They're coming in."*

"I'll be there right away. I'm going to figure out how—"

From outside the opening band's trailer came a strange vibration, followed by a series of earthquakes above and below us that shook the room and knocked the television off the wall. Something was wrong with the Dark Matter Foloptopus.

Thighbone ran inside the trailer and snatched the phone away from me.

"The dam is *coming apart*," he said.

I ran out of the trailer and stared at the structure. It was crumbling, on fire. I heard the *VRUMP* sound of the Perfectly

Reasonable stopping their set short, followed by Skark speaking to the crowd.

"Okaaaay . . . everybody stay calm," said Skark, his voice muffled by the gooey walls of the Foloptopus's stomach. "Seriously, don't worry about the dam. I *assure* you trained technicians are fixing it right now. The band and I are going to take a quick intermission and we'll be back to finish the set. . . ."

Skark turned to Cad and Driver but didn't get far enough away from the microphone, which picked up what he said next: "We need to get out of here *now*. That wall is about to come down. Head for the bus."

When the crowd saw the band turn and run, there was hysteria. Hordes of concertgoers trampled each other as they sprinted for the lot where their shuttles and spacecraft were parked—a lot located behind where I was standing, which meant the mob was rushing directly at me, howling for me to *get out of the way.*

On the other side of the stomach, I could see the Interstellar Libertine lift off from behind the stage. The band had made it inside, but I was nowhere near them and they didn't seem to care. I didn't know what to do. I couldn't push my way *against* the onrushing swarm, because I'd be knocked to the ground and crushed. But if I ran *with* the throng, I would just be moving farther from the bus.

Both options seemed terrible, so instead of picking either, I ran *away* from the mob sideways and pressed myself up against the lining of the Foloptopus's stomach, which smelled like a slab of meat that had been left out in a powerful sunbeam, rancid and old and foul.

There was a series of *pop*s from the dam, and I watched it split. A flood of bile poured through the break, dissolving concession booths and fans as it filled the Foloptopus's stomach cavity.

I had bought myself a few extra seconds of life by getting away from the path of the bile, but it would soon reach me too. I attempted to climb the walls of the Foloptopus's belly, but there were no handholds on the slick surface, and the creature was thrashing too violently for me to keep my footing.

I saw the Interstellar Libertine rotate in the air, heading in the opposite direction from where I was standing, searching for the exit.

Nobody on the bus had spotted me.

"Hey!" I shouted.

The bus drifted away.

I watched as a tidal wave of stomach acid consumed the metal lighting fixtures at the front of the stage and the merchandise stands hawking bootleg Perfectly Reasonable T-shirts and beer koozies. In the parking lot, it gobbled up the vehicles that had been unable to get off the ground before traffic snarled, and it gobbled up the vans that had crashed together in the rush to escape. The wave devoured Thighbone, who appeared to be in the middle of an argument with his ex-girlfriend, which seemed like a silly way to spend one's final moments.

The bile pooled near me in the dents and craters of the Foloptopus's stomach, steadily getting closer.

It was all deeply unfair. I had always considered high school a purgatory that I had to endure while waiting for real life to begin, but if I was to perish *here,* it would turn out high school *had* been my life. That was it. I had gotten *so far,* found my way into space, figured out where Sophie was being held, and made *contact* with her. Part of me was beginning to believe that I was going to be a hero, but if this was the way things ended, I would exit outer space the same way that I went into it—thinking about a girl.

The bile lapped against the toes of my shoes, melting the soles. The smell reminded me of Gordo High seniors peeling through the parking lot in their cars trying to run over frosh—and occasionally me, if they were in the mood.

Then the bile dissolved the rest of me. There's no other way to put it. Perhaps I was in too much shock to feel any pain, but it was actually a warm feeling, like going to sleep from my toes on up.

I died. It's not a pleasant memory.

If the first kiss of my life had been something like a dream comprised of pure, pharmaceutical-grade joy, my second kiss made me never want to do it again. My eyes were closed when I was overcome with the smell of stale makeup and the sensation of having two alcohol-lubricated slugs pressing against my face.

I heard Skark's voice, which sounded very far away, like he was speaking to me through a long tin tunnel.

"Just to make it clear," he said. "I didn't *want* to do that, but I've often been told my kiss is magic, so get up. You've cost this band almost all the money it has left, so the least you can do is awaken. And my God, put on some ChapStick once in a while. Not for my benefit, but for yours."

I opened my eyes, whereupon I saw Skark's painted eyes a few centimeters from my own, his long, pointed face filling my field of vision like an out-of-focus head shot.

"And . . . he's back," said Skark, waving a bottle of Spine Wine above his head. "I *told you* my lips have life-restoring powers. My father was a mortician. When I was bored when I was young, I used to kill time by bringing corpses back to life."

"That explains a little bit," said Cad.

"All art has to come from somewhere," said Skark.

". . . How long have you been doing that?" I said groggily. I still wasn't sure where I was or what was going on.

"A minute or so," said Skark.

"A full minute?"

"Barely a heartbeat compared to my normal Tantric indulgences," said Skark. "Don't act like this is something I found *pleasurable.* I have *always* preferred ladies, but when a little pro bono medical attention is required, I don't mind stepping up to do my part. Plus, you were *dead,* so a little *thanks* would be appreciated, *particularly* because you're uninsured, as we've discovered."

"I'm on my parents' insurance," I said.

"Do you really think they take Blue Cross Blue Shield of New Mexico up here?" said Cad.

I looked around and saw I was in some sort of hospital room—there were squiggly charts hanging on the wall, and a variety of ominous, pointy metal instruments on a side table next to my "bed," which was less a bed than it was a receptacle coated in the dregs of a gooey pineapple-colored liquid. A pair of thin broadcloth scrubs covered my otherwise naked body. Skark, Cad, and Driver were standing under a lamp that was emitting a bright lime-green light, making everyone in the room look vaguely puppetlike.

"What . . . happened?" I said.

"It was *Ferguson* who sabotaged us," said Skark, sounding even more unstable and emphatic than usual. His eyes were dilated, and it seemed like he was on something stronger than just Spine Wine.

"Ferguson had nothing to do with it," said Driver. "We know you went searching the hospital for pills during Bennett's operation. Whatever you took is increasing your paranoia."

"I heard *explosions* before that dam came down," said Skark. "Ferguson's letters used to describe *fantasies* about him watching me perish in the stomach of a giant beast while he played his triangle, *ding*ing it slowly as he enjoyed the sight of my body being eaten away. I swear I heard those *ding*s today."

A doctor poked what I assumed was his head into the room. He was round-bodied and unclothed except for bands of fabric around his chest and waist. It looked a bit like he was wearing a woman's bathing suit, but perhaps that was just what surgeons wore up here. His head was a set of jaws opening and snapping shut, like the snout of an alligator, but missing the rest of the skull. I couldn't figure out where his eyes were located, and the only reason I knew that he was male was that Cad said *hey, man* when he entered the room.

"How are you doing in here?" said the doctor.

"A little rattled, but fine, I think," I said.

"Good boy," said the doctor. "I kept thinking that I was getting your proportions wrong during the rebuilding process, but your genes were saying that's actually the way you're *supposed* to look. Amazing."

The doctor's jaws opened and closed rapidly as he cackled to himself, and he ducked out of the room.

"What happened to me?" I said.

"You were dissolved inside the Dark Matter Foloptopus, and we brought you back," said Cad.

"What do you mean, brought me back?"

"We were coming to *get* you in the bus when all of a sudden we saw you get swallowed up by the bile," said Cad.

"If you had stayed alive another few seconds, it would have saved us a lot of money," said Driver.

"We used this really high-end Tupperware we keep around for some of Driver's more disgusting meals to scoop up a little of the stomach acid from where you disappeared, and we brought it here," said Cad. "It was pretty foul. The doctors had to reconstruct you from your DNA."

"Personally, I think they did a great job," said Driver. "The new cells really cleared up your complexion."

"Wait . . . this isn't even my *real body*?"

"Oh, like you would have been able to tell the difference if we hadn't told you," said Skark, rolling his eyes. "The doctors said it was actually a fairly simple reconstruction—none of your thoughts or memories were particularly profound, so they were easy to recover from what was left of your cells."

I spotted another chart tacked up on the wall. It appeared to be a page that had been ripped from an extraterrestrial anatomy textbook, with an illustrated figure of a human male in the middle of the sheet, surrounded by arrows pointing to sensitive parts of the body and cryptic symbols that I couldn't understand. The aliens had clearly learned something from all the people they had abducted, though I saw that the figure had no nipples, which concerned me. I put my hand on my chest to confirm mine were there.

"Yeah, I made sure the doctors gave you your nipples back," said Cad. "They weren't going to do it because it wasn't in their chart, but I showed them mine, and they figured it out."

"Thank you," I said.

"Speaking of which—the doctors said there's a *chance* that some other DNA got mixed up with yours," said Driver. "There were a lot of fans getting dissolved, a lot of acid sloshing around—you were there, you understand."

"If you start feeling strange or develop any abnormal powers, that's probably why," said Skark. "Just ride it out and try not to get too *angry* about things—that's normally when odd conditions flare up."

I pulled my body to a sitting position. It seemed great—all my parts *felt* new, like I'd received a head-to-toe tune-up. Dying wasn't so bad if this was what you got to come back to.

Skark produced another bottle of Spine Wine from somewhere, and with a series of *glug*s emptied its entire contents down his throat. It was the most that I'd seen him consume at one time. His movements were frantic one moment, lethargic the next.

"Another," said Skark. "There must be alcohol somewhere in this hospital. Somebody find me another bottle. I hate hospitals. And I hate it even more when I have to be in one because of *Ferguson.* Thank God I found those pills in a *drawww-errrrr. . . ."*

He started slurring. I watched him use the edge of my tub to keep himself upright.

"You shouldn't have taken those pills," said Driver. "You don't even know what they were."

"I'm *fiiiine . . . ,"* said Skark. "By the *waaaaay,* did the *rooaadieeees* make it *oouut?"*

Driver frowned. "They made it out, but they quit their jobs, citing dangerous working conditions. And they took our gear as payment for lost wages."

"So we don't have our instruments?" said Cad.

"That's correct," said Driver. "We have nothing, except Skark's wardrobe, which none of the roadies wanted."

"At least there's *thaaaaat.* This is all Ferguson's *faaauuult,*" said Skark, and with that, he passed out and fell to the ground, mouth stained red.

"Good *Lord,* he's got a drinking problem," I said.

"Not even Skark's body can handle Spine Wine combined with whatever pills he took," said Cad. "This isn't the first time we've seen this. He'll be out for hours."

"Hours?"

"Most likely," said Cad.

"As in, *many* hours? Enough time to make a side trip?"

I looked at Cad and Driver. They could see what I was thinking.

"Any pit stops, and we'll be cutting it close getting to Dondoozle, if we make it in time at all," said Driver.

"This is his *prom date* we're talking about," said Cad.

"It'll really piss off Skark," said Driver.

"Reason enough for me," said Cad.

"All right, everybody grab a limb—we're going to have to get Skark out of here," said Driver. "Bennett, you need to wear those scrubs until we find you another outfit. We couldn't track down any underwear for you, but you'll have to deal with it for now."

It was then that it occurred to me that I'd just been totally *remade,* and therefore all my *appendages* were new.

I peeked under the scrubs to make sure everything was fully intact down there.

"How does it look?" said Cad.

"Honestly, maybe better than before," I said.

"Good," said Cad. "When the doctor was doing the reconstruction, I told him to give you a little extra *pop*. Glad he listened."

"I am forever grateful," I said. "Truly."

Driver grabbed Skark's arm.

"Help me lift him," he said. "It's time to get your girl."

WEDNESDAY

Before we got to Jyfon, home of the Ecological Center for the Preservation of Lesser Species, Driver gave me the background on Certified Receipts, which were important in space due to widespread smuggling between planets. Because a lesser creature on one planet might be considered a pet or food on a world with larger, more aggressive organisms, the Certified Receipt was the only way to prove you *weren't* somebody else's property.

Apparently in the rest of the universe all creatures were issued a Certified Receipt when they were born, and every creature was supposed to carry it around for his or her or its entire life, or until he or she or it gave it to somebody else. Because of the disparity of economic conditions in different galaxies, it was common for aliens to rent themselves out as indentured servants on other worlds, which meant handing over their Certified Receipts. If somebody had your Certified Receipt, they had you.

When I pointed out that nobody issues Certified Receipts on Earth, Driver explained that backwater planets like Earth weren't part of the standardized Certified Receipt program because they had no affiliation with any larger governing body, so everybody tended to look the other way. However, not adhering to the Certified Receipt system didn't exempt humans from having to show proof of self-ownership. In most situations, showing a legal birth certificate would suffice—I guess a birth certificate *is* just a receipt, in a way—though it might take some time to check with the proper authorities back on Earth and verify that such a document was authentic.

"Are you telling me I'm supposed to be carrying around my birth certificate to prove that I own *myself*?"

"That's exactly what I'm saying," said Driver. "All of us have to."

"Do you have yours, Cad?"

"Wouldn't be caught dead without it," said Cad. "Shore Memorial Hospital in Somers Point, New Jersey. We picked it up before I came on tour. Have to be careful—you know how much some aliens would pay for a handsome human blessed with the gift of music?"

"What about you, Driver?"

Driver showed me his Certified Receipt—it was a laminated rectangle of green paper, resembling a bookmark, with a bunch of words and numbers I couldn't read.

"It's a pain to carry around, but not as much of a pain as trucking across the galaxy to the Office of Documentation and Proof of Ownership if you lose it."

"The system seems broken," I said.

"What system doesn't?"

The Interstellar Libertine vibrated and popped out of its latest space rift, and Driver took his foot off the accelerator to make sure we didn't overshoot our destination. As we drifted toward Jyfon, we began seeing what appeared to be three-dimensional billboards promoting the Ecological Center for the Preservation of Lesser Species.

The boards—if I can call them that, because they weren't made of any solid material—were free-floating, high-resolution, mile-long pixelated images that changed form every few seconds, their atoms artfully arranging themselves into mirages of odd creatures sitting in open fields or underground caves. All of the animals had looks on their faces like they were being forced to sit still and smile for the camera. I even thought I saw the tip of a weapon at the edge of one photo, but it might have just been somebody's finger on the camera lens.

An image of a greasy ball of nervous lemon-lime fur melted into a shot of a silver-skinned brick of an alien wearing a head-dress made of strawberry-colored animal skins. The picture liquefied again, and I knew the subject of the next shot even before all the particles snapped into place.

It was an image of Sophie, wide-eyed and looking over her shoulder as she ran past the front door of an Olive Garden.

Apparently the Jyfos hadn't been able to coerce her into the same kind of fake-casual photo as easily as they had the other residents of the Ecological Center.

"Looks like Sophie's become a tourist attraction in her short time here," said Cad. "Which won't make it any easier to get her out."

"Thanks for making that point," I said.

"I'm just saying, it would be hard to roll into the San Diego Zoo and ask them to hand over a penguin," said Cad.

"Maybe the rules are different for research centers," I said.

"It would be just as difficult to show up at Princeton and ask for one of their study monkeys," said Cad.

"Is that some kind of passive-aggressive Princeton comment?" I said.

Cad and Driver stared at me.

"What are you talking about?" said Driver.

"I got wait-listed at Princeton," I said. "I thought I already told you guys about that."

Cad and Driver shook their heads.

"As long as you get into other places, being on the wait list isn't such a big deal," said Cad.

I didn't say anything. Cad and Driver looked at me.

"You didn't get in anywhere else?" said Driver.

"I didn't apply."

"You didn't *apply* anywhere else?" said Driver, incredulous.

Cad and Driver were stunned. As far as I knew, neither of them had even been to college, and *they* couldn't believe I had only applied to one place. I didn't even know how Driver *knew* about Princeton. Maybe Cad had mentioned it to him before because of the New Jersey connection. I felt humiliated.

Our final descent toward Jyfon was what I imagine approaching Vegas would be like—rows of lights hanging in the sky guiding the way, more boards featuring strange creatures interspersed with the occasional unflattering candid shot of Sophie, and finally the distant panorama of a city rising up out of the blackness of absolutely nothing. It was easy to discern the location of the Ecological Center—80 percent of the planet was gray skyscrapers and grids of electricity, in the middle of which was an egg-shaped wilderness of magenta and malachite fields. At the bottom of the reservation was a building shaped like an X.

"Guess that's the welcome center," said Driver.

We plunged through the atmosphere, down into a lot that was—to our surprise, given the amount of promotion hanging in the ether around Jyfon—completely empty, like a theme park in a ghost town. I would have thought the place was closed, except for the fact that through the windshield, I could see the front doors of the Ecological Center for the Preservation of Lesser Species rising up over us, thirty feet tall, utterly open.

"And here we are," said Driver. "Good luck in there."

"You're not *coming*?"

"We need to find some instruments," said Driver. "We brought you where you had to go, but this is still a tour."

"Just go in there, tell them what you want, and if they ask about the Certified Receipt, give them this," said Cad, putting a brick of cash in my hands.

The bills looked like euros—brightly colored, different-sized paper rectangles featuring ink-drawn portraits of illustrious aliens. I've never been to Europe, but whenever the news does a report on a crumbling economy over there, I've found myself admiring the aesthetic of the currency.

"I thought you spent the money from the Foloptopus gig on my medical care," I said.

"This isn't from the Foloptopus gig," said Driver. "This is Skark's personal nest egg."

"He hides his money in one of his platform heels," said Cad. "He thinks we don't know about it, but we do, and we need gear and you need your girl."

"What if paying them off doesn't work?" I said.

"We'll swoop in and help you out," said Cad. "Just hold on, we won't take long."

Driver slid open the door to the bus. I tucked the brick of cash into the pocket of my scrubs. Driver had given me the choice of some of Skark's other jumpsuits, but the scrubs were more comfortable and looked less ridiculous, so I had kept them on. I stepped outside onto the paved earth of Jyfon, and immediately I was hit by the scent of animals—hair, saliva, waste. This was the place.

I walked through the entrance to the Ecological Center for the Preservation of Lesser Species, which led to a long hallway where a female Jyfo was sitting behind a counter, flipping through a magazine and occasionally adjusting her glasses. She looked a bit like Driver wearing a wig, which I took to mean that the Viking dogcatchers who had snatched Sophie had to be nearby.

She looked up at me as I walked toward her, fake smile on my face, attempting to seem casual.

"Welcome to the Ecological Center for the Preservation of Lesser Species," she said. "Can I help you?"

I didn't respond, just kept smiling while I thought about what to do. Because I didn't actually have a Certified Receipt for Sophie, I figured I only had a few options:

I could lie and say that I had lost the Certified Receipt but I still wanted her back, which—in a best-case scenario—would lead to them taking me out to see her, at which point she would run to me and leap into my arms and the Jyfos would recognize that we were supposed to be together and let us go. This seemed unlikely.

If the Jyfo behind the desk insisted on seeing the Certified Receipt, I could subdue her by force, hijack whatever kind of vehicle they used in the facility, and hope I managed to find Sophie and get her back to the bus before the Ranger and the scientists tracked me down and made me part of the center's ecosystem. This was my least favorite option, both because I wouldn't know where I was going and because I didn't like the idea of manhandling a lady, even one who weighed several hundred pounds more than me and who was holding my date hostage.

Finally, I could bypass the Certified Receipt situation entirely and simply offer my bribe in exchange for Sophie's release. The problem with *this* option was that I knew Sophie had become a popular attraction, and a low-level employee might not want to subject herself to the kind of scrutiny that came with letting a star exhibit go. Nor might she even have the power to do so.

None of the options were good. I was going to have to wing this.

"Can I help you?" said the woman behind the counter once again, impatiently this time. I recognized her voice—she was the Jyfo I had talked to on the phone.

"Yeah, we spoke before. I've come to pick up Sophie, the new human."

"Right right. I've already let the Ranger know that you're coming. I can't guarantee he'll be in a good mood when you see him. You've thrown quite the kink into his research."

"I'm sure he'll be able to continue his research without her. It seems like you've got a well-stocked facility."

"Sure, but we've never seen anybody run like her. We never could have *imagined* a human could be so wily—she's rewriting our opinion of your species."

"She does mud runs."

"I don't know what those are."

"It's not important."

"Show me your Certified Receipt and I can start processing the paperwork for her release."

"About that Certified Receipt . . . I *have* a Certified Receipt for her. The *problem* is that I had to leave Earth in a hurry, and I left the Certified Receipt at my *house,* so I don't have it *on me.* But I do have it, and I can *send* it to you later, for your records. If you have a fax machine, something like that . . ."

"The center is very particular about paperwork."

"I'm sure, and I was *hoping* I could make a *donation* to the park in order to make up for the fact that I perhaps wasn't as prepared as I could have been, and to facilitate the documentation process."

"It's rare that we take donations at the gate."

"If a donation to the park isn't satisfactory, maybe I could make a donation to a charity of your own *personal* choosing. Or I could just *give* you the money and allow you to donate it as you see fit. I'm not from here, so I'm not familiar with your causes."

"You'd want to give me the money directly?"

I put Skark's brick of cash on the counter in front of her.

"Are you trying to bribe me?" she said.

"No no no. Forgive me for giving you that impression. Again, I'm not from here, so I'm not familiar with the customs. I'm thinking of it more as an expediting fee."

The receptionist eyed the money and then looked up at me.

"I see," she said. "An expediting fee. We don't call it exactly *that,* but I understand how you would want your friend returned immediately."

"I appreciate that."

"And it is a *generous* donation," said the receptionist, looking at the money. "Will you be reporting this contribution on your taxes, by any chance? I'd prefer to not deal with any extra forms."

"Of course not," I said. "I choose to keep my charitable donations private. You can do with it what you like."

She smiled.

"Well then, I don't see any problem with you sending me the Certified Receipt at a later point," she said.

"Thank you for understanding my situation. If it ever happens again, I'll make sure I have my paperwork in order before my arrival."

The receptionist took the money off the counter and surreptitiously slid it into the desk in front of her.

"I'll call the Ranger and tell him you showed me your Certified Receipt. Just make sure to keep your hands inside the vehicle. Remember—there are a lot of exhibits here, and out in the open you're food. There's a reason nobody comes anymore."

"It's not safe?"

The receptionist leaned in close to me.

"Visitors don't come here anymore because of *him*," she said. "I suggest you get your girl and get out as quickly as possible, or you might not be leaving at all."

I waited for the Ranger in a clearing behind the welcome center, standing next to a garden filled with iridescent roses and mother-of-pearl bonsai trees. Beautiful. A small section of the enclosure had been set aside for exotic grasses, so I plucked a handful and shoved it into an inside pocket of my scrubs to give to Walter later on. I had no idea if the grasses would be good for him or not, but I remembered seeing some rams at a farm when I was young, and it seemed like they could digest anything.

After a few minutes, I saw the Ranger driving toward me in a vehicle that was a cross between an amphibious duck boat and a Sherman tank. What looked like a surgeon's mask was hanging from his neck, but instead of a lab coat, he was wearing a suede jacket with thin strips of leather hanging from the elbows. He resembled a combination of mad scientist and western-wear enthusiast. The horns on his skull were catching the sun, and his forehead was as polished as a leprechaun's pot. No doubt—this was one of the Jyfos I had watched kidnap Sophie.

The Ranger accelerated as he drew closer, threatening to run me over. At the very last moment, he turned the wheel hard, skidding to a stop a few inches from my feet. I'd seen the bullies in my high school use the same intimidation technique.

"Are you the guy who had the Certified Receipt?" he said.

"Yeah. I already gave it to the front desk."

"I have to say, I'm deeply disappointed you showed up. I've never seen a human able to run like this female, but she's starting to tire. We all wanted to see what would happen when she had to make a stand."

"You realize that using a girl as bait in a game of death isn't normal human behavior, right?"

"*Bait* sounds so crass," said the Ranger.

"It's true, though."

"From our studies, your culture seems to love violence, love the chase. We're just giving the rest of the universe a chance to see it play out."

"You shouldn't have taken her."

"My actions were all in the name of science. Get in. I'll give you a tour of the place and get you out of here."

"I don't want a tour. I want Sophie."

"*Everybody* gets a tour. We do good work here, and we like to show it off. Who doesn't like a tour? Feeling the wind whip through your scrubs. What's the deal with those anyway?"

"I lost my other clothes," I said.

"That's too bad," he said. "It's good to have a little more protection from the elements out here."

It was a ghastly ride. The park's unpaved roads were peppered with craters shooting hot air that scorched my skin and dried my eyes, and the Ranger seemed intent on driving his vehicle over every one of them. Each time the front wheels smacked into a new pothole, I thought the ground would crumble beneath us and we would disappear into a pool of boiling water.

"Is this road safe?" I said.

"Nooooo, but I take tourists out here all the time as a special treat," said the Ranger. "There's some wildlife I want to show you, since your visit is so unexpected and unique."

"I don't need to see any new things," I said.

"I don't know what is with your species's reluctance to travel and have new experiences," said the Ranger. "You go back and forth to your moon a few times a couple generations and you think you have the right to call yourselves adventurers. It's tremendously arrogant."

The Ranger's vehicle approached a field of glass littered with circular cracks, as if heavy stones had been dropped on it from high above. A sign depicting a Jyfo being eaten by a blood-drenched monster was posted in front of the area.

"Here at the Ecological Center for the Preservation of Lesser Species, we care for over ninety thousand endangered animals from forty thousand worlds," said the Ranger. "Our primary goal is to save these species from climate problems, wars, and poachers—and in your case, *yourselves*—while also preserving the animals for future scientific research. You never know when a species that might have gone extinct will turn out to be the cure for one of our diseases or something helpful like that."

"Are you talking about grinding up humans and using them for medicine?"

"Or applying them topically—you can't foresee what the use might be," said the Ranger. "I'm not saying we *would* do that, because we're a conservation society, but when an inhabitant passes away—"

"The bait, you mean."

The Ranger rolled his eyes at hearing me use the word *bait* again. He pointed at the field of glass. There didn't seem to be anything out there. I didn't know why we were stopping.

"Here we go. I wanted you to see this," said the Ranger. "Because we slowed down, it's going to *think* it's feeding time, so I suspect it won't be long before we witness some activity."

"Who's *it*? What do you mean, feeding ti—"

VOOSH. The field of glass sucked up into itself and shot upward, twisting into the air to form a monster as tall as a church and made entirely of mirrors.

In a single violent movement, the beast leaped forward, coming to a hard stop directly over us. I could feel it staring at me, but I didn't know where its eyes were. Every part of the mirrored creature was reflecting the image of the Ranger and me sitting in the vehicle back at us.

"That," said the Ranger, "is the Palapar Glass Cloduron of the Cloverleaf Quasar. Extremely dangerous, incredible appetite, extraordinarily low IQ, which makes it impossible to reason with once its emotions overtake it. Needless to say, we should *truly* not be here, but I thought you might want to check it out."

"Bragh," said the Cloduron, rearing up on its haunches. Its teeth were shards of broken quartz and its breath smelled like burning sand.

"Thanks for the *opportunity*," I said. "But I think I don't need to check it out any more than we already *have,* so let's *go.*"

"Come now, don't tell me you can't appreciate the *beauty* of the Cloduron. The sheer *unlikelihood* that evolution would somehow produce a hundred-foot-tall killing machine made of glass. Even in a universe with an almost infinite number of worlds . . . it's remarkable."

The Cloduron straddled our vehicle, its head hovering above us. Abruptly, a glob of diamond mucus the size of a football fell from its nose and landed on the vehicle's grille, smashing a headlight.

"Ah, *dammit*," said the Ranger. "Sometimes that happens when the Cloduron is feeling under the weather. Its nose gets runny, but no vets will come out to see it because it kills all of them instantly."

"Bragh bragh," said the Cloduron.

"You're probably wondering why you can't understand him even though you've no doubt had your share of Spine Wine by now, since you can understand me," said the Ranger.

"I was wondering why we're not *leaving*. I don't *care* why I can't understand him. I have *no reason* to talk to this thing."

"The answer may surprise you," said the Ranger, ignoring me. "You see, Clodurons have no formal language. We think that they communicate with each other by reflecting patterns of light, but we're not sure. It's hard to do research on them for the same reason it's difficult to get vets to see them—they're psychopaths."

"Bragh bragh bragh," said the Cloduron, lunging at our vehicle with its open mouth, serrated tongue lashing forward, about to cut my head clean off. I jumped back in my seat and covered my eyes when suddenly bullets rang out around me, shattering the Cloduron's elbow and three of its teeth.

The Cloduron howled, retreated from the shots, and collapsed back onto itself. As quickly as it had come to life, it flattened out and once again became a field of glass.

"Exciting stuff, huh?" said the Ranger, holstering the enormous black-and-blue pistol he had pulled out of his belt.

152

"Does that happen every time you drive past here?" I said. Sweat was drenching my scrubs.

"Yes, most of the time, the Cloduron gets a little pissy when I ride past," said the Ranger. "Today was a particularly showy display."

"And you shoot it every time it rears up?" I said. "Isn't that a little counterproductive to conservation?"

The Ranger grew somber, and stared at the puddle of mirrors stretching out in front of him.

"I have no sympathy for it," said the Ranger. "This beast ate my partner."

And that's when I said something I shouldn't have.

"The guy with the orange clipboard?" I said.

The question just popped out. Having watched the Ranger and his partner take Sophie away, I must have gotten excited at the thought that one of them might have met his fate in the jaws of another specimen they had kidnapped.

The Ranger trained his eyes on me.

"How, exactly, do you know my partner carried an orange clipboard?"

"I don't know," I said, scrambling for a way to cover my tracks. "I just thought since you're doing research . . ."

Recognition crossed the Ranger's face.

"I *knew* it—you were *there* the night we picked up the girl, weren't you?" he said. "I thought I remembered seeing you on our scanner while we were flying over. It was you and the girl, but we only took her. Our readings said your brain wasn't fully developed."

"My brain is developed."

"No no, we definitely got a reading that your decision-making skills were subpar."

"You can't know that from a scan. I've always done great in school."

"If I remember correctly, our equipment said you only applied to one college. Anybody whose brain was fully developed would never do that kind of thing."

Impressive technology.

The Ranger tapped his fingers on the steering wheel and then gripped it tightly. I could tell he was boiling inside at having me in his vehicle, and I anticipated him lunging at any moment. I pressed my back against the door, which felt icy through my scrubs.

"You don't mind if we head back to the front desk so I can check out your Certified Receipt with my own eyes?" said the Ranger. "Not that I don't trust you. It would only be to cover my ass for administrative reasons, of course."

I paused a moment too long.

"And there it is," he said. "I *knew* you were lying about the Certified Receipt."

"Whether I have a piece of paper or not, I want my date *back,*" I said. "You had no right to do what you did. She's not *bait.* She's important to me."

"As someone who did a graduate thesis on human culture, let me say this—we have as much of a right to do what we did as humans have when they haul a gorilla out of the jungle or a lion off of the plains. We do this for the preservation of your species."

The Ranger fell quiet for a moment, thinking. He loosened his grip on the wheel.

"But I appreciate that you've come so far to get her, and I believe you when you say her return holds a special importance to you."

"Thank you," I said warily. He was changing his tone, but something wasn't right about this.

"We Jyfos may have pleasant exteriors, but I'll tell you a little secret—our hearts are even warmer than our smiles," said the Ranger, not grinning. "I'll take you to the female right away."

"If you want, another ranger can take me," I said. "It's a big park—I'm sure you've got extra staff."

"Oh, I'm the only Ranger," he said. "This is my world."

He put his foot on the gas, and the vehicle zipped down the path, though this time he avoided the potholes he had been crashing into on purpose before, and his mood seemed to be lighter—maybe all I really had had to do was be honest with him.

I briefly allowed myself to think that he might have a wife or a girlfriend at home and could probably identify with not wanting to see somebody you care about abducted by a race with superior technology. My heart rate slowed, and against my better judgment—or against any judgment at all—I relaxed slightly.

"Thinking about all of this, I've got to say—I didn't realize she was your *date*," said the Ranger. "A date. Wow. That's much more important than a Certified Receipt, in my opinion. It's just that she's so much more *attractive* than you, and it seems impossible to wrap my head around how you ended up with her. I'm not even human and I can tell she's *way* out of your league."

"I guess the heart is tough to study."

"Nah, you just cut it out of the chest cavity," said the Ranger. "Where are you two going on this date?"

"Prom."

"Prom . . . that's dancing, right?"

"There's dancing."

"And a fruit beverage."

"Sometimes there's punch, sure."

"I read about this in one of my grad school textbooks. The males dress in black and look the same, while the females wear bright colors and paint their faces and smear color on their lips."

"Guys wear tuxedos and girls put on makeup, if that's what you mean."

"Fascinating. I'm not just saying that."

We reached a tall fence, beyond which were the boxy buildings and tasteful Spanish tile roofs of the massive mall complex. I could see a fountain illuminated by neon lights in the entrance's circular courtyard, behind which was a Bloomingdale's and a Tiffany. The buildings nearby held a Gucci and—most impressive to me—the largest Brookstone I had ever seen. I couldn't help but think how good a vibrating massage chair would feel at that moment.

I had to hand it to the Jyfos—kidnappers or not, they had faithfully reconstructed a high-end mall.

A plump man in a ripped polo shirt was hitting golf balls, practicing his short game on the manicured lawn near the gate.

The Ranger stopped his makeshift jeep, hopped out the side, and walked over to a door in the fence. The golfer began lumbering toward him, curious about the reason for his visit.

"Are we going in there?" I said.

"Of course we are, that's where your date is."

"Can't you call her over? I'm not sure I want to get in a cage with a man holding a golf club who is used to hunting down whatever new person you throw at him."

"A man who thinks about golfing when he could be participating in the hunt isn't someone you have to worry about," said the Ranger. "Besides, your girl is too deep in the enclosure to just call her over. We have to go to the source and root her out. She's a spunky one."

The Ranger whistled as he unclipped a ring of keys from his belt and unlocked the gate.

"Come on now," he said. "Nobody waits in the car on my watch. That's no way to experience *nature.*"

I climbed out of the vehicle and cautiously joined the Ranger, keeping an eye on the golfer, who had stopped walking and was tapping his club on the ground threateningly, staring at me.

"How about this—if you can go in and get Sophie by yourself, I'll wait out here," I said to the Ranger.

"Don't you want to see what we designed for your fellow humans? It's quite authentic. I'll call off the hordes, I promise."

"From where I'm standing, it looks like you did an amazing job, and I am *glad* to check out any literature that you have. . . ."

The Ranger opened the gate, pulled his pistol, and fired pot-shots at the feet of the golfer—*bang bang bang*—forcing him to retreat from the fence. The golfer jumped away from the bullets and scurried off, looking back at us as he went.

"So just to reiterate, if I could wait out here, that would be great," I said.

The Ranger picked me up by the back of the neck and looked at me.

"Then you should have brought a *Certified Receipt.* Don't you understand we're trying to *help* your species? Someone needs to think about you if you won't think about yourselves," he said, and chucked me inside the fence.

I never actually made it inside the mall; instead, I was forced to take shelter at a freestanding McDonald's, where the Jyfos had constructed the most impressive PlayPlace I had ever seen. It was a solid square mile of climbing walls, four-story slides, zip lines, underground tunnels, foam castles, and—fortunately for me—a ball pit the size of an Olympic swimming pool, where I was hiding.

But let me backtrack for a moment.

Upon my initial entry into the enclosure, the golfer chased me until he exhausted himself, after which I was followed by a

Boy Scout troop that had obviously been abducted years ago and outgrown their uniforms, parts of which they now wore stitched to the back of their Gap jean jackets like some sort of motorcycle gang. They tried to corner me near the entrance to a Macy's, but it had been a long time since their hiking days, and they ran out of breath quickly. I left them behind.

I had never witnessed such an unhealthy group of individuals as those trapped in the enclosure. Jyfo scientists must have looked at the fact that fast-food restaurants could be found in any city and concluded they were a basic food source. As everyone in the enclosure became overweight and sweaty and aggressive toward their fellow inhabitants, the Jyfos perhaps concluded this was a matter of course for the human race.

Before I go on, let me make it clear that in *no way* do I have anything against people who are out of shape. And had I been stuck in the mall with the same food choices to which these cooped-up residents were subjected, I'm sure I too would have eventually found myself sitting around, staring down at my soft, ever-growing belly made of concentrated boredom and saturated fat.

Running through the enclosure, my pursuers reminded me of dogs barking at each other to give warning.

"New arrival on the way."

"Coming in your direction."

I sprinted toward the yellow McDonald's *M* for no other reason than that it was the tallest thing around, a towering sign outside the main mall, standing like a roadside beacon.

As soon as I dove in, I knew that taking refuge in the

PlayPlace ball pit was a poor strategic choice—if my pursuers found me, they would have the high ground, and the lack of secure footing meant I wouldn't be able to quickly escape. But I was getting tired, and for the moment I thought I had created enough distance from my antagonists to buy a few minutes to catch some labored breaths among the plastic spheres.

Peering through the spaces between the balls, I could see an old hippie holding a wrench lumber out of the fast-food restaurant, responding to the commotion. He looked like a man who had been abducted straight from 1960s Haight-Ashbury—tie-dyed T-shirt, ratty gray beard, chewed-up sandals. A burnout on an epic scale. I wondered if he knew he was actually in space, or if he thought he was really, really high. If he had survived this long, he must have been doing something right—but then again, he might also just be an old guy who had disappeared, and now here he was.

"I think I saw him running toward the McDonald's," said a voice in the distance.

"He's not over here, man," said the hippie. "I checked out the entire *restaurant,* and it's clear."

"You checked the playground too?" said the voice.

"I checked *everything.* I am the *manager* of this McDonald's. When an outside element has been introduced, I can *feel* it."

"Hanging out at a fast-food restaurant all day doesn't make you the manager. Get out here and help us look."

The hippie grumbled to himself and toddled off to join the other idiots.

I was trying to figure out how the dynamics inside the enclosure actually worked. It seemed the society here was built from a mixture of cliques—for instance, this hippie was clearly part of a group for which he was guarding the McDonald's, though he must have been the low guy on the totem pole to so willingly slink off to join the others when summoned. Everywhere you looked, there were individuals and allied twosomes doing their own thing. That the man who had greeted me was a *golfer* casually practicing his chipping appeared to be indicative of something—the Jyfos had set up a game to the death, and from what I had seen on television, Sophie was definitely being pursued, but it seemed like a great number of the inhabitants were too lazy to *really* get involved. Maybe they were just too comfortable to want to go home.

I bided my time in the ball pit, making sure the orbs were completely covering the top of my head so I couldn't be seen, and pondered where Sophie might be and what to do next.

I heard the voice of the Ranger blaring out of the speakers installed around the mall.

"Creatures! There are two new inhabitants of your terrarium—the girl, of whom you are already aware, and the girl's dancing date, believe it or not. If you eliminate one or both of them, you will get to return to Earth on our next expedition, and choose a friend to come along. How fun for you. I'm not too happy with these two individuals, if you couldn't have guessed."

I heard hooting and shouting—the barbarians were pleased now that they had two targets instead of just one—but the commotion was coming from far away. I realized I might be alone. I listened again, waiting until I was sure *nobody* was around before poking my head out of the ball pit. I opened my mouth to suck in an unobstructed gulp of oxygen . . .

. . . and nearly choked when a French fry shot at me out of nowhere, bounced off my tongue, and lodged in my throat.

"*Ghag,*" I coughed, trying to hack it out.

A whisper: *"Bennett . . . is that you?"*

It was her voice, no question.

"Sophie?"

I looked around, but I couldn't find her.

"Shhh," she said. *"Sound carries out here. It's because of all the damn stucco and tile. . . ."*

I scanned the playground, but I couldn't see her. Wherever she was, she was well hidden.

Another French fry bonked me on the forehead, this one covered with ketchup, which I felt dripping down my nose.

"Look up, *Bennett,"* she said.

I looked up at a red-and-yellow foam castle that was the highest point in the PlayPlace. The turret on top had a small rectangular window cut in it.

A hand appeared in the window and gave me a *come here!* gesture.

Sophie was inside.

I checked the PlayPlace a second time to make sure I wasn't being watched, then crawled out of the ball pit and scurried over to the rope ladder leading to the tower, feeling a bit like

Rapunzel's prince. At the top of the ladder was a plastic door made to look like a drawbridge, which I nudged open with the top of my head.

As soon as I was through, Sophie pulled me inside and hugged me.

"Bennett," she whispered.

"Garhmpf," I replied, because she was crushing my face against her body.

"Sorry," she said. "Oh my God, I can't believe you're here. This is *hell.* I'd kiss you, but it probably wouldn't be sanitary."

She was right. There was a deep cut on her lip where dried blood had crusted. The knees of her jeans were ripped. Her hair was frayed. She had zits underneath her mouth—no doubt due to the grease from the fast food on which she'd been subsisting. There were bruises on her arms. One of her earrings was missing, and she had a puncture wound in the cartilage where she had pulled out her tag. Her nail polish had chipped off. She kept running her tongue over one of her teeth, and I could see it was loose.

She was the most beautiful thing I had ever seen.

"I can't believe you're *here,*" she said.

"I wanted to make sure we were still going to prom."

And there it was: *"HA . . . hehhhhhh . . ."*

Everything I'd been through was worth it to hear that laugh. She covered her mouth, and a concerned look crossed her face.

"The jerks out there didn't see you come up here, did they?" she said.

"They're on the other side of the mall, searching for me. And you."

"I hate them. They're like these dim-witted, slow-moving hyenas. I've been running from them for days. I think they're trying to kill me."

"Whoever hunts you down gets to go home," I said.

"I assumed there was some kind of prize, but I couldn't understand any of the announcements over the loudspeakers."

"It's because you haven't had Spine Wine."

"Is that the booze I see these freaks drinking? I've been avoiding it because this doesn't seem like the best time to get drunk, though a lot of them certainly seem to actively partake of it."

"I'd say that's the right move on your part."

"This isn't even a great mall, by the way. If there was a pharmacy, I would have treated these cuts by now. There's nothing useful here."

We heard voices muttering underneath us.

"I wish this McDonald's would bring back the McRib like the rest of them. . . ."

"Do you remember the McLobster? I used to love the McLobster."

"Never heard of it, but it sounds delicious. No way it had real lobster in it, though."

Sophie shook her head at me and whispered: "All they ever do is talk about food. They're *legitimate* morons."

Beneath us, the discussion escalated.

*"What do you mean, no way it had real lobster in it? You call-
ing me a liar?"*

"I'm saying what you're saying don't make any sense."

"So you ARE saying I'm a liar."

There were the *umph*s and *smack*s of a brief fistfight, followed by calls of *knock it off* from a chorus of male and female
voices. I heard the door to the McDonald's open and shut and
then another group approaching.

The greater the number of pursuers who gathered at the
McDonald's, the more silent the group became as a whole.
From the *hmmm*ing and the cop-show exhalations of *now
that's interesting*, it seemed like they were investigating something.

"Why are there balls scattered outside the ball pit?"

"Ask Catfish. He thinks he's the manager and all."

Catfish must have been the hippie.

"Hey, before I came to help you guys look for her, there weren't
any balls outside of the pit, man," said Catfish. *"I would have remembered something like that."*

"You sure?"

"I take pride *in keeping that ball pit nice. That is the centerpiece of my establishment. I'm the manager."*

"You're not the manager. And is that a fry in the pit?"

"Crap," whispered Sophie. "They're going to figure out
we're here. We'll have to run. Wait for me to say when. . . ."

*"If there's a fry in the ball pit, it means the new guy must
be around here somewhere. Two of you start digging. Everybody*

else, help me check the rest of the playground. Make sure you look inside the slides."

"Keep your eyes on me and wait for my signal," whispered Sophie, looking back and forth between my eyes and the ball pit. "I want them to space themselves out a little more before we go. They always separate in stupid ways."

"Fan out toward Starbucks Number Eight. I want us covering as much ground as possible."

"Told you they'd separate," whispered Sophie.

We heard a gaggle of idiots hustle away. Sophie looked at me.

"Three . . . two . . . one . . . *go,*" said Sophie, throwing open the tower door before the remaining stalkers could trap us inside. Before I'd even moved, I watched her jump the rope ladder entirely, land on a plastic bridge, and make *another* leap, to a bench where a statue of Ronald McDonald was sitting with a frozen grin on his face.

She was already down from the tower, once again running too fast for me to keep up. It was a repeat of that awesome/awful night in the Roswell desert.

"Bennett, go," she said over her shoulder.

I bolted out of the tower and free-fell down the rope ladder, threads of twine puncturing my palms. On the bridge, I tripped and scrambled over the planks to keep my momentum going forward, and barely managed to escape the outstretched hands of my pursuers as I shot past the Ronald McDonald statue and out of the PlayPlace.

Up ahead, I could see Sophie make a hard turn away from

the mob into the outdoor courtyard of the mall. While the fastest of the louts had taken off in pursuit of her the moment she had emerged from the PlayPlace, the slowest of the bunch were now after me, wheezing so hard I could hear them as I ran. I looked back and saw nothing but twisted faces—women wiping sweat off their cheeks as they pushed themselves onward, men foaming at the corners of their mouths, triple chins bouncing on everyone. If I ever got back to Earth, I resolved to start a regular fitness routine.

By the time I reached the courtyard, my pursuers were spots in the distance, with their hands on their knees, sucking wind.

I looked around the corner into the courtyard. It was packed shoulder to shoulder with flannel-wearing lumberjacks, mental patients in hospital scrubs, loonies huddled in dirty blankets. It seemed that everyone in the enclosure had gathered for the excitement. I couldn't actually *see* Sophie, but I knew she was in danger from the kinds of things her pursuers were yelling: *Reach up and grab her. . . . Kill her. . . . I want to go home. . . .*

The fountain in the center of the courtyard appeared to be the focus of their attention, but if Sophie was there, I couldn't see her through the thicket of degenerates, some of whom—suddenly finding themselves pressed up against their rivals in such close quarters—were taking the opportunity to fight each other as gangs, violently acting out whatever intra-enclosure rivalries had been building among them. I saw eyes being gouged and limbs being broken and bits of hair with the scalp still attached flying through the air, in addition to the mists of spit and sprays of blood normally associated with a melee. If the Jyfos were getting this on camera, their ratings would be going through the roof.

I probably could have figured out a more strategic course of action than the one I took, but when I realized that Sophie was somewhere in that mass of kinetic flesh, I snapped. I pushed my way to the center of the horde, taking elbows in my chest and getting my clothing ripped as the members of the mob clawed at me with their fingertips, trying to position themselves closer to the fountain. They waved bats and field hockey sticks and meat pounders from Williams-Sonoma above their heads. As focused as they were on the fountain and on beating each other up, they didn't appear to even notice that their other target was moving among them.

In the pandemonium of swinging arms and stabbing scissors and people stomping on each other with Foot Locker soccer cleats, I managed to see Sophie climb to the top of the fountain. The men and women clogging the basin of the structure were climbing toward the faux Venus de Milo statue at the top, reaching for Sophie's legs as she kicked at them and trying to pull her down.

"Get *away* from me," she said, stomping on the hands of a thick-armed, dirty-overalled hayseed, causing him to tumble backward into the sweating, shouting multitude, where he was stepped upon and beaten as the others tried to get closer to Sophie.

"Leave her *alone*!" I yelled, charging into the fountain and pulling her pursuers off the statue. If they had lost track of the fact that I was among them before, the sight of the two of us together ignited them into a frenzy: *There he is. . . . They're both mine. . . . Stop pushing and let me do this. . . . It's time for me to go home. . . .*

"*Bennett,*" said Sophie.

Before I could reply, the mob was upon me, yanking my legs out from under my body, knocking me into the fountain basin, and forcing my head under the inch or so of water that hadn't been splashed away. I flailed and thrashed to get them off, but they were all too large, there were too many of them, and they had the leverage.

They smashed my nose against the concrete foundation. I saw rivulets of my blood float through the water in front of me, and I heard Sophie screaming above as the mob finally managed to pull her down. More hooligans stepped on my back, pushing out the last of my breath. My vision distorted. I felt time slow down and my heart beginning to beat erratically.

But then . . .

BRRRANNNG!

A *deafening* guitar chord rang out over the courtyard. The men and women drowning me threw their hands up over their ears, allowing me to sit up and suck in the longest gasp of air I'd ever inhaled.

BRRRANNNG!

I looked at the sky, where, epically slowly, the Interstellar

Libertine was lowering itself over the mall courtyard. Cad was standing on top of the bus with a new guitar hooked up to an amplifier, grinning proudly.

"Stay *away* from those teenagers," he yelled. "*Look* at you fat asses. This is a *sea* of losers as far as the eye can see. You should be *ashamed* of yourselves. You *know* that this isn't what Earth is like."

BRRRANNNG!

Cad hit another chord, and everybody in the courtyard covered their ears again, giving me a split second to force my way to my feet and climb the fountain. Sophie grabbed my arm and pulled me up.

"What *is* that?" said Sophie.

"That," I said, "is the Interstellar Libertine."

"You were right, Bennett," said Cad, looking over the side of the bus. "She *is* hot. I thought maybe it was just a trick of the television, but in person—even better."

BRRRANNNG!

"You told that guy I was *hot*?"

"You talk about a lot of things when you're trapped on a bus with a band."

"You all right down there?" yelled Driver out the window.

"We won't be unless you hurry," I said.

BRRRANNNG!

The Interstellar Libertine hovered in front of the fountain, and Driver threw open the door.

"What *took* you so long?" I said.

"We found this secondhand music store that was having a massive sale and lets you shop on credit," said Cad. "We weren't going to stay long, but I got wrapped up playing around with this old Moog synthesizer—"

"Tell me about it later," I said.

Driver grabbed Sophie and me and pulled us into the bus. The residents of the enclosure who had survived the melee were staring up at us, button eyes looking out of their doughy faces, covered in scratches and bits of gristle and streaks of snot from ripping each other apart. I could see fallen bodies in between the survivors, some of whom were waving their arms at the Interstellar Libertine, as if they thought that after everything we had been through, *maybe* we would still give them a ride. Others were starting to creep away, putting some distance between themselves and their rivals while they still had a chance, like animals slinking off to lick their wounds.

Cad gave his new guitar a final strum.

BRRRANNNG!

"You've been a terrible audience and I hope to never play for you again," said Cad. "Do some sit-ups. *Good night.*"

Sophie was ravenous after days of subsisting on French fries scavenged from the Dumpster, so Driver stopped at a Chinese food place we found sitting on a floating platform that was zipping past Jyfo. A reasonably priced restaurant that visited you instead of the other way around—what an idea. The entrance to its dome quickly opened as we approached and snapped shut behind us just as fast.

Instead of ordering takeout, we decided to have a sit-down meal and regroup. We left Skark on the bus, still passed out, crumpled in his sleeping pod.

At the table, Driver shoveled buckets of fried rice into his face, while Cad ripped at his spareribs. Sophie choked down a glass of Spine Wine so she could understand what Driver was saying, after which I watched her gobble a heap of chow mein and pot stickers.

"This food is pretty great," said Sophie.

"It's not bad, right?" I said.

"A little salty."

"That's the only issue."

After the noodles, she finished a huge portion of Szechuan pork. Color came back to Sophie's complexion, and her body started to relax.

"You should at least chew a couple of times before you swallow," said Cad. "Nobody in the band knows the Heimlich maneuver."

"I know the Heimlich maneuver," I said. "I took first aid to earn extra credit in gym class."

"I think you've saved me enough times for the day, Bennett," said Sophie, smiling. "All I want is to go home and shower."

Cad and Driver looked at each other. Sophie picked the last few grains of rice off her plate.

"When are we leaving to go back home?" she said, licking her fingers.

"Bennett?" said Cad. "Would you like to explain our itinerary to your girlfriend?"

"Wait—have you been telling them I'm your girlfriend?" said Sophie.

"I made it clear you were my prom date, not my girlfriend."

"I'm *pretty* sure you said *girlfriend*," said Cad. "Kinda strange you would lie about that, if it wasn't true."

I stared at Cad.

"I didn't lie about it, because I didn't *say* it."

"Huh," said Cad. "I guess I remember things differently."

Though I was new to the dating world, even I could recognize what he was doing. From the moment we'd saved Sophie, I'd seen Cad checking her out—looking at her legs, putting a comforting hand on her back as he showed her the bus, offering his personal toiletries so she could clean some of the dirt off her skin. Now he was trying to make her feel uncomfortable around me by suggesting that I'd been calling her my girlfriend when I hadn't.

There wasn't a doubt in my mind—Cad was trying to move in on Sophie.

Which—if you'll allow me to step back from the story and try to be objective about that moment and the journey as a whole—was within Cad's rights, if not a little brazen and untimely. Yes, Sophie was my prom date, but it wasn't like a date to a single dance was some sort of binding lifetime commitment that would *warrant* the type of sinister jealousy bubbling up in my gut as I watched Cad eyeing her from across the table, turning oh so slightly to the side each time he took a drink to make sure that she saw the ropy muscles in his arms. Just because you saved someone didn't mean you just *got* that someone—if that was the case, every lifeguard in the world would have fifty spouses—and Sophie was her own girl, single and free as the wind, with the exception of those couple of hours on Friday when she was supposed to dance with me.

But sitting at that Chinese restaurant, having endured Skark's bullheadedness and survived the Jyfos' misguided environmentalism, I was finding it impossible to be objective about the extra attention Cad was paying Sophie. I could save her from the dangers of the universe, but keeping a handsome bassist away from her was another matter entirely.

"Go ahead, Bennett," said Cad. "Tell her the news about the rest of the trip. We've got to get on the road."

"Sophie," I said. "I know this is annoying, but we've got one more stop. It's a music festival."

Sophie shook her head and gave me a look. "Are you *kidding*?"

"I'm not."

"While I'd *normally* be up for partying, I think I've had enough *fun* in the last couple of days," said Sophie. "Can you drop me off *before* you—"

The sentence wasn't even out of her mouth when Skark burst in through the door of the restaurant. He was clutching a velour cape over his skeletal shoulders and scraping crusty makeup from his face. He looked like some hideous, cracked-out demon.

"What in *God's* name is going on here?" he yelled, shuffling toward us.

Sophie yelped at the sight of him.

"Oh, *shut up,*" said Skark. "I almost had the same reaction, looking at your outfit."

"I have been running for my *life,*" said Sophie.

"That's all life is, rapid movement and trying to stay alive—get used to it," said Skark. "*God,* what a headache I have. What did I *take?*"

A waiter scrambled out from behind the counter and began waving his hands in front of Skark, trying to get him to leave.

"Customers only," said the waiter. "Leave now."

"Customers only? Who do you think is *paying* for this meal, apparently straight from my personal savings?" Skark looked at his bandmates. "You don't think I check my boots to make sure my nest egg is safe whenever I wake up? And now it's *gone.*"

"We used the money for instruments," said Driver.

"You spent *all* my money on instruments?"

"And a bribe," said Cad.

"A bribe?" said Skark. "Were we detained at a border?"

"It was for Sophie," said Cad.

Skark stood at the front of our table, staring at Sophie, too twitchy to sit down. His eyes were bloodshot and he was sweating, residue from the booze and pills exiting his body any way it could. "Would someone mind telling me *who this is*? With all the *strays* that come onto the bus, sometimes it feels like I'm the owner of an *orphanage* instead of a legendary front man."

"This is Sophie," I said. "My prom date. Sophie, this is Skark Zelirium, lead singer of the Perfectly Reasonable."

Skark thought about this for a moment. I could see him working out what it meant in his mind.

"Hold on," he said. "You went to Jyfon while I was *sleeping*?"

"We went to Jyfon while you were *passed out,*" said Cad.

"We have *Dondoozle* to get to. How far off course are we?"

"I'm going to use a shortcut to make up time," said Driver. "We'll get to Dondoozle with time to spare."

"What shortcut?"

"Through the Hyperbolic Back Roads. It's the only thing that makes sense."

Skark petulantly stomped on the ground, grabbed Cad's chopsticks, and broke them in half.

"Being *swung* from the orbit of *one* world to the next as slowly as possible," said Skark. "What a *pleasant* way to travel. You *know* I get motion sickness, especially when I'm feeling a bit hungover. I can't take this. I'm getting rid of this girl."

Skark took a fast step toward Sophie, but as I got to my feet to protect her, I felt Cad's hands on my shoulders, forcing me to sit back down. Cad stepped around me and got in Skark's face. He was stealing the moment.

"If you're going to do anything to Sophie, you'd better be prepared to throw *me* out first," said Cad.

"Fantastic," said Skark. "I would *relish* the opportunity to be rid of you."

"Make the first move, then," said Cad.

Skark and Cad stared at each other until Skark's body shook involuntarily, still trying to process the booze and drugs. He was weak. He pulled his cape tight around his shoulders.

"I'm feeling too ill for this," said Skark. "Ridding the bus of these leeches will have to be delayed. New girl, Sophie, whatever your name is, know that one way or another, I'll be through with you soon. Bennett, I've been told that deep space smells a bit like burning metal and barbecue. I look forward to you confirming this for me imminently. You can just give me a nod before you lose consciousness as I'm waving to you through the window."

Skark hobbled back toward the parking lot, shuddering and looking into empty bottles to see if there was any alcohol left.

"Thank you, Cad," said Sophie.

"Thank you, *Cad*?" I said. "I was *trying* to stand up to defend you, and Cad held me *down*—"

"Sophie, I just want you to know I'm taking a personal interest in keeping you safe," said Cad, ignoring me.

"*I'm* the one who saved you from Jyfon," I said. I knew that my protests might come across as touchy—after all, the most important thing was that Sophie was safe, not who got credit for her life—but now I understood the manner in which Cad was going to move in on my territory. He would present himself as Sophie's protector, a bulwark.

"Technically, Bennett," said Cad. "And I don't mean to be a stickler here, but I'm the one who came to the rescue with the bus while you were being overrun. So it wouldn't be unreasonable to say that *I'm* the one who saved her."

"You *both* saved me," said Sophie. "Why is this some point of contention?"

"I followed you into *space,*" I said.

"I'm fully *aware* of that," said Sophie. "I'm here in space right now too, remember?"

"Again, I don't mean to be picky," said Cad. "But it wouldn't have been *possible* for you to go to space had I not invited you along as the guest of this band, would it? Which sounds to me like more evidence that I'm the one who rescued Sophie. But it's déclassé to fight for credit."

"Did you just use the word *déclassé*?" I said. "I've barely heard you use anything but single-syllable words up until now."

"Maybe I was just waiting for someone who could handle a higher-end conversation," said Cad, faking being smart. "Come on, Sophie, I'm sure you've got questions you'd like answered."

Cad and Sophie got up from the table and walked out of the restaurant side by side. Through the window, I watched Cad put his arm over Sophie's shoulders and whisper something just before they disappeared into the Interstellar Libertine, and then I heard her laugh.

"HA . . . hehhhhhhh . . ."

Cold rage swelled through me. I rolled an egg roll around on my plate with a fork. I could feel Driver staring.

"Cad's stealing your lady, man," said Driver. "This is the

same thing he did to Sheila and me after we got married. I mean, *right after.* As soon as we exchanged rings, he seduced her. She was still wearing her dress. They spent my honeymoon together."

"And you forgave him?"

"Who said that I forgave him?" said Driver. "We're in a band together. I don't have to like him."

"But you and Cad aren't even the same *species,*" I said. "Why would he go after your girl?"

"Cad doesn't care. That man will hit on anything. Unless you do something, Sophie is going to be on his arm, regardless of how far you traveled for her."

I was in shock. One minute I had traveled *billions of light-years* to save the girl whom I wanted more than anything, and the next, she had been snatched from me by a sleaze I had thought was my friend.

Driver got up from the table and shook his head as he passed my chair, disappointed in me. I was alone. The same waiter who moments before had tried to shoo Skark away from the premises came over and began cleaning up, picking up the plates with one hand and wiping down the table with the other.

"That guy's girlfriend is *hot,*" said the waiter.

"She's not his girlfriend," I said. "She's with me."

"I would *not* have thought you were together," said the waiter. "I was looking at her the whole time."

"It's weird you were watching."

"We don't get many girls who look like *that* up here."

"How did you even get up here?"

"My parents were born here," said the waiter.

"Don't you ever get the urge to go to Earth?"

"Everyone says it sucks."

"Yeah, it can. They're not entirely wrong."

I got up from the table and walked to the door.

"You forgot this," said the waiter. I turned around, and he tossed a plastic-wrapped fortune cookie to me.

"I'm not a big believer in fortune cookies," I said.

"It seems like you need advice."

I picked it up and cracked it open. I read the message:

DON'T LET OTHER GUYS TAKE YOUR GIRL, BENNETT

"You've *got* to be joking," I said.

"The guys who write fortunes out here have a machine so they can travel into the future to see what's what," said the waiter. "They're always pretty accurate."

I saw the bus lift off the ground outside the restaurant, and I ran for it. Inside the bus, I heard Sophie again: *"HA . . . hehh-hhhh . . ."*

Cad and I were going to have a chat.

THURSDAY

"Here you go, Walter," I said, extracting the grass I had taken from Jyfon from my inside pocket. "It was all I could take with me, but I figured it might be a nice break from Chinese."

Walter's eyes went wide. I thought he was going to cry.

"You brought me *grass*?" he said.

"I wish I could have brought you more."

I set the grass in front of him on the floor of the closet.

"This is the nicest thing anybody's done for me in *years,*" said Walter.

"My pleasure."

I watched Walter lean down and—methodically, savoring each individual blade—chew on the end of each piece, slurping it up into his mouth as his eyes fluttered in satisfaction.

"Thank you. So much."

"Enjoy it," I said, closing the closet door to give him privacy. I could hear his snorts of pleasure through the wood.

Sophie had been sleeping for a couple of hours on an oversized ottoman at the back of the bus, snoring lightly. Exhausted. The snores sounded like a miniature variation of her laugh, but instead of a *"HA . . . hehhhhhh,"* it was more of a *"WER . . . werrrrrr."*

I might have found it adorable had I not been so irritated. I was listening to Cad tinker on Skark's guitar, trying to write a song.

"Oh, pretty girl, I met you far from home . . . ," he sang.

With every new lyric, I grew more annoyed.

"Now I know why I've been flying around. . . . Sophie Sophie . . . But only with you have my feet left the ground. . . . Sophie Sophie . . ."

"You sound ridiculous," I said. "You're thirty and she's still in *high school.* It's a good thing there aren't age-of-consent laws in space."

Cad looked up at me.

"She's already told me she's *eighteen,* and *you* told me yourself that you're graduating in a couple of weeks," he said. "What's the problem? Picasso had a teenage muse, why can't I?"

"She's not *your* muse. She's *my* muse. I don't want to hear you using Sophie's name in your songs. *I* use Sophie's name in songs. You've been with a million girls, leave mine *alone.*"

"You write songs?"

"I write songs. Yes. Of which Sophie is a *dominant* part."

"Can I hear one?"

I paused.

"I've never actually completed one," I said. "I'm not always great at finishing what I start, but that has nothing to do with this."

"I see. How about we make a deal, then. *You* feel free to use Sophie's name in song *fragments,* and *I'll* use her name in *real* songs, and then someday you can release an album of *couplets* that you can sell down at the local open mike night. I'll handle the proper album, thank you."

"It's going to be hard to release an album if your band hasn't written a new song in five years."

"*Skark* hasn't written a song in five years. I've written hundreds, he just never uses them."

"I don't blame him. I'm listening to you working on this, and it's terrible."

Cad lifted the guitar strap over his shoulders and rested the instrument on the chair beside him.

"If you're sore about this girl, I'd like to point out you said she was your *date,* not your girlfriend. If you aren't official, it's game on."

"How official do things have to be for you? Driver said you went home with his wife on the *day* they were married."

"I regret that decision. Sometimes at weddings you hook up with women you wouldn't expect."

"She was the *bride.*"

"And Skark wrote a hit song about it: 'Forbidden Cake, Forbidden Frosting.' Top ten in fifty-three galaxies. That's what you *do* with these awkward situations. You channel them into *art*."

"I don't *want* Sophie channeled into your art. I want her back in New Mexico with *me.*"

"I hear you, but the fact remains, you two aren't technically together. As far as I know, she might just be your neighbor who agreed to go to the dance with you or something."

I didn't say anything.

"She *is* your neighbor who agreed to go with you, isn't she? It gets better and better. I'm sorry, but the gloves are off."

"I came to *space* to rescue that girl, and the *moment* I get her back, you swoop in."

"It's not my fault she and I are hitting it off."

Something in my brain snapped.

"Leave her *alone!*" I yelled. I leaped at Cad, knocked him to the ground, and stared into his eyes while squeezing his face with my fists.

"Stay. Away. From. Her," I said, punching him in the side with each word.

Cad tried to block my blows. "Not if you ask me like that . . ."

"I *mean* it," I said, pulling him toward me by his shirt and slamming him back down onto the ground again and again. I was prepared to kill him. I wasn't sure what the penalty for murdering somebody in space was, but I was willing to go before whatever tribunal was in charge and defend myself. A crime of passion.

"If you don't *back off,* you and I are going to have *problems.* I will stay awake until you fall asleep. I *will* chop you up and I will *eject* you out of here, and I will make sure that we're *near* a planet so I can watch you *burn up* in its *atmosphere.* You got that, Cad? Are we *clear?*"

Cad thought about this.

"You sound like Skark," he said.

"I've been having to listen to him a lot," I said. "I'm not surprised some of his personality has rubbed off."

"Does Sophie have any cute friends?"

"She's not a big socializer at school, but I can check," I said.

"If you do that for me, I'll call off the pursuit," he said. "You know, I didn't think your body could be any stranger than I already thought it was, but having you on top of me is like being mounted by an angry Slim Jim. Now get *off.*"

I rolled off Cad and collapsed out on the floor next to him, out of breath, my heart pounding. I wasn't used to such physical confrontations.

"You're stronger than you look," said Cad. "You don't look like you have any natural athletic ability."

"I didn't think I did," I said. "I must have a lot of unused adrenaline saved up from my youth."

And then . . .

"Um," said Sophie.

Cad and I looked up, and saw her staring at us from the ottoman.

"When did you wake up?" I said.

"As soon as you tackled Cad. It was pretty loud."

"I see," I said. "So . . . did you hear all of that?"

"You were practically shouting," she said. "And we're on a bus. So yeah. I heard all of that. Did you really think I was interested in Cad?"

"You're not interested in me?" said Cad.

"What is *wrong* with you two?" said Sophie. "You have all the glories of the universe in front of you and you're arguing about a girl. Grow *up*. I'm using the restroom, and you *better* stop being creepy by the time I get out. I'm so *tired* of being here."

Sophie got up, opened a door, and yelled.

"Hello," I heard Walter say.

"*Why* is there a *ram* in the bathroom?" she said.

"That's the closet," said Cad. "The bathroom is the next door down."

"This bus is *psychotic,*" said Sophie, slamming the closet shut and opening the door to the bathroom.

Cad looked at me.

"Man, she's attractive," he said.

"I can still *hear* you," said Sophie from the bathroom. "Let's just get to this festival and get home. This is a nightmare."

Sophie was looking out the window, arms around her knees, tracing the paths of the passing comets with her eyes. She'd slept as much as she could, I guessed. Though her environment had changed, she was just as stuck and not in control of her fate as she had been a few hours before. I felt bad about my own actions. It wasn't much of a heroic rescue if you didn't get the girl you rescued home safely. And it was even worse if you immediately jammed her into the middle of a love triangle to boot.

I walked over to her.

"Mind if I pull up an ottoman?" I said.

"If that's what you want to do," she said.

I dragged the puffy, circular piece of furniture next to her and joined her in just looking outside. I could see why she'd been staring out the window so long. Driver was coasting, and she was watching a meteor shower from above, comets raining down on the red atmosphere of a planet below us, bursting into pools of fire as they split apart.

"Do you think anybody lives down there?" I said.

"I don't know. It has a bunch of those swirling red Jupiter spots, which I think are unpleasant places to be."

"Probably better than living on a bus with three guys and a ram," I said.

"Four guys and a ram," she said. "You're forgetting to include yourself."

The Interstellar Libertine soared out of view of the planet being assaulted by comets, and once again everything looked far away—blinking pinwheels and atomic crayon streaks of magentas and blues swirling together.

"I'm sorry that you heard us fighting over you," I said. "But to clarify, I never said you were my girlfriend. I know that we're just going to a dance, and that's it."

"I can't believe you came after me," she said.

"Those aliens really ruined the night we were having," I said. "It made me mad."

"It was a good night up until that point."

"It was the best night I ever had," I said. "Plus, going after you seemed easier than explaining the situation to your parents."

Sophie rubbed her eyes.

"I bet they're freaking out right now," she said.

"You're fine," I said. "I'm sure they just think I kidnapped you. I walked out of the desert alone and abandoned my truck in the drive-through of an In-N-Out Burger."

"After I was abducted, you went and got *food*?"

"I know how that sounds. But it was In-N-Out."

"At least it was In-N-Out," she said. "Those burgers are great. I would have done the same thing."

"That's where I met these guys."

Sophie turned and looked at the band. Skark was scrounging in the seat cushions, mumbling something about missing his stash. Cad was tuning his bass. Driver was tapping on the controls of the bus with his drumsticks, giving a good *whack* to what appeared to be very sensitive equipment every time he came around to the downbeat.

Due to Driver's habit of drumming while driving, the dashboard looked like it had been shot up by a Gatling gun. The glass protecting the digital readouts was covered in spiderweb cracks, and several gauges were permanently unlit because the bulbs had been broken so many times. I could only assume that Driver was piloting the bus mostly by feel at this point.

Driver shoved the drumsticks into a space next to his seat and nonchalantly started flipping through a fashion magazine.

"I can't believe this is where I am right now," said Sophie. "This is the first time in my life I've actually missed home. Boring, terrible Gordo, New Mexico."

"If you want, you can stay there and I'll go to Princeton for you," I said.

"You'd have to wear a wig."

"Small sacrifice."

She looked down at her arms.

"All my scratches are really going to screw up our prom pictures."

"I'll appreciate those pictures no matter what they look like, if they mean we got back."

Behind us, Cad began humming and mucking around on a guitar again, but as his humming turned into words, I could hear that this time the song had nothing to do with Sophie. It was a simple melody—a few chords, a little bit of whistling here and there—the subject of which was looking for a home when you no longer feel like you belong where you grew up. *The house was there, but home was somewhere else. . . . My life was there, but I wasn't myself. . . .*

We listened to him finish the song, whistling and humming for the outro.

"What's that one called?" I said.

"'Home,'" he said. "It's an old one."

"It's great," I said.

Cad took his hand off the strings. "I don't need you ridiculing my songwriting any more tonight."

"I wasn't kidding. It's a great song."

Cad tapped the body of the guitar, examining my face to determine if I was telling the truth. "I've always thought it might be good. Skark hates it."

"Skark is a drunk," said Sophie.

Cad gave us a small smile.

"That might be the first time in a decade somebody has told me one of my songs is good," he said. "Groupies excluded, of course."

"Of course," I said.

"I guess I'll work on it a little more. I'll keep it down. Thanks, guys." He went back to strumming the melody, and we went back to looking out the window.

Sophie examined my face.

"What?" I said.

"I'm sorry, but I still can't believe you only applied to one school," said Sophie. "I kept thinking about it when I was hiding in the mall."

"*That's* what you were thinking about?"

"It popped into my head a few times," she said.

I stared out at a cloud of wintergreen-gum-colored space dust in the distance, which to my eyes looked like it was forming a distinct letter *L. Loser.* Even the universe was mocking my collegiate decisions.

"What else did you think about out there?" I said.

She paused for a moment.

"I thought about how bananas are technically classified as herbs."

Obscure facts. I loved her so much.

"Bananas are herbs?"

"Banana trees aren't actually trees. They're made up of a center stem with a bunch of leaves protecting it all over the place, which means that the bananas are essentially just the top of the stalk popping out. Ergo, the fruit is technically an herb."

"If you tell me that parsley is a meat, I don't think my mind will ever recover."

"Parsley's not a meat. But giraffes sleep less than an hour a day."

"You're kidding me."

"No joke. I was glad to be able to zone out and think about weird stuff at the enclosure. I don't know what I would have done if I had had to actually acknowledge my situation."

"I'm so glad you're here," I said.

Sophie put her arm around me and gave me a hug.

"I hope you get into Princeton," she said. "If you came to outer space for me, it means I know I could call you to save me if I ever got drunk at a party or something."

"I'll save you no matter where you are," I said.

"I know you'll get in," she said.

It was nice of her to say so, but I knew I was doomed. It had crossed my mind that there must be a number of good universities up in space—somebody had to be teaching youthful extraterrestrials how to engineer all these advanced technologies. Maybe I could stay and get my education that way. However, I rejected that idea when I realized whatever degree I managed to earn probably wouldn't be accepted back on Earth, and after having gone four years without a social life in Gordo, showing up on campus in a strange galaxy would have likely just made me a bizarro foreign exchange student with even fewer opportunities to fit in.

I leaned against Sophie and she embraced me. She helped me put the future out of my mind. I wished I could just major in her.

The Hyperbolic Back Roads that Skark had been dreading so much weren't all that bad, to be honest. In fact, they reminded me of a lazy river ride at a water park. An artery of heavenly bodies lined the sky in front of the bus—red giants and yellow dwarfs and a few basic water-covered blue planets that reminded me of home. The orbs' proximity to each other created a kind of natural gravitational slipstream, which pulled in the Interstellar Libertine as soon as the bus entered the orbit of its first sun.

We rode the orbit until we were plucked out of space by the overlapping gravitational pull of the *next* celestial object, which passed us along to the next, and so forth. Driver had his hands on the wheel to steady the bus, but his foot wasn't on the accelerator. There was nothing to do but go with the flow. It was nice to be moving at a different speed, though Skark was pacing up and down the center of the bus, looking nauseated from this undulating mode of travel.

"Are you *sure* there's no way to get us through this part of the trip faster?" said Skark. "I'm sick, this is *boring,* and I'm tired of looking at these stowaways."

"If I hit the gas, all we would do is break out of the orbit and have to find our way back in," said Driver. "Gravity is out of whack in this part of space, so we can't skip it. Breathe. When we get to the other side, we'll be almost there."

"Never tell me to breathe," said Skark. "I allow air to come into me when I choose."

Skark paced some more, giving me an angry stare every time he walked past. Eventually I got tired of it, so I stopped looking up, prompting him to smack me on the back of the head. He didn't like being ignored.

The final star in the Hyperbolic Back Roads was the largest and brightest. I held a cushion from the couch in front of my face to protect my eyes, causing Skark to scream at me to stop touching his furniture. The star dragged us around its orbit until Driver gently guided the wheel to the left, popping us out into open space.

By the time we were through, Skark was green. His motion sickness must have been terrible, because he wasn't even consuming his Spine Wine.

On the other side of the Hyperbolic Back Roads, we saw a strange comet. At first we thought it was just another point of light hanging in the blackness, hurtling past us. It was always peaceful to watch the comets wafting past—they reminded me of the outer space equivalent of birds, long tails streaming behind them, wandering from their places of birth but planning to return someday.

Normally, Driver was excellent at avoiding the comets, so what happened with *this* particular comet couldn't be considered his fault. Initially the rock was a far-off speck, silhouetted against a swirling purple-and-white nebula. It was streaming toward us, but it wasn't going faster than any other comet we had seen, and Driver didn't even look at it twice as he pulled back on the controls, lifting the bus to safety.

He peered into the back of the bus, where I was eating an egg roll I had found in a Styrofoam to-go container. I was hungry again.

"Hey, back there," said Driver. "Good-sized glower should be passing underneath us in a couple of minutes, in case you want to take a look. I don't know how many comets you've seen up close, Sophie, but it's worth checking out."

"I wouldn't like to see *any* comets up close," said Sophie. "I'm done with danger."

"It's coming right past," said Driver. "But don't worry, I'll keep us comfortable."

Sophie glanced out the window, then quickly pulled back, startled. She yelled to the front of the bus.

"I thought you said that the comet was going to be beneath us," she said.

"It is."

"It's changing directions," she said.

"Impossible," said Driver. "Comets don't change trajectory unless they hit a gravitational field or some other object. They're just chunks of burning ice . . . *whoa.*"

Driver yanked the wheel just as I was about to pop the nub of my egg roll into my mouth. It slipped from my hand and hit the floor, gathering dust as it tumbled to a stop. I decided not to try to eat it again.

"What's going *on* up there?" yelled Skark.

"Sophie's right," said Driver. "Somehow this thing changed its course and is heading toward us. Hold on, I'm going to try something else."

I looked out the window and saw that the comet was *close.* Driver was maneuvering out of the way when it abruptly dropped, cutting off our path. Driver jerked the bus to the side, but again, the comet was there, coming at us at full speed. Each time it moved, streams of superheated air shot out of various spots all over its surface, and as we got nearer, I could see that it looked like it was made of metal rather than ice.

"It's not a comet, it's a *ship,*" said Driver. "I'm going to back us up."

But there was no point. Before Driver could put the bus in reverse, the comet had zipped underneath us and was trembling, as if it was staring angrily at the Interstellar Libertine.

"What's it doing?" said Sophie.

"It looks like it's getting ready for something," said Cad.

Hooks shot out of the comet and lodged in the side of the bus.

"That was *totally* unnecessary," said Skark. "They could have contacted us without damaging the exterior. Do they have any *idea* how much it costs to have this thing detailed?"

"At least the hooks didn't break through the hull," said Cad.

There was a drilling sound outside the bus.

"I think the hooks are breaking through the hull," said Sophie.

A glittering, angry-looking obelisk punctured the wall. Its tip folded back on itself, sealing the hole while at the same time leaving a tubelike protrusion at its end. Liquid began sputtering from the tube and pooling on the floor of the bus. The dribble became a spray that drenched the walls, furniture, and ceiling, splattering the band and slathering the inside of the bus.

"What is this stuff?" I yelled, covering my mouth with my hand so I didn't swallow any of the goo. It stuck to my skin, cold and gelatinous.

"It's *awful,*" said Sophie, squinting her eyes against the torrent. "Make it *stop.*"

"Everybody *get away* from the tube," said Driver, trying to clear the glop out of his eyes.

"Does this *stain*?" said Skark. "This *better not* stain my couch. I feel like it's going to stain."

The goo was solidifying on our arms and legs, making it impossible to get away, not that there would have been any place to run even if we could have moved.

I watched the goo turn Driver into a petrified lump as he tried to take shelter underneath the steering wheel. It glued Cad to his bed as he tried to shield himself with a blanket. It froze Walter as he was jamming himself beneath the kitchen sink.

Sophie was closest to the tube when it started spraying, which meant she was hit the worst, rapidly mummified by thick layers of the goo. I could no longer see her face, but I could hear her struggling beneath the heavy cover. *"Mmmmmff."*

By the time the spray stopped, one of my eyes was somehow still mostly uncovered, with just a clearish coating on it that was turning my vision purple, like I was all of a sudden looking at the world through Prince's eyes. The Interstellar Libertine started to shake, and for a moment I thought that we were going to be towed toward the comet.

Nope.

The drill sent out thin blades that cut a jagged rectangle in the side of the bus. The panel fell out of the wall and drifted into nothingness, and—frozen like statues—everybody aboard tumbled outside.

Which was how I ended up floating in space.

Weightlessness.

I tried to yell, but the goo was sticking my mouth shut; I tried to breathe, but it was clogging my nose.

The eighteen years of my life played in front of me, and it was nothing but an endless series of homework assignments interspersed with scenes of sexual and songwriting frustration. I wish I could say that having been given a second chance to prepare for my own death, I thought about my parents and my family and approached my end with dignity, but this wasn't the case—I thought about myself, cursing creation for allowing me to die a virgin, and sniveled and whimpered inside my mind.

But after a few minutes, I realized something—I had been blubbering and mourning my passing, but I *wasn't dead.* The coat of goop was silencing me and restricting my movements, but it was also saving my life. In addition to protecting me from the subzero temperatures of space, it seemed to be *breathing* for me; I could feel it forcing oxygen through my skin into my blood. It was an odd sensation, not needing my lungs anymore.

When I realized I wasn't going to die—at least not immediately—I started to relax, and the floating became soothing. I looked around. Nothing else to do. I saw stars slowly rotating below my feet, and above my head I saw red blankets of cosmic debris.

My brain was having difficulty wrapping itself around the vastness of space, and the incomprehensible distances between where I was drifting and the wonders that I was observing. The thought popped into my head that all of creation looked a bit like a computer screen saver from the early nineties, which was a manageable concept that allowed me to temporarily get a grip on myself.

Everybody from the bus seemed to be gliding in the same general direction, covered in their own coats of goop, with the exception being a lump I assumed was Walter the ram, who was spinning a different way entirely. I watched him become smaller and smaller until he was just a splotch far behind the empty husk of the Interstellar Libertine, indistinguishable from any small piece of detritus.

Goodbye, Walter.

I had no sense of how long it took for the comet to finally come and scoop us up. Ten minutes? An hour? It sailed toward us to begin its collection process. I couldn't imagine what Sophie was thinking—just when she thought she had been saved, she had to deal with *this*.

The comet positioned itself over Cad, opened a portal in the bottom, and—*shloop*—sucked him inside. The comet repeated the process with Sophie next—*shloop*—and I felt a wave of relief wash over me to know that she was okay.

Driver was sucked up next—*shloop*—and then it was my turn.

The comet came to a stop above me, opened its portal, and—as if invisible hands were cradling my body—I felt myself being gently pulled toward it. I didn't know if it was chemicals in the goo or steady vibrations coming from the ship itself, but I suddenly felt like everything in my life was going to be totally fine.

Then I realized, nope. Not fine at all.

While the sensation of being coaxed into the floating rock

was pleasant, the *angle* at which I was being brought up was askew. Instead of being sucked into the *middle* of the portal, I was positioned way over to the *side* of the hole.

"*Mmff,*" I said, or rather attempted to say—no sound in space—trying to signal to *somebody* on the comet to readjust my trajectory, but I couldn't move my arms to gesture for them to stop. I also couldn't shut my goop-covered eye, which meant I had no choice but to watch the rocky edge of the portal get steadily closer and closer and . . .

CLUNK

I hit my head on the ship, and for the second time in less than a week, everything went black. If I ever got home, I was going to start wearing a helmet.

The basement room where I woke up was clearly some sort of recording studio, given the amount of hi-fi equipment around, though to my blurry eyes it more closely resembled a sloppily constructed madhouse. Ripped foam padding covered the walls, there were deep cracks in the temporary-looking floor, and harsh fluorescent light shined down from naked bulbs hanging from the ceiling.

Promotional photographs and posters of younger incarnations of the Perfectly Reasonable were haphazardly tacked up everywhere. In each picture, the faces of the band members were scribbled out or graffitied or had nails driven through them. We were clearly in the hive of an individual *obsessed* with the group.

The band's instruments were lying in a pile on the floor. The comet-ship had saved them from space as well, though I had been blacked out when this salvage mission happened. All of the band's other possessions seemed to be gone, lost to the void.

Driver, Cad, and—to my overwhelming relief—Sophie were all there, while in a corner of the room there was a glass vocal booth in which Skark was sitting in a straitjacket, looking like he'd been zapped with electric currents. I later found out this had actually been the case—when he refused to enter the studio, he was zapped by our captor, and when he refused to sit down, he was zapped again, and then he was zapped a few more times so he wouldn't be such a pain in the ass going forward.

A heap of stained rags was piled against the wall, next to a can of solution that smelled like turpentine. It appeared that this combination was what Sophie and the band had used to wipe the goo off their skin, though nobody had done a particularly thorough job, and purple specks dotted everybody's face and clothing. I figured that Sophie had been the one who had de-gunked me while I was unconscious, given that she left behind her gooey *SG* initials on my arm.

"Thank God you're up . . . ," said Sophie. "I can't listen to any more of Cad and Driver's asinine conversations."

"What were they talking about?" I said groggily.

"They were playing I Spy with My Little Eye," said Sophie. "And Cad kept spying *me.*"

"Cad . . . ," I said.

"Sorry," he said. "I didn't mean to be sketchy. It was just boredom."

Skark was sitting in his booth, ogling us in catatonic shock. His mouth was moving, but we couldn't hear him because of the egg-crate insulation in the tiny vocal booth. A music stand with lyric sheets was positioned in front of him, and a microphone was pointed at his mouth.

On the other side of the room, behind a sheet of protective glass, hunched at a mixing console covered in knobs and switches, was a man with curly red hair. He was wearing a torn Perfectly Reasonable T-shirt, and each time he turned his head, I could see the heavy curve of his scoliosis-gnarled backbone.

There wasn't a doubt in my mind. This was Ferguson, the triangle player exiled from the band nine years before.

Ferguson pressed a button on the mixing console, and his voice rang out through an intercom.

"Finally *finally*," he said. "Looks like we're all up and alert now. You know, when you guys kicked me out of the group, you told me I'd never be in the same room with you again . . . and yet, here we are. Back together, happily. The music press is going to flip out."

"The band was *already* together, Ferguson," said Driver. "You're not a *part* of the band anymore."

"Since you fired me, you've been a glorified cover band," said Ferguson. "You have no idea how disappointed I've been, watching what you've become. One billion sixteenth in the universe. Disgusting. When I was in the band, we were *twelfth*. Now let me think for a second. What is the missing link here?"

"It has nothing to do with you no longer being in the group," said Cad.

"The time line says otherwise," said Ferguson. "You might as well be busking in some red-light district for Spine Wine and loose change."

"You think that someone playing a stupid *triangle* has an impact on a band's popularity?" said Cad. "That's how far gone your spongy little brain is. Anybody can play the triangle. I could train an *ape* to play the triangle."

"*I was the most talented triangle player this universe has ever seen.* And you dropped me without consideration of the *work* I had put into my craft, into this *group.* And now—here we are again, all together, and the triangle solo will be part of the Perfectly Reasonable once more."

In the reflection of the glass partition that separated the control room from the rest of the studio, I could see that there was a contusion above my left eye where my head had smacked into the bottom of the ship. It was a cloudy purple, and speckled with smooth, blood-red bubbles. Every time I moved, I could feel my brain sloshing around inside my head, banging into the interior of my skull.

"Where are we?" I said.

"We're in Ferguson's basement," said Driver. "You can tell from the lack of style."

"This studio is about music, not comfort," said Ferguson.

"I have a question," said Cad. "How are we supposed to play when you won't even let us *talk* to our singer?"

"I'll let Skark out of his booth when you learn the sheet music in the folders," said Ferguson. "Until you know the new song I wrote, there won't be any music for him to sing over, so for now he's staying in his vocal booth. It's a little time-out as punishment for his past deeds, and a moment to reflect on what he's going to say in your press release stating I'm back. When you're done, I'll come in and lay down some triangle."

"Skark is our guitarist," said Cad.

"Oh, give me a break," said Ferguson. "Everybody plays guitar. Have the guy with the welt on his head do it. You probably play guitar, right, new guy?"

"A little," I said.

"Then learn the song," said Ferguson. "I'll be back after I take a bath and do a mask. I need to look good for my reemergence onto the universal stage."

Ferguson got up from his engineering console and left the room.

"What a *dick,*" said Sophie.

"He's always had an inflated sense of his importance to the group," said Driver.

We looked at the booth. Skark's hair was falling out in handfuls, clustering on his shoulders. He was shaking.

"That is awful to see," said Driver.

"Can you help him?" said Sophie.

Driver was silent for a moment, examining Skark.

"You might not believe me, but I think what's happening to Skark is actually good," said Driver.

"Why?" said Cad.

"I think he's *detoxing,*" said Driver.

I had noticed that Cad also wasn't looking so great. He was

grinding his teeth, and his cheeks were sunken and corpselike. Runnels of red capillaries were polluting the whites of his eyes, and he kept pulling at his shirt like he was overheating.

"I'm feeling a little off myself," said Cad. "And look at you, Driver. You're sweating everywhere. It's disgusting."

Cad was right. Perspiration was pouring out of Driver's temples, down over his ears, and onto his shoulders, forming sweaty pools in the indents of his collarbones.

"I thought my body was readjusting from floating in space," said Driver. "But you may be right. Perhaps we're all detoxing, but Skark has it the worst."

Hands trembling slightly, Driver picked up the paper with Ferguson's song. "Does anybody know how to read sheet music?"

Sophie nodded. "I do."

"You can read music?" I said.

"I play violin," she said. "My parents made me learn in middle school."

"There is *so* much I don't know about you," I said.

"My family also has a harpsichord in the attic," she said. "I'm weirdly good with any kind of baroque instrument. Too bad there are none here."

Cad looked at me.

"She's amazing," he said.

"I'm aware," I said.

"Shut up and let's start," said Sophie. "The sooner we do this, the faster we leave. Give me a B major."

There was silence in the room.

"What's a B major?" said Cad. "I just play by feel."

"Okay, this is going to take some finessing," said Sophie. "Just play something that sounds like this. *Hmmmmmm.*"

Cad plucked a note that sounded like Sophie's humming, and we were off.

Cad, Driver, and I did fifteen run-throughs of Ferguson's terrible "Explosion of the Heart"—Sophie humming the song's notes as we figured them out on our instruments—before Ferguson made his way to the studio wearing a towel and holding a pair of scissors. He made his way to Skark's booth, and with a quick *snap* of metal he cut the straps of his straitjacket.

"There," said Ferguson. "You once cut me loose, and now I'm returning the favor. I know it must be hard to be a front man when you know you have no control. So, so sad."

Ferguson gave Skark a shove with his foot. Skark fell from his stool and began crawling across the floor, jumpsuit soaked with perspiration, groaning and stopping every few feet to make sure he didn't throw up. His limbs were spasming because he'd been bound too long, and he was shaking from the Spine Wine withdrawal. Every time he opened his mouth to speak to us, I could hear loose phlegm blocking his throat. *"Gack,"* he said, again and again.

Ferguson stepped into the control room and locked the

door to make sure we couldn't go assault him, watching Skark as he made his way toward the rest of the band.

"That is both a pathetic and a very satisfying sight," said Ferguson.

We got out of our chairs and lifted Skark to his feet. His legs were flailing, so Driver plunked him down in one of the folding chairs. He raised his head and looked at me, and his voice was a rasp when he spoke.

"How—*cough*—did you get that horrible bump about your eye?" said Skark. "It looks like your brain is trying to escape from your head."

"Hanging out with you guys, it must know it's being underused," I said.

Skark smiled and coughed again. "*Gack.* Probably true."

"How you feeling, Skark?" said Cad.

"Terrible," he sputtered. "But sober, for the first time in about ten years."

"This might be the first time the band has been together without *somebody* having some sort of liquor in his system," said Cad.

Ferguson rapped on the control room glass to get our attention and pressed the intercom button.

"All right, there you go, you guys are reunited with your singer," said Ferguson. "*Hurrah,* good vibes all around. Let's lay this thing down."

"I have a question," said Skark. "Were you the one who blew up the dam inside the Dark Matter Foloptopus?"

Ferguson smiled.

"I thought a good scare might get some of your creative juices going," he said. "It makes me physically ill seeing what you are now, compared to what we used to be."

Ferguson opened a cabinet inside the control room and reached inside to remove a triangular case. Reverently, he unclicked the latches and extracted a polished metal triangle and a brightly burnished wand.

"Hello, my treasure," whispered Ferguson. He kissed the triangle, and I could hear the wet smacking sound through the studio microphone. "Time to make a classic."

"You're kidding me," said Driver. "Look at Skark. He's in no condition to sing. He hasn't even *practiced* with us yet."

"The point of being a professional is that you're always ready to perform," said Ferguson, pressing a button in front of him. "I've waited long enough. Tape is rolling."

"You're not going to come in here?" said Driver.

"I'm comfortable laying down the track from the control room for now," said Ferguson. "I realize you're probably feeling a little *tense* toward me, and I wouldn't want you to lash out irrationally."

"You'll have to wait," said Cad. "We're not playing until Skark is ready."

Ferguson angrily looked around the room, his eyes flicking to each of us before landing on Skark.

"The Skark I used to know would record no matter what kind of shape he was in," said Ferguson.

"And the Ferguson I used to know was always inconsiderate to his guests, so I guess I've changed and you haven't," said Skark. "I'm not singing or listening to your atonal *banging* until I catch my breath, so begone with you, amateur."

Ferguson placed his triangle back in its case.

"Just gives me more time to put some lotion on my hands before the fireworks," he said. "Enjoy your night together, but I wouldn't try to leave. The doors are locked and it's a bit of an *inhospitable* area, so you wouldn't get far."

Ferguson exited the control room, and once again we were alone.

"Hate that guy," said Skark.

"His songs have always been unlistenable," said Cad.

"I'm going to try to see where we are," I said.

Although we were in a basement, there was a small window at the top of a wall of heavily marked Perfectly Reasonable fan photographs. It looked out over the ground level of the property, and I stood on the seat of Driver's drum kit to peek outside.

Ferguson had told the truth about the remoteness of the area. It appeared we were at the top of a treeless, snow-covered hill in the middle of a viscous, half-frozen green lake. Ferguson's comet—no longer glowing, now just a ship with its LED lights turned off—was parked on a flat piece of land at the bottom of the hill, with the Interstellar Libertine still latched to its back. It appeared that he had repaired the hole through which we had been extracted, soldering a panel of alien metal to the side of the bus. I couldn't think of a reason why he would have fixed it up, other than thinking he was eventually going to be traveling with the band, which seemed optimistic in the wake of him imprisoning us.

I put my hand on the glass for a split second before my arm reflexively pulled backward. It must have been a hundred below zero out there. I looked at my fingers—they were turning blood-red.

"I can see the bus out there," I said. "But holy *crap* it's cold."

"Ferguson has always lived in these terrible places," said Driver. "He thinks it makes him more of an artist to be isolated."

"If you'll indulge me in a bit of *I told you so,* considering our present situation," said Skark. "Would you please admit I wasn't being paranoid when I said Ferguson was after me, given that he just confirmed he caused the dam to fall?"

"I'll admit you were right, if you admit that it may have sounded like just another one of your drunk complaints," said Cad.

"We've all made drunk complaints," said Skark.

"Yours were constant," said Driver.

Skark thought about this.

"Let me say something while I'm thinking clearly, which I know doesn't happen often," he said. "I realize that I've always been difficult, and my behavior has become a bit more erratic in recent years, perhaps, I admit, due to my affection for wine. It's not easy for me to acknowledge that character flaw, but I do. I care about this band, and it's been hard for me to see its decline. Perhaps it was easier to drink than to recognize, as the songwriter, that our path to irrelevancy is my fault. The Dondoozle Festival is tomorrow, and the thing that breaks my heart the most is that people aren't even going to miss us if we're not there."

Nobody said anything. Cad and Driver seemed to agree with Skark, and I did too. The band's fans had barely been turning up for shows where the Perfectly Reasonable was the *headliner,* and at Dondoozle they would be just another group on the undercard, hoping somebody would pay attention. And in an early-afternoon slot on the opening day, at that. Even in a best-case scenario, only a handful of people would be there to see them anyway.

Skark reached down and picked a guitar up off the ground.

"We're obsolete . . . ," he hummed, strumming a gentle melody. *"And it's all done. . . ."*

Cad plucked at his bass.

"We're terrible . . . ," sang Cad. *"It's been a long dry run."*

Driver tapped out a beat on his chair.

"Oh, the Perfectly Reasonable are ending . . . ," sang Driver.

I picked up another guitar and joined in, playing rhythm over Skark's lead guitar.

"All our deaths are pending . . . ," sang Skark.

"And our prom we won't be attending . . . ," I sang.

Sophie laughed: *"HA . . . hehhhhhhhhh."*

It was the first time I had ever sung in front of another human being on purpose, and certainly the first time I'd sung in front of a couple of nonhumans, but I couldn't help myself. The rhyme was there.

"You don't have a bad voice, Bennett," said Skark.

"I think we just wrote a new song," said Cad.

"First in five years," said Driver. "All we had to do was sober up and be held captive."

"Shall we write another?" said Skark. "If the goddess of music is asking us to dance, let us take her hand. What say you, young Bennett?"

"What about Sophie?"

"There doesn't seem to be a violin or harpsichord around for her," said Skark. "Which is unfortunate. I went through a chamber-pop phase in the mid-eighties, which culminated in our minor masterpiece 'Scarves of Cashmere.'"

"How about I help with the lyrics?" said Sophie.

"Of course," said Skark. "This band is a democracy, after all."

Driver chucked a drumstick at Skark, who dodged out of the way, smiling. For the first time, I heard him laugh, once again just a skinny guy in a band.

And with that, we started to jam.

Pinkish light filtered through the slats of the window, casting our shadows on the studio floor. Outside, I could hear the cold wind blowing and the ominous thundercracks of the lake's alien ice moving and splintering. Hours had passed.

"Come here, Bennett," said Skark. He was sitting against a wall, posture upright, looking over an old photograph of the band that he had pulled down. The picture featured the three beaming faces of the current core of the band—Skark, Cad, and Driver—along with Ferguson over to the side, slumped in a chair, recovering from whatever debaucheries he had committed the night before.

I couldn't believe how *young* Skark, Cad, and Driver looked in the photo. It was more than the fact that the picture had been taken when they were at the height of their careers—their skin was clear, their chests were out, they were grinning. More than anything, they were *leaning into each other.* Buddies. There was no distance between them, no tension, no sense of the epic manner in which everything was going to be falling apart for them in the next couple of years. There wasn't even a bottle of Spine Wine in the photo. They were just happy.

"Have a seat beside me," said Skark.

I plopped down next to him. He continued to look at the photo.

"I barely recognize myself in this photo, you know," he said. "I know it's me, of course—I'm the only one who could pull off that tight of a trouser leg—but anytime I've looked in the mirror in the past few years, that hasn't been the man looking back at me."

"What do you think is different?"

"When this photo was taken, we had a future. Now I don't know what's going to happen to me. It's one thing to lose your record distribution deal in some tiny world where it doesn't make a difference one way or another to your career. But to lose your record deals everywhere in *creation*—it's hard to bounce back from that. Where do you go?"

He looked at me. He actually wanted my opinion.

"I can't say I've ever been in the same kind of position as you," I said. "I've never had any success at all—aside from getting Sophie to go to prom with me, I guess—but I think the idea is that you just move forward and focus on making yourself as good a person as you can and stop worrying about what everyone else is thinking or saying. I know that's what I did in high school when I felt like things were hopeless—I just put my head down and studied and hoped if I worked hard enough things would get better."

Skark stared at me. He looked skeptical.

"How did that work out for you?" he said. There was a flat tone in his voice, like he was afraid of bringing up some conspicuous bit of information.

"You know something, don't you."

"I may have . . . talked to the guys. About your general approach to the college application process."

Fantastic. Now even *Skark* knew that I had screwed up my college future. I pictured a universe in which my gaffe was passed from mouth to ear from world to world, until every sentient being in creation would look at me with pity and shake their head at my lack of foresight.

"I never went to college, but I may have some advice for you," said Skark. "When you don't get something you want, give yourself a moment to feel terrible about yourself, and when that's over, remember that all rejection means is that every other possible path has just opened up to you. It's freedom."

"I haven't been totally rejected yet."

"It's always pretty hard to get off a wait list," said Skark. "I'm still on a list to get into the Patarto Venturai Country Club. They said it could take eight hundred years, and I doubt I'll even live to more than five hundred, the abysmal way I've treated my body."

"That's . . . too bad."

"It's fine, I hate stuffy environments," said Skark. "I was only doing it because there was a waitress there I used to fancy. I got her eventually when she came to a show. But look. In the past few days, you have become one of the few humans who have definitively learned that *not only* are you not alone in the universe but there are *literally* almost an infinite number of options out there. All problems are small, and remarkably solvable."

"What about *your* problems?"

"Mine are huge, but that's because I'm huge," he said. He took a moment to think about this, then exhaled. "Was huge, I should say. I know it's just in my head these days."

Across the room, I noticed that Driver had fallen asleep behind his drum kit, exhausted from the all-night jam. As he slumbered, he made small twitching movements with his hands, his fingers making what looked like controlled, repetitive scooping motions. Skark saw me looking.

"He's dreaming," said Skark.

"About what?"

"Sewing. He loves music, but when it comes to what really touches his soul, it's always been clothing design."

Driver's subconscious must have heard us talking about him, because his eyes quivered and popped open. He looked at us looking back at him.

"Was I talking in my sleep?" he said.

"No, but you might have been designing a cardigan," said Skark.

"How do you know that?"

"It looked like you were using a tuck stitch," said Skark. He winked at me. "I know a little bit about clothes too."

On the other side of the room, Sophie was sleeping against the wall. Next to her, Cad was tuning his bass strings, trying to get them right after a night of banging and pulling at them in a kind of manic freedom.

Abruptly, Sophie gave him a quick kick with her heel and looked over her shoulder at him.

"Could you *please* do that somewhere else?" she said. "We were up all night. I deserve twenty minutes of sleep without having to hear a bass."

"I'll move if you promise not to kick me again," said Cad.

"I'll take it under consideration," said Sophie, rolling over and closing her eyes once more. Cad climbed to his feet and walked over to Skark and me.

"How do you think Ferguson is going to react when he realizes that we stopped practicing his song?" said Cad.

"We had more important things to do," said Skark, grinning. "Music is about *chemistry,* and we have discovered it again. It will take us ten minutes to lay down the song when the time comes."

"You might want to rest your voice in the meantime," said Driver.

Driver was right. Skark had been singing new lyrics—most of which were Sophie's—over our improvised playing all night, and now his voice, already raspy from detoxing, sounded positively gravelly.

"My voice will be fine," said Skark. "It has never let me down before, and it certainly won't so close to Dondoozle. Some hot water with honey and I'll be fine."

"I've never heard you ask for something other than booze," said Cad.

"It's been a long time since I've desired anything else."

I looked out the window to see if anything had changed. The bus was in the same place, but there was nobody out there we could flag down to help us. Because of the good vibes resulting from the band putting aside their differences and playing music together again, nobody had said what I was sure we were all thinking—that unless something extraordinary happened, there was no way we were getting out of here. Ferguson could keep us prisoners until he was satisfied with his song.

Then, through the window, I saw something peculiar—an object in the lake was *moving*.

At first I thought it might be a piece of debris, but then I realized it was changing direction—every time it came to a large slab of ice, the odd dot would slowly paddle its way around the chunk and keep pressing on, getting closer to our island. When it was confronted with an unbroken sheet of snow, I saw it dive, disappearing for perhaps half a minute before reemerging through a fissure near the shore, where it remained motionless for several seconds before beginning to paddle again. As it got closer, I could see it was purple, and as it finally climbed up onto the bank and slumped on its side, catching its breath, I knew what the thing was.

"It's Walter," I said. "He's *outside.*"

Skark, Cad, Sophie, and Driver joined me at the window. Walter had begun trudging up the hill toward the house, still covered in purple gunk.

"How did he *get* here?" said Skark.

"Rams are known for being resolute," said Sophie.

"Walter!" yelled Cad. He hit the glass with the side of his fist, then quickly pulled it away. "Man, it is *cold* out there."

"Don't get frostbite from the glass—we need your fingers for Dondoozle," said Skark. "I have an idea."

Skark held up his rings to the window, attempting to reflect the morning sunlight to get Walter's attention. Halfway up the hill, the ram winced and stared straight at us.

"Walter!" shouted Skark.

Walter put his hoof underneath his beard and made a slicing motion across his neck, like he was telling Skark to knock it off. His fur was slicked down with the purple goo, but he had clearly managed to gain some degree of flexibility in his joints, and he continued stiffly trudging up the hill.

Walter walked up to the door of the Interstellar Libertine and gave it a firm *whack* with his hoof. The door opened. He climbed the steps one at a time, getting his feet set before each jump like he was scaling a cliff, and then disappeared inside the bus.

"Does he know how to drive?" said Sophie.

"I don't see how he would," said Cad. "He has no hands."

The door of the control room opened and Ferguson walked in. He pressed the intercom button, and his voice rang through the speakers.

"Your bandleader has arrived," he said. "Let's lay the song down so we can move on to the next one. We've got a lot of time to make up for."

"We?" said Skark, outraged.

Skark straightened his back and slowly walked up to the control room, showing Ferguson his full eight feet of height. Overnight, he had sweated out the chemicals in his system, and what I supposed was his normal pinkish-purplish color had returned to his skin. Apparently his pallid countenance had had more to do with what was going into his body than with heredity.

Skark put his palms on the window of the booth and stared down at Ferguson, looming over him like the specter from Ferguson's past that he was.

"You will *never* be in this band again," boomed Skark. "We *fired* you because you could no longer balance your lifestyle with your commitments to this band. We *fired* you because you embarrassed us in front of our fans. We *fired* you because you were a *pestilential* presence on the bus, draining us before and after shows. We *fired* you because you thought you were *bigger* than the rest of the band."

Skark looked back at Cad and Driver.

"All right, I *realize* that I did those things as well, but please forgive a bit of megalomania in your front man. Once again, I'm sorry."

"Glad to hear it," said Cad.

"You *can't say* that my new song isn't good," said Ferguson.

Skark focused his gaze back on Ferguson.

"Isn't good?" said Skark. "I would wish *deafness* on this entire *universe* so that nobody would have to hear your song. I would destroy every instrument in *existence* if it meant your song would forever go unplayed. Last night the Perfectly Reasonable became a *band* again, wholly and magnificently *without* you. If I had a choice between this barren, worthless little planet exploding beneath me or putting you back in the band, I would *select* that fatal boom—"

CRUNCH!

On cue, Ferguson's house was ripped apart by the out-of-control Interstellar Libertine. The bus was spinning through the air, pulling a large piece of metal behind it where it had broken free from Ferguson's ship.

Apparently Walter's plan had been to just hit the gas and see what happened.

Because we had been in the process of watching Skark reaming out Ferguson, nobody was prepared for the bus to come crashing through the house or for the foam walls to tear open or for the subzero air to bite our skin. It felt like we had stepped into a twister. I grabbed Sophie and was holding her tightly, trying to shelter her from the collapsing house, when Skark collared us with his thin hands and tossed us into the bus. Driver climbed in behind us, breathing heavily and carrying Cad, who seemed dazed, with dilated pupils and pieces of foam in his hair—he'd been whacked in the head by some sort of debris.

"Skark, come *on!*" yelled Driver, but Skark was waving him off. He was searching the rubble for instruments. I watched a guitar fly into the bus, followed by Cad's bass and most of Driver's drum set.

"Your cymbals are somewhere out here," said Skark.

"*Forget* about the cymbals," said Driver.

"The cymbals make things *funky,*" said Skark.

Skark pulled a high hat from the debris and was about to toss it in the bus when—*DING*—Ferguson appeared on the other side of the combat zone, covered in dust, ice in his hair, gripping his triangle.

"You're *not* leaving here," said Ferguson.

Skark looked at him and shook his head.

"I'm sorry, Ferguson," said Skark. "I don't have the time it would require for you to tap me to death with your wand. If you get out of this, I'll have a pair of tickets waiting for you at Dondoozle so you can enjoy the show, provided you're the one wearing the straitjacket this time. Good day."

Skark stepped onto the bus, where Walter was sitting in Driver's seat, hooves still on the controls, covered in purple goo, looking woozy from the crash.

"I had to turn the ignition with my mouth, and I couldn't stop the bus without hands," said Walter apologetically. "I was trying to just *nudge* my way through the wall."

"I've got it from here, Walter," said Driver. "You did well."

Walter and Driver switched places, Walter falling out of the driver's seat and stumbling to the back of the bus. I looked down at Sophie, who was lying next to me on the floor where Skark had thrown us inside.

"You all right?" I said.

"About half a second from frostbite, I think," she said. "Same as you, apparently." Our exposed flesh—our faces, my chest, her neck—was blotchy with deep blue spots, where the skin was trying to keep itself alive.

I looked around for a blanket, but there weren't any. I was shocked at how empty the Interstellar Libertine was. When Ferguson had cut the hole in the side of the bus, everything had been sucked out of it—the furniture, the kitchen appliances, the beds, Skark's sleeping pod, the secondhand amplifiers the band had purchased outside Jyfon, the contents of the wet bar, and the entirety of Skark's wardrobe. The only thing left was a pair of Driver's drumsticks, stuck in the armrest where he stored them while he drove.

Driver pulled back on the controls and the bus lifted off the smashed floor of Ferguson's recording studio, pointing its nose through the broken roof. He hit the accelerator. It felt like a normal takeoff, but then there was a burst of heat and the sensation of suddenly being jerked *downward.*

"Dammit, that chunk of Ferguson's ship we're pulling is too heavy," said Driver. "Somebody open the emergency door and get rid of it *now.*"

Skark ambled toward the back of the bus, lumbering like an old-time Hollywood monster to keep his balance. He looked dazed, which maybe made sense considering he had just learned his entire wardrobe had disappeared. All he had left was his jacket and the jumpsuit on his bony back.

Slipping and careening, Skark made it to the emergency exit, where he crouched and yanked the lever of the door, throwing it open with a sweep of his arm. A blast of icy air shot through the bus. Skark swung his leg in a powerful arc, kicking the cable that was tethering the bus to the piece of Ferguson's ship. The cable snapped through the air like a snake, and the Interstellar Libertine lurched forward ferociously, liberated from its anchor.

And then we had another problem to solve.

Straining against the heavy anchor had caused the engine to overheat, and with an ominous *VVVTT,* the Interstellar Libertine stalled. The interior lights went black, and the bus began to drop from the limited altitude we'd struggled to achieve. Driver was pounding on the wheel and the dashboard to no effect. We were about to crash back down into Ferguson's house.

"I can't get it to start," said Driver. The bus was already starting to tip on its side. When it hit the ground, it was going to roll.

"Let me try," I said. "I have a trick for whenever my pickup stalls."

Driver stared at me. He could see I wasn't kidding.

"Whatever you're going to do, do it *fast,*" Driver told me, bolting up from the chair and hanging on to the railing of the door to steady himself. I took his place, and through the windshield I could see the ground roaring toward us.

I stared at the wheel. Then I reached forward, rubbed its underside three times, and whispered to it.

"I love you," I said.

I turned the key, and the bus roared to life, gaining altitude and tacking sideways, righting itself.

Driver was staring at me, stunned.

"How did you *do* that?" he said.

"Sometimes all a car wants is a little appreciation," I said. "Your turn to take over."

Driver switched places with me behind the controls, and I made my way to the back to see if Sophie was okay. I found her gripping the frame of the closet, holding Walter.

"You used the *I love you* trick, didn't you?" she said.

"Cars are the same everywhere," I said.

Behind Sophie, I saw Skark grab the handle of the emergency door, twist his body, and bolt it shut with an authoritative *clang.* The Interstellar Libertine shot toward the outer reaches of the planet's atmosphere. Sophie lost her grip on Walter, who slid on the floor past me and crashed into the wall. Cad hung on to his pull-up bar as the bus rapidly ascended. As I seized the frame of the bathroom door and Sophie clutched the sink, I saw Driver's drumsticks whiz past at a hazardous speed.

"We're almost out," said Driver. *"Hold on. . . ."*

We skyed upward. I looked out the window and saw a coat-less Ferguson standing in the rubble of his broken island home, taking pained steps as he tried to make his way toward the shelter of his ship. I couldn't fathom how in that cold, without any protective clothing, he was going to survive. I watched him bend over to pick something up—from the shape of the object, it might have been his triangle case—but soon he was too small to see and all I could make out was the remnants of his home, haloed by the frozen pond and endless meadows of snow. He had the entire hemisphere to himself, and it seemed like that was where he was going to stay.

He would not be rejoining the band.

There was a thud of impact and the sound of warping metal as the Interstellar Libertine's front grille crunched its way through the atmosphere, and then we were drifting again, sequined stars and pinpoints of light all around us. I saw Driver slump back in his seat and shift the bus into a lower gear.

"Never much cared for that guy," said Driver. He glanced into the back of the bus. "Skark, stop being so quiet. It's time to celebrate. Looks like you'll get the chance to play Dondoozle after all."

There was no response.

"Skark?" said Cad.

Everyone turned to look at Skark, who was sitting against the back wall of the bus, pointing to his neck.

"Mrmrff," he said.

One of Driver's drumsticks was stuck through his throat.

⭐ ⭐ ⭐

Nobody was sure what to do about the piece of wood protruding from Skark's neck. There wasn't time to go to a hospital and still make the gig, but he clearly needed some sort of medical attention. Cad wanted to pull the stick out and see what happened, while Driver offered to use his thick hands to break it off at the base but leave the rest of it where it was, if only to make sure that Skark didn't accidentally hit it on something and push it in farther. Sophie was rolling her eyes at the scene, pointing out that it was *probably* better to skip the festival and get Skark the help he needed, but each time she repeated the suggestion, Skark shook his head. He wasn't missing Dondoozle.

Skark was sitting against the wall that Ferguson had bolted to the side to cover the hole, staring brokenly at the bald interior of the bus. Even the rugs were gone. The mobile opium den that I had encountered when I had first climbed aboard now resembled the kind of abandoned clunker where a hobo might hide from the rain. Skark touched the skin around the drumstick with his fingers and winced. He opened his mouth and tried to speak, but nothing came out but spittle and air.

We stood around, looking at him. Walter was next to me, banished to the closet no longer, contorting his body to pull the last bits of goop out of his fur with his teeth.

"What do you think we should do?" said Driver.

"I already solved one of your problems," said Walter. "You're on your own for this one."

"How did you *find* us?" said Cad.

Walter told us that he had been picked up by a couple of teenagers going to Dondoozle. When he had said he had also been going to the festival—against his will, but still going—the teenagers had asked who he wanted to see. Walter had replied that he didn't want to see anybody, and that he had been a prisoner of the Perfectly Reasonable.

The teenagers had never even *heard* of the Perfectly Reasonable, so they had looked up the band on their phones and spent several minutes mocking old promotional photographs of the group, dissecting song lyrics, and generally treating the band like the prehistoric oddity they considered it to be. Walter had joined in the fun, finally getting a chance to expunge himself of years of resentment.

"One of the band photographs had Ferguson in it," said Walter. "I said to myself, *Huh, that's the guy I saw creeping around while I was staring out the window at the Dark Matter Foloptopus gig.*"

"You *saw* Ferguson?" said Driver. "Why didn't you tell us?"

"Why would I ever tell you *anything*?" said Walter. "That's when I put it together that Ferguson might have been the one who hijacked the bus, since Skark is talking about him all the time. The teens looked up where Ferguson lived on their phones and dropped me off. Simple as that. They set me down in the wrong spot, so I had to *swim* across that horrible lake, but I made it."

"Why did you come back?" said Cad.

Walter nodded to me.

"Bennett was the first one in four years to pay attention to me," said Walter. "He gave me grass. I figured I owed it to him to at least try."

"So if it wasn't for Bennett—" said Cad.

"You would still be there, absolutely," said Walter. "Forgive me, Sophie. I'm only talking about the band here. You seem sweet, and I don't mean to sound like I'd intentionally maroon you somewhere."

"Don't worry, I wasn't taking it that way," said Sophie.

"Ghack," said Skark. It was the first noise we'd heard him make.

"I'm willing to take that as a positive sign," said Cad.

"As am I," said Driver. "Skark, save your strength. Everybody think of ways to disguise that stick in his neck."

"You could hang a white surrender flag from it," said Sophie.

"Ghack ghack," said Skark, his distressed eyes momentarily flaming to life. Regardless of the woebegone nature of his situation, he was clearly insulted by the idea that someone thought he wouldn't find a way out of this.

I had to say, it was kind of admirable. As *unaccommodating* a presence as he had been my first few days on the bus, over the past twenty-four hours I'd come to like him. Stripped of his wine, his voice, and all his possessions, he still wanted to get to the gig and do his job.

He gripped the end of the drumstick and wiggled it around. I heard it squish.

"Relax, Skark," said Cad.

But Skark did not relax. He gave the drumstick one more jiggle, then defiantly *yanked it out,* leaving a bottle-cap-sized hole in his throat.

"Oh my *God,*" said Sophie.

Skark might have looked somewhat human from the outside, but it was clear that his insides were nothing like ours— the tissue on the other side of his skin was white and had the consistency of Styrofoam. There was no blood, no fluid, no tendons, just *nothing* but a hole in his voice box. He looked like a smoker who'd had a tracheostomy but forgotten to ask for the speaking valve.

That said, his decision to pull the thing out seemed to have had little effect on his ability to talk—he was still making the same wheezing, *ghack*ing sounds, except now there was an unsightly neck crater as visual accompaniment to the gasping and croaking.

"You could have given a heads-up that you were going to do that," said Cad, looking a little disturbed. "Kind of messed up."

"Ghack," said Skark.

The band was in trouble.

FRIDAY

The Dondoozle Festival took place on a largely abandoned, sod-covered planet in a remote galaxy known as Dnarp 229, which Cad informed me was considered a kind of galactic Wild West—if you killed somebody in a more civilized region and wanted to make sure you were never found, you came to Dnarp 229. Except for one weekend a year, that is.

Not only was Dondoozle the largest music festival in the universe, it was the only one that really mattered. A good performance here, and your name was on the tip of every in-the-know tongue in creation. A bad performance, and you never got invited back.

The fact that the Perfectly Reasonable had given a strong performance at the festival years before was the only reason they were able to play Dondoozle again. They had been the headliners a decade earlier, when they had been in total command of their powers, and it was this magisterial performance that had catapulted them to the height of their stardom. At the time, they had been coming off *The Perfectly Reasonable Is in Your Kitchen and They're Hungry,* which was their biggest-selling album to date. Cad had just joined the group and had been burning for success. Driver had been in better physical condition, which had provided him greater power in his drumming. Skark had thought he was about to change the universe with his music.

But today, the fans at the festival were there to see anybody *but* the Perfectly Reasonable. They were the first band playing—always the least desirable time slot, because attendees were still arriving and wanted to check out the schedule, stretch their legs, and generally get settled. The only reason the band was being allowed to play at all was that the festival programmer was doing them a favor as a nod of respect to their triumphant gig years before. How big a favor was debatable, given the way they had been buried in the schedule.

The festival was located on a borderless stretch of flat, burned ground, and the lack of vegetation meant that it was possible to see the ten stages that had been set up, stretching all the way to the dead mountains on the horizon.

Due to the lack of cover, it was *hot,* and to stay cool the fans milling about wore little clothing, which made for a crash course in alien anatomy. Because of the nature of the festival—bands from all over the universe coming to one place—it was *by far* the most diverse place I'd ever been. I saw wood-colored clouds disappearing from one side of the festival and materializing at the front of the lines at the busy beverage stands. I saw sheets of water whooshing through the crowd, avoiding overheated sand trolls that were trying to leap through them to cool off. I saw sentient chunks of asphalt rolling unsteadily along, and enthusiastic chairs walking about, carrying their girlfriends, who were also chairs, which was kind of cute. I saw lime-green shadows swooping down and snatching pretzels from the hands of patrons who actually looked like oversized pretzels, which made me wonder if some sort of cannibalism was going on. The grounds were crowded and the heat was oppressive, and yet everybody seemed to be in a jubilant mood—hugging, chatting, drinking, eating, comparing terrible tattoos.

But I saw all these things from a distance, because I was backstage, trying to help get the band ready for their performance. Driver was caking makeup on himself and Cad to cover the bruises, cuts, and signs of exhaustion they had accumulated over the previous couple of days—but no amount of makeup was going to bring back Skark's voice.

Skark was sitting in front of the vanity mirror, wheezing through his throat hole, willing his voice to come back. He was still going through the motions of getting ready, putting makeup on over his eyes while the rest of us stood around, unsure what we should be doing in the meantime. The Perfectly

Reasonable had made it to the festival, but they weren't going to be able to play.

A stage manager poked her head into the dressing room. She looked like a tote bag turned upside down—canvaslike skin propped on top of a pair of spindly legs, eyes in the middle of her body like two buttons.

"Fifteen minutes, guys," she said. "You know, I don't normally interrupt bands as they're getting ready, but I'd just like to say I'm a longtime fan and I can't *wait* to see Skark in person. I hadn't heard anything about you guys in *years*—to be honest, I thought you were dead—and then I saw you on the bill. I figured it was a mistake, but the promoters said no, they're really playing. I couldn't believe it. Where have you been?"

Skark made a hacking sound: *"Ghack."* Bits of phlegm escaped from his mouth, landing on the stage manager's headphones.

"Guess that's why you're never supposed to meet your heroes," said the stage manager. "Fourteen minutes until showtime." She hustled away.

Skark silently finished painting his customary stripe over his eyes. His jumpsuit was streaked in grime. I watched him open his mouth, wheeze, shake his head, and run his hands through his hair. I'd never seen him look so desperate.

"What are we going to do?" said Cad. "Push him out onstage and have him hack into a microphone? Who's going to sing?"

Skark leaned back in his chair, looking at the ceiling, gathering his thoughts. He pointed at me.

"Bennett doesn't know our songs," said Driver.

Skark grabbed a tube of lipstick and wrote on the vanity mirror:

DO YOU HAVE A BETTER IDEA?

"I've never sung in public before," I said.

Skark wrote again:

FIRST TIME FOR EVERYTHING

"Not to be a stickler for rules," said Driver. "But *contractually* I don't think we can trot out a new lead singer when they're expecting *you,* our famous front man."

Skark thought about this, then leaned forward and wrote on the sliver of mirror that was still clear:

DRESS HIM UP LIKE ME

HE'S ALREADY TALL AND WEIRD-LOOKING

"I can't sing like Skark . . . ," I said.

"If we say that you're slightly under the weather, I'm sure nobody will begrudge you a few high notes," said Driver.

"I really don't think—"

Sophie grabbed my face and *squeezed.*

"*The faster* you get out there and do this, the faster we get to prom," she said. "Now be a man—or actually, be whatever the hell Skark is—and get out there and *sing.*"

Message received, but there was still something I wanted to mention to Sophie before I did this.

"I don't have a tux," I said.

"What?"

"For prom. I don't have a tux. It's been weighing on my mind."

"We can worry about that *later,*" said Sophie. "Priorities, please."

"Fine, I'll do it," I said. Skark got up from his makeup chair and offered it to me. I sat down, and he began drawing a stripe across my eyes.

"This is such a bad idea," I said.

Over the next ten minutes, Driver used foundation to make my skin the same pale hue as Skark's, while Skark completed the fetching metallic yellow stripe across my eyes. Sophie used a chemical solution from an on-site first-aid kit to dye my hair orange, then spiked it with some of Driver's spit, which had the stickiness and consistency of Elmer's glue and smelled a bit like sausage.

Skark removed his sweat-stained jumpsuit and filthy tiled jacket, stripping himself naked except for a Dondoozle Festival program he was holding over his nether regions. He offered the clothes to me in an unappealing wad, and I put them on. I gave him my scrubs; the pants ended halfway up his calves, like a pair of out-of-style capris.

We shoved pages of the festival program into his size-20 shoes to help them fit me more snugly, but the extra stuffing was little help. I have no idea how women walk in high heels—I felt like I might tip over in *any* direction at any time, and I had no idea where to put my weight.

Sophie and the band looked me over.

"It's actually not a bad style," said Sophie. "If you'd done this in high school, you definitely would have gotten more attention."

"Think it's enough for him to pass as Skark?" said Cad.

"If nobody comes to see us, it doesn't matter what he looks like," said Driver.

Skark hacked a few times and shrugged. Apparently he thought the resemblance was good enough.

"Ladies and gentlemen . . . welcome to the Dondoozle Festival. And there is nobody we'd rather have starting us off than our next band, making their comeback. Please put your hands together for Dondoozle veterans and current one billion fiftieth greatest band in the universe . . ."

"When did we drop to one billion fifty?" said Cad.

"Universal Beat released new rankings last night," said Driver. "I found out about it when we landed, but I didn't want to say anything."

". . . the Perfectly Reasonable!"

The band waited for applause to welcome them to the stage, but none came.

"The announcer and us are the only ones who know we're making our comeback," said Cad.

Driver looked at me.

"Time for you to be a star," he said.

Driver walked out onto the stage, followed by Cad, but when it was time for me to make my entrance, I couldn't move—my stomach was knotted and I could feel sweat cutting streaks through my makeup. I had never been onstage before.

On the back of my leg I felt a supportive hoof that nearly sent me toppling from my platform boots to the ground.

"You can do this," said Walter.

From behind his drum kit, Driver was imploring me with his sticks to *come on*. I took a few steps . . . and then fell over into the base of the public-address system mounted at the front of the stage.

"Fantastic," I heard Cad say.

I stumbled again as I tried to get up, nearly knocking over the drums this time, then tripped a third time, whereupon I decided to cut my losses and crawl across the stage to the microphone. I grabbed the stand, pulled myself to my feet, and straightened my guitar.

The positive thing about my botched entrance was that nobody was there to see it except Sophie, who had no *choice* but to watch us play and had—intimidatingly—positioned herself in the open field *directly* in front of the stage. The only festival-goers looking in our direction were a few by the food carts in the distance, killing time as they covered their hot dogs with ketchup or mustard or Minotaur blood or whatever it was that aliens used for condiments.

"Hello, Dondoozle," I said into the microphone, my voice echoing over the empty lot in front of us. "I am Benn—I'm Skark Zelirium."

I glanced over at Cad and saw him giving me a *hurry it up* gesture.

"All right. Okay. I'm doing it. It's great to be here. *One, two, three, four,"* I said, because that's what confident rock stars did. Driver and Cad began playing behind me, shooting vibrations up my back . . .

. . . and I froze.

I couldn't remember a *note* of a Perfectly Reasonable song. I mean, I'd only *heard* the songs once or twice, and I had just the *vaguest* idea of the lyrics.

Cad stepped away from his microphone and walked over to me, plucking his bass.

"What the *hell* is going on?" he hissed.

I stared at him.

"Play," he said. *"Sing something.* We'll play over you—nobody will be able to tell the difference. What's wrong with you?"

I looked down at my guitar, then up at the vacant field in front of me. Sophie was still the only one there, imploring me to get it together.

"Come *on!*" she yelled.

The stage manager motioned me on from the side of the stage, waving her tote-bag tendrils around to show her concern.

I looked at Sophie. I was malfunctioning. She was standing in the middle of the dusty field, hair sticking out in all directions, arms blotchy with bruises and lined with scratches, shielding her eyes from a strange sun, having been through hell. She was here because of me. I didn't want to fail in front of her.

"Pretend like you're in your bedroom!" she yelled over the drums. "You can do this!"

And with that . . . a strange feeling came over my fingers, which started to move like they were doing what they wanted without my conscious control. They knew just where to go, which I guess made sense, since I was playing one of my own songs. I leaned into the microphone.

"I'm going to call a little bit of an audible for our first number," I said into the mike. "This song is called 'Sophie and Me Under the Waterfall.'"

Sophie's mouth *dropped.* I turned to Cad and Driver, who were equally shocked.

"What the hell is 'Sophie and Me Under the Waterfall'?" said Cad.

"Just follow my lead," I said.

Having spent hundreds of afternoons alone in my bedroom with my guitar, I had mentally collected the fragments of a million songs I didn't have any idea how to finish, which until now I'd always thought was a flaw in my character. Every time, I would hit that point where I got discouraged, and give up.

But with Sophie standing in front of me, I wasn't going to give up this time. I started to sing.

> *Love is gonna run, but I'm gonna chase*
> *Sophie's gonna win, but I'm gonna place*

As I began, it felt like I wasn't Bennett anymore—I was just another note hovering above the stage, channeling ideas. From my perch, I watched a crowd start to come, approaching with the sandwiches and drinks that a few minutes before had been a more enticing option than watching the first show of the festival.

I tried not to look at Sophie—I knew she was shocked, which was understandable, considering that *every song* I was playing was clearly about her, and I was using her real name in all of them. Less than a week ago, when I had spotted her through the telescope and we had started this journey, I had assured her that I wasn't a stalker. These songs *really* weren't going to help my cause.

The fifth song in the set was the long-in-development "Sophie and Me Up in Those Trees," about us living together in the Amazon jungle. Halfway through, I realized the stage manager had turned on the video screens on either the side of the stage. For the first time in my life, I caught a glimpse of myself fifty feet tall and singing:

> *You're swinging up there and I'm looking up at you*
> *Can't wait to come home to a tree house made for*
> *two. . . .*
> *Oh!*

It was the first time I'd ever shouted *oh!* I could see why singers did it all the time. It was satisfying.

The video screens, the growing crowd, and the *songs* attracted bigger crowds, and by the seventh number—"The Time Sophie and I Got Locked in a Target"—we weren't getting only snack-gobbling curiosity seekers, we were getting fans who were *showing up* already dancing, pushing their way to the front for a better view.

By the eighth song, I figured it was time to try something else, so I eased the band into a song that had no title, which we had worked on together in Ferguson's basement, words courtesy of Sophie.

As was the case with everything she did, writing lyrics had seemed to come to Sophie with ease, and throughout that night I had watched Skark repeating her rhymes to himself as they popped out of her head, laboring to commit them to his newly sober working mind.

These particular lyrics were patently about being trapped with a bunch of people you didn't want to be stuck with. Because they were fresh in my mind, they rattled off my tongue: *"Nowhere to go but out in the snow, nowhere to hide with these guys as my guide."* Propelled by the *thump* of Driver's drums, they poured out of me, and I could see Sophie grinning and looking around at the crowd roaring behind her.

For the ninth song, my brain went back to one of my own compositions, just called "Sophie," which I knew was uncreative. I couldn't see where the crowd ended, and they were all *moving*. Or at least jumping—by now, the crowd was too tightly packed for any individual to be doing a solo dance number.

That's something I forgot to mention about the songs— while they started out with me strumming a guitar alone in my bedroom, with Cad's bass and Driver's huge backbeat, they had somehow morphed into *dance songs*. And I *liked* watching the crowd move out there.

This was why I needed a band. I had always thought my personal musical style would end up somewhere in the Bob Dylan / Jeff Buckley / Van Morrison song-as-confessional mold—but it turned out that in my heart, in true seventies funk-lord style, all I wanted to do was make the people *dance.*

As we began the tenth song—"Sophie at the End of the Telescope," which was another number that wouldn't help my *I'm not obsessed with you* case—I looked at Sophie to see her reaction, but all I got was the back of her head, because she had turned around and was pushing back against the crowd pressing her up against the stage.

> *I see you through my glass viewfinder*
> *Let me be your lovin' next-door minder*

I reached down from the stage and pulled Sophie up to keep her from being crushed. I didn't even lose my balance—three songs in, I had become one with my platform shoes, and by this point I thought I might never take them off again.

She yelled into my ear over the music. "Every song is about *me*. I think you owe me royalties," she said, smiling.

"Sorry about the surprise," I said.

"It wasn't a surprise," she said. "I've been listening to you singing about me for *years.*"

Well, that solved that mystery. She *had* heard me singing

about her through my open window. I didn't have time to feel self-conscious about it. There were a hundred thousand eyes—grouped in twos and threes and fours—staring up at me from the field.

I turned to make sure Sophie made it safely to the wings of the stage. And there, for the first time since I'd started performing, I noticed Skark.

He was rubbing his throat and pacing back and forth barefoot, miserable. This was supposed to be his moment, but there I was in his shoes, fronting his band, playing to the entire ticket-holding population of Dondoozle.

We finished the last song. "Thank you and *good night!*" I yelled. "The Perfectly Reasonable loves you."

I hustled offstage and immediately began taking off my boots as the audience stomped and clapped and screamed for the obligatory encore.

Skark gave me a gesture of *what are you doing?*

"*You're* going out there," I said. "But you can't do it naked, so you're going to have to put all of this back on. Fast."

I looked at Sophie.

"A little privacy, please," I said.

"Let me point out that I've just been watching you jump around in the tightest jumpsuit *imaginable,*" she said, turning around and covering her eyes. "So there isn't much *mystery* between us anymore."

"That's not true," I said. "You're still totally mysterious to me."

I saw Sophie smile. She liked that.

I took off Skark's jacket and peeled the jumpsuit from my body while Skark pulled off the scrubs and handed them back. It was a little odd standing face to face with a naked man who had a body kinda similar to my own, like I'd stumbled into an abstract black-and-white photograph from the 1970s, but there was no time to dwell on it.

"*Hackkk,*" said Skark, rushing to put the jumpsuit back on. Dressing him up wasn't going to solve the issue of him not being able to speak.

There was still one thing we hadn't tried, maybe because we hadn't had the right kind of spackle.

I pulled a sweaty wad of balled-up festival program out of my boot and shoved it into the hole in his throat.

"*Garumpf,*" said Skark, shocked.

"See if that helps," I said. "I *know* you've got one song in you."

Skark rubbed his stuffed voice box and looked at me.

"A little better . . . ," he croaked.

I held the top of the platform boot open, and reluctantly he lifted his callused foot toward me.

"You know what?" I said. "Your foot is bugging me out, so I'm going to let you put on your shoe yourself."

One after the other, he jammed his feet into his boots and laced them himself. He stood, checking his balance, and put out his hands to me.

I gave him his guitar.

"Thank you," he whispered, barely forcing it out. "I'm glad you came on the bus."

"Me too," I said. "Good luck."

With that, Skark smiled at me and walked onstage for the encore. The applause was deafening, and I was pleased that it was partly mine.

If anyone in the audience had questions about why the Skark who walked onstage for the encore was taller, had slightly different colored hair, and carried himself in an alternate manner than the Skark who had walked *off* the stage two minutes earlier, they forgot them once the real Skark stepped up to the microphone.

"Accckkk," he hacked, willing his throat to do what he wanted. *"Accckkk . . .* dammit *. . . accckkk."*

It was disgusting, but the crowd thought it was part of the theatrics of the show, and they loved it.

Skark grinned at the crowd, and I saw him relax. If they were going to cheer for him for simply *clearing his throat,* then he already had them where he wanted.

Before Skark got up there, I'd cockily been thinking that my own performance had been rather showstopping—my singing was in key, my songs were embraced by the audience, my fingers knew what to do with the guitar strings without me having to tell them—and then Skark went up there and proved how a true legend owned a stage.

"*Accckkk.* Aha. There it is. You'd *forgotten* how good the Perfectly Reasonable could be, hadn't you?" he said. "I assure you that after tonight you won't forget us again. This next song is called 'You Can't Hide'—perhaps you've heard it before."

They launched into the song, and it became evident that I had exploited only a *fraction* of the energy the audience had pent up inside their bodies. I might have *started* them dancing, but Skark took it from there, whipping them into such a froth I was fearful they'd rush the stage and rip the Perfectly Reasonable to shreds, which would have perhaps hindered their comeback. But it would have been a glorious way to end a career and would have no doubt received some exceptional press.

"I think I'm turned on," said Sophie, watching Skark.

"Turn off," I said.

I'd never seen Cad and Driver *smile* while they were playing music together onstage, but now they looked like thirteen-year-old kids who'd just started a garage band and were realizing it was a lot of fun to make a lot of noise.

The ground was shaking as Skark stood on the amplifier at the front of the stage and soloed over the crowd, then fell backward into the audience and allowed his adorers to catch him. He played horizontally as he was passed from hand to hand, his clothing being torn to ribbons. By the time he was returned to the stage for his final song, he was naked aside from his jacket, which was fortunately *just* long enough to keep the concert from turning pornographic.

Skark stood at the microphone, fixing his hair. "You could have *waited* until I was done with the show before stripping me to the skin. You know I've always had an open-door policy regarding fans coming home with me, and I'll need your help to keep in shape until the next tour."

"When is the next tour?" shouted somebody from the crowd.

"We're planning it as soon as we finish this, so silence thy-selves and pay attention. For the rest of your days, you'll be gloating about this next performance to your friends who aren't here, for you're about to witness the solo debut of our bassist, Cad, playing his own song."

Skark took off his guitar and handed it to an astonished Cad.

"The only reason I never let you play before now was that I wanted to give you the largest possible audience," said Skark, smirking.

"How *thoughtful* of you," said Cad, putting down his bass and strapping on the guitar.

Skark took the bass and retreated to the rear of the stage, graciously gesturing Cad to the center microphone. Cad looked out at the audience.

"The last time we were here, it was the best gig of my life," said Cad. "Now this is. You've given this band new life. This is a song I wrote called 'Home.'"

The moment Skark said Cad was going to play a song, I had hoped it would be 'Home.' His lyrics about looking for something but not wanting to go back to the place you came from—*born on the coast but never saw the ocean again, knew*

I'd meet you but I never knew when—ran over and underneath and through the endless sea of crowd members raising their arms, embracing him from where they were standing. The first part of the song was just Cad and his guitar, but when the chorus kicked in—*made it here with you,* repeated several times— Driver fell into a groove behind him and hammered through the rest of the song like he'd been playing it his entire career.

Even though I had a strained relationship with my hometown, when I first met Cad, I had thought it was odd that he had never gone back to New Jersey. I may have desperately wanted to go to Princeton, but I couldn't imagine never going back home to see my family. Cad didn't have a family, but from the way he was grinning at Skark and Driver before turning back to an audience that was in the middle of really loving him, it seemed like he had made a home right here. Maybe some people could really just totally get away and be happy.

I knew the band had never played Cad's song together before, but it sounded like a permanent part of the encore. When Cad finished, he tossed his guitar pick into the roaring audience, watched them fight over it for a few satisfied seconds, and handed the guitar back to Skark with a *told you so* nod.

"You've made me fear for my job," said Skark. "Where did *that* come from?"

"Years of frustration about you telling me to shut up," said Cad.

"You need shut up no longer, friend," said Skark. "But I'm

going to have to ask you to surrender the stage for a few moments. It's time to end this engagement properly."

Cad put his bass back on while Skark walked to the microphone and raised his hand. "Perfectly Reasonable, on my signal."

The band stared at Skark as they waited for him to give them the go-ahead, knowing it wasn't coming anytime soon. Skark was going to milk this. For ten seconds, Skark left his hand hanging in the air, staring at the audience as the volume of their screams increased, wiggling his fingers at the crowd to taunt them.

Finally, he dropped his hand to start the next song . . . but instead of playing, Cad and Driver simply took off their instruments and left the stage. Cad smiled at me as he walked into the wings.

"This is how we used to end our shows," he said. "Watch."

Skark stood alone, the video screens flanking the stage showing him from every angle, pressing in on the makeup melting off his face, the wild tangles in his hair, and the wet plug of paper damming up the hole in his throat. He removed his guitar and turned back to the microphone.

"Ah, at last, private time with the people I love most. Thank you so much for tonight. I can't tell you what it means to the band and me. It's been a long road back."

With that, Skark closed his eyes and incanted a single haunting note, letting it drift over the audience, making it dip until it was so low that I felt it rumbling in my belly and then rise until

I couldn't hear it at all, though I knew it was still there, hanging in the air. It sounded like the music that plays in movies when a virtuous hero is taken up to heaven—seraphic, soothing, completely his own.

When he had expelled the last of his breath, Skark closed his mouth, bowed to his audience, and walked offstage to complete silence. The audience was so dumbstruck that they couldn't even raise their hands to slap them together.

"That should give us enough time to get away," Skark said, winking at Sophie and me as he rapidly walked past. "Come on."

Sophie and I followed, weaving our way around roadies for other bands who were standing in place, holding amps and drums, also entranced by the sound of Skark's voice. We hustled past the stage manager, who was gripping a pen in her canvas tendril, having just put a check mark next to the Perfectly Reasonable's name on her band lineup—gig, finished—before she too heard Skark and froze. We grabbed cookies from the catering station, where a chef had paused in the middle of rotating some sort of oversized amphibian on a spit and was staring in the direction of the stage in astonishment.

We piled onto the bus.

"It's so important to leave before the audience does, both for the mystique and so the bus doesn't get overrun," said Skark. "Driver, kindly take us out of here."

Driver piloted the bus upward. Beneath us, we could see the stage. No one in the audience had moved.

"That should be enough time," said Skark. *"Listen."*

All at once, the crowd snapped out of their collective trance to deliver an eardrum-ripping thunder of applause that caused the bus to vibrate. They were waving up at us, screaming for Skark, stomping their feet, demanding another encore.

"That," said Skark, "is the sound of *rebirth.*"

Skark ran through the bus, sweatily embracing everybody. He lifted Cad out of his seat and gave him a bear hug, holding him against his chest a foot off the ground.

"I take back everything I ever said about your lack of song-writing talent," said Skark, straight into Cad's face. "I'm still shaking from your performance. Please tell me you have other songs. We will record them all."

"I have a few," said Cad.

"Fantastic. We'll put your head in a vise and squeeze them out one by one. I can't wait to discover what's in there. I'm disgusted that I never knew I was in the presence of such a master."

Skark lifted Walter, who immediately struggled to get out of his arms, whacking him with his hooves. Skark didn't even seem to feel it.

"Walter, thank you for all your spiritual advice over the past four years," said Skark. "Thank you for rescuing us. We're taking you home tonight."

"I'm still not your spirit guide, but if it gets me back to Nevada, you're *welcome.*"

Skark took my cheeks in his hands and planted a wet kiss on my forehead.

"If you let me record the songs you played tonight, I'll give you part of the album sales."

"You'll have to ask Sophie. It's her name that'll be all over the universe."

The band looked at Sophie. She was thinking.

"You can record the songs if Bennett and I each get twenty-five percent of the total gross," she said. "Half of the money for us, half the money for you."

"A *shrewd* businesswoman when it comes to publishing rights," said Skark. "I'm impressed. If Bennett is happy with the deal, so am I."

"There wouldn't be any songs without Sophie," I said. "I'm happy with the deal."

Hovering far above the stage, we could still hear the shouts and demands for another encore from our audience.

"You'll get your encore when we're *headlining* next year!" yelled Cad, looking out the window at the crowd.

"Always leave them wanting more," said Skark, winking at me. "We're *back*."

PROM

I spent the ride back to Earth holding hands with Sophie and staring out the window. We knew we'd never get to see All of Everything from this angle again. She put her head on my shoulder as we passed a nebula that looked like clouds of white cotton, and she squeezed my fingers as we watched a group of stellar jets spitting out neon blue bubbles like great cosmic snorkels. We were trying to remember everything, so we didn't talk much. There was time for that later.

Driver and Cad were stripped to the skin, having donated their own ragged clothing to the cause of making me a tuxedo by the time we got back to Earth. Driver had needles in his mouth as he put the finishing touches on the garment. He had made the tuxedo pants out of my scrubs. For the shirt, he'd cut around the sweat stains of one of his enormous tank tops to create a simple white button-down, fashioning the buttons from porcelain chunks of the toilet, which Walter had chipped off the rim of the bowl using his hooves. For the coat, Skark just let me keep his jacket.

"The jacket will do whatever you tell it to do," said Skark. "If you want it to look like fireflies, it will. If you want it to look like it's made of ice, it will. The controls are here." He pointed to a series of buttons inside the sleeve.

"I'm probably just going to need it to match these white pants," I said.

"It can do that," said Skark, tapping a couple of buttons. The coat grew warm, and in one movement the panels from which it was built flipped over, revealing their lustrous white undersides.

"Sophie, what color is your evening dress?" said Driver.

"Yellow."

"Spectacular," said Skark. "You two will stop *time* in your outfits."

Driver took a brief break from stitching the tuxedo to get behind the wheel and guide the Interstellar Libertine through the Kuiper Belt at the edge of our solar system, weaving the bus between celestial icebergs and clusters of comets that came at us like shotgun pellets.

Familiar planets soon came into view—Saturn, with its annular disks, and Jupiter, with its Great Red Spot. Mars wasn't particularly captivating—after what Sophie and I had seen, it was hard to care about whether NASA ever put a human on such a dead rock, considering there were so many other interesting places to visit. No reason to be there.

Finally, we saw the blues and greens of Earth, which—even more than the thought of *we're finally home*—gave me the feeling of staring at a quaint country house. I was perfectly okay with the fact that the rest of the universe regarded us as unsophisticated and potentially doomed. It was nice being tucked away in our own secluded, comfortably climated sliver of the universe, far from everybody else. We popped through the atmosphere and descended toward the snuff-colored landscape of the American Southwest.

I didn't know what was going to happen next, but I was feeling pretty good about myself in that moment, I have to say. I had gone after Sophie, and one way or another, I'd finished the task. I'd brought her back.

When we arrived in Gordo, I had Driver land the bus near the town dump so we wouldn't be seen falling directly from the sky onto Sophie's front lawn, and from there we drove the roads to her house. It was night, and the bus's headlights kept shining on *Sophie Come Home Soon* signs in people's yards and on ribbons imploring her return tied around tree trunks. For a while, I wondered why there weren't any signs supporting *me,* and then I realized, *Oh, it's because people think* I *kidnapped her.*

Although my parents were vacationing in Vietnam and presumably had no idea that I had been gone, this was *not* the case with the Gilkeys. They not only were *home* but had spent almost a week in a state of catatonic worry about their missing daughter, who had last been seen fixing her motorcycle in her driveway . . . a motorcycle later found in the back of my truck in the drive-through of the In-N-Out, which meant there were news trucks parked outside *both* our houses.

The reporters assigned to the kidnapping beat nearly passed out when they saw the platypus-shaped bus roll up in front of the Gilkeys' house, park, throw open its doors, and eject Sophie. They yelled questions, but she was inside before they could get her to answer anything. We heard them pounding on the side of the bus, shouting questions about where we'd taken her, but Driver refused to open the door while he was making the final adjustments to my tux.

They were probably having a field day with the story— "Loner Teen Kidnaps Beautiful Neighbor"—but despite photographers snapping pictures of the Interstellar Libertine and the throng of journalists amassing outside the Gilkeys' front door, trying to get at Sophie inside, I hadn't been spotted yet. The bus had tinted windows for a reason.

A police car pulled up outside, and I heard a cop's voice through the speakers.

"Please exit the vehicle."

"No way," said Driver, thread in his mouth, making a few last stitches to my tie, which he'd made from the leather shell of the bus's steering wheel.

We heard more police sirens.

"Get out of the vehicle now."

"Hurry up, Sophie," I muttered. "We're already late. . . ."

I knew that Sophie's parents had been waiting almost a week for information about where their daughter had gone, only to have her suddenly come bursting through the front door. No doubt they were currently all over her, hugging and crying and asking questions and phoning relatives with the good news and checking to make sure she wasn't hurt and generally making it difficult for her to get ready for the dance.

But—and I know this is going to sound insensitive—I was getting impatient. We had prom. In due time, I was sure she and I were going to have to explain everything, but right now . . . I wanted to put all that off and get to where we were supposed to be. We were going to be late.

I saw the door opening and Sophie sprinting for the bus, and in that short, glorious run, all the strange situations I had endured over the past week ceased to matter.

She was wearing a floor-length yellow gown with spaghetti straps and a plunging neckline. When she turned to look at the reporters chasing her, I saw that her back was bare down to her waist, and the sheer fabric outlined her long legs from the curves of her hips to just below her knees. She had somehow managed to pull her hair away from her shoulders and twist it into a stylish bun, which showed off the length of her neck.

"Wow," said Cad.

"Makes me wish I was human," said Walter.

"Me too," said Skark.

"Perfect match for the tux," said Driver proudly.

Sophie's parents trailed her down the footpath leading from the house to the road while reporters snapping pictures swarmed. A cop stepped in front of her, only to be faked out by a quick two-step shake and bake.

"How does she run like that in heels?" said Walter.

"You get used to it," said Skark.

Driver smacked the button to open the door of the bus, and Sophie barreled inside.

"Get us *out* of here," she said.

"On it," said Driver, turning the ignition. I heard the *whoop* of the police siren.

"How do I look?" said Sophie.

"Like every star we've seen in the past week, amplified," I said.

She smiled. "You do clean up well, by the way. And Driver, the tux is a masterpiece."

Driver grinned back at us from the front seat. "I was inspired," he said. "Maybe I'll start my menswear line after all."

Sophie turned to me and spread her arms, showing all of her dress. Her body.

"Incredible," I said.

"Do you mean that? I didn't have a chance to do my makeup because my mom kept crying and hugging me and my dad was searching for a baseball bat."

"Why a bat?" said Skark.

BOOM BOOM BOOM. There was a pounding near the wheels of the bus, followed by shouts from Mr. and Mrs. Gilkey.

"Give me *back* my daughter. You're *not* taking her again."

"We'll need to leave the bus in the shop for a month after this trip," mumbled Skark.

"I'm sorry about the damage. Let me handle this," said Sophie, rolling down the window and poking her head out. "*Dad.* Everything is *fine.* This is my ride. I'll be back after prom. *Relax.*"

Mr. Gilkey lowered his bat.

"Who's in there with you?" he said.

I opened a window and looked out.

"Hi, Mr. Gilkey."

"Bennett."

"I promise everything is okay. There's nothing else to worry about—we got Sophie back in one piece."

"Who's *we?*" said Mrs. Gilkey.

Cad, Skark, Driver, and Walter poked their heads out of the window around me, which may have been a tactical error. The sight of their daughter on a bus with two aliens—who were essentially naked, though I don't know if her parents could tell that from their vantage point—a thirty-year-old bassist, and a ram couldn't have been comforting.

"Gotta go. *Love you.*" Sophie closed the window.

"Driver, get us to the high school as fast as you can," I said. "They're going to be coming for us, but we can get in at least one dance. . . ."

"Do you want to drive or fly?" said Driver.

"I'd say drive," I said. "But *fast.* If you fly, we'll have even more questions to answer."

"Actually, we have one more stop first," said Sophie. "I know we're cutting things close, but it's necessary."

Driver gunned the bus down the road before the news trucks could even start their engines. We were late, but I knew what Sophie required to complete her outfit. I had been thinking about it too.

Though my tuxedo matched her dress terrifically, Sophie still needed a corsage. Cad—perhaps momentarily forgetting the romance of prom—suggested grabbing a carnation from a graveyard to save some time, but when Sophie protested at the thought of having ghosts inhabiting her dress, we decided to pull into a supermarket instead.

The flower shop was closing as Sophie and I walked inside, but the woman working the counter took one look, saw our outfits, and knew why we were there. Fortunately, she didn't seem to recognize us from the press coverage. I guess flower-shop ladies live in their own worlds.

"I think your dance has already started, darlings," said the flower lady. "I know making an entrance is important, but you might have mistimed matters."

"Do you have any corsages left?" I said.

"If you're in yellow, that means you need something pink or white. Come over here."

We went with the pink, because Sophie said it was more promlike. I thought I'd be able to slip the corsage over her wrist, but she wanted it fastened next to her neckline. The flower lady gave me the long pin.

"Keep your hands still, now," she said. "You don't want to pop that bosom before you get to use it."

I froze.

"I can't really pop it, can I?"

"You're an idiot," said Sophie.

"I don't have much experience with this sort of thing," I said.

Despite my brushes with death—despite actually *dying* at one point—this was the most stressful moment of the past five days. I was sweating. I took a breath, reached back carefully with the pin . . . and stabbed Sophie.

"Are you *serious*?" she said, recoiling. "I *cannot* believe you did that."

After my repeated apologies, the flower lady gave Sophie a tissue to dab up the small spots of blood on her chest, and she handled the rest of the pinning herself.

"You found the *one* spot on my body that wasn't hurt, and you injured it," she said.

"I'm so, so sorry."

"I'm kidding," she said. "Do you really think I would care about one more little nick at this point? Let's go."

When we got to the parking lot, we found Cad, Skark, and Driver standing outside the bus, wearing stained white butcher coats, which was unsettling.

"I see you've found terrifying new outfits," said Sophie.

"They were outside the back door of the deli, waiting for the cleaners to pick them up," said Driver. "They still smell like meat, but it's better than nothing."

"I feel that it is important for us to be matching if we are playing a formal," said Skark.

"What *formal* are you playing?" I said.

Skark, Driver, and Cad grinned at me.

"Oh, *come on,*" I said.

"One song," said Skark. "'Wonderful Tonight' by Eric Clapton. I promise, that's all I'm going to do. It's a classic. My voice is in splendid form, and we've never gigged at a prom before."

"Can we stop you?" I said.

"Absolutely not," said Skark.

"This is gonna be epic," said Cad.

A banner hung from the exterior of the gym—*Gordo High School Welcomes You to a Winter Wonderland in the Desert*—and a silver carpet stretched from the curb to the front door, flanked by blue and white balloons. The parking lot closest to the school was crowded with waiting limos, so Driver eased the Interstellar Libertine into a spot adjacent to the basketball courts, near a van with windows steaming up from the inside and a bench where a few prom goers were drinking cans of beer.

I opened the door and offered Sophie my arm to help her down to the pavement, where the beer drinkers greeted us with shouts of *great ride* and *we thought you were dead.* To which we answered *thanks* and *we're not.*

As we strolled the silver carpet, we could hear the *boom* of music filtering out from the gym.

"Good, it's still going on," said Sophie.

Hand in hand, we walked inside the gym and over to the ticket table, where my French teacher, Mrs. Jolivet, was sitting reading a gossip magazine and drinking a Tab.

She looked up at us, bewildered.

"Bennett . . . Sophie . . . ," said Mrs. Jolivet.

"We're late, but we made it," I said.

"Everybody has been looking for you. . . . Parents . . . the cops . . ."

"We know."

Mrs. Jolivet got a strange look on her face.

"Who are *those* guys?" she said.

Behind us, Skark, Cad, and Driver were holding their instruments, wearing their butcher coats, friendly smiles on their faces.

"Musical chaperones," said Cad. "To make sure everyone gets home safe."

From inside the gym, we heard the DJ: *"Snuggle up with your dates or whoever else is left and desperate, because we're getting ready for tonight's LAST SONG."*

"Mrs. Jolivet . . . I know everybody has questions about where we've been, and I know our friends look a little strange, but right now we need our tickets. We've come a *long* way for this, and I *promise* that everything is going to be fine."

"Go in, go in," said Mrs. Jolivet, waving us inside. "Whatever secrets you're hiding, they can wait five minutes. But the rest of you have to stay out there."

Skark took Mrs. Jolivet's hand in his own and gazed into her eyes.

"Madame," he said. "If you let us in there, you have my word that nothing will happen. We are professionals, and we would never try to upstage such an important occasion. I would never lie to a beautiful woman, unless I had ulterior motives, of course."

Skark winked at Mrs. Jolivet, and I saw her swoon. It didn't matter that he was eight feet tall, it didn't matter that he was in a deli coat covered in splotches of liverwurst and ground beef—he had put her under a spell. *That* is true charisma. He was even more charming without Spine Wine in his body than he was when he was buzzed.

"We can always use more chaperones," said Mrs. Jolivet, spellbound. "Go."

Sophie pulled me through the doors of the gym straight to the dance floor, allowing me only the briefest glimpse of the wintry décor. The room was bathed in blue light, with snowflake-shaped lanterns hanging above us and fake pine trees scattered around. Silver stars covered the walls, and fake penguins stood atop the bleachers.

Skark, Cad, and Driver made their way to the DJ stand.

"We're here to close out the night," Skark said. "Made it just in time."

"Close out the night?" said the DJ.

"Haven't you been to one of the proms in this town before?" said Cad. "They always bring in a band to play the last song. It's like a closer in baseball. It's tradition."

"Nobody told me," said the DJ. "I've done plenty of proms. . . ."

Skark stared at the DJ, unblinking.

"Cut. The. Music," said Skark. "Let us do our job." With the touch of a button, the music was off. Skark took the microphone.

"Good evening, Gordo High School," he cooed. "My name is Skark Zelirium, and as a unit, we are the Perfectly Reasonable. Thank you for inviting us to sing you out on this romantic evening."

My classmates were looking back and forth between Skark and Sophie and me, trying to figure out the connection.

"So, gents, grab your ladies. Without further ado . . . this is Eric Clapton's masterpiece 'Wonderful Tonight.'"

As Skark strummed the opening chords to the song, Sophie draped her arms over my shoulders. Five days earlier, being this close to her—her stomach pressed against me, her hair tickling my chin, her fingers running down my arms—would have scrambled my senses and caused me to pass out on the dance floor. It still made me feel light-headed, but I was at least able to stay upright.

"I'm not sure our outfits go with the Winter Wonderland theme," she said. "At least you've got some *white* in your outfit. There isn't a *speck* of yellow in this room."

I pressed a button in the sleeve of my jacket, and—*schloop*—the miniature tiles turned yellow.

"Now there is," I said.

"Slick."

"Thank you," I said.

I looked over her shoulder as she looked over mine. The entire school was standing around watching us dance, their eyes panning from Sophie to me. I couldn't tell if it was because we'd been missing and now here we were, or if it was because of the incongruity of seeing a girl as hot as Sophie with *me*.

I overheard my classmates' theories as I held Sophie tight.

"He must have drugged her."

"Maybe it's one of those Stockholm syndrome situations where the girl falls for her kidnapper."

"He's probably been brainwashing her for the past five days."

Sophie looked at me.

"Want to mess with them?" she said.

"Desperately."

I leaned in and kissed her. All around me, I heard female gasps and male grumbles.

"There's no way they actually ran away with each other, is there?"

"Does that look real to you? It kinda looks real."

"Way to go, Bennett. Can't believe what I'm seeing."

Skark finished the song, improvising lyrics over Clapton's melody. I saw a few girls gripping their boyfriends, willing them to complete the traditional last dance of the night without getting distracted by the overwhelmingly strange band that had invaded the ceremony, but everybody else in the room had stopped in place and was just *gawking* at the musical intruders who had taken over the makeshift stage, all of whom were clearly not from New Mexico.

Skark brought the song to an end.

> *Don't Bennett and Sophie . . . look stylish . . .*
> *tonight. . . .*

"Thank you, Gordo High, and good night," said Skark. "Be safe out there. The weirdness of life sneaks up on you quick. Just want to put that out there—good thing to learn when you're young."

I could hear our classmates heading for the exits—Sophie's and my return from the dead might have been interesting, but there was beer to drink outside and hooking up to do, so they left us alone. It wasn't until I felt a tap on my shoulder that I stopped kissing Sophie. Skark, Cad, and Driver were standing in front of me.

"I hate to interrupt," said Skark. "But I'm afraid this is goodbye."

"That was the best rendition of 'Wonderful Tonight' I've ever heard," I said.

"Of course," said Skark.

"You guys going to stick around at all?" I said.

"Not long," said Skark. "We have to visit In-N-Out. Everybody is hungry, and Dondoozle just wired us our fee."

"Plus, we've got to drop off Walter," said Driver.

"Why didn't he come in?"

"He's in the soccer field bingeing on grass," said Cad. "Behaving like an absolute swine, but he's earned it."

"Am I going to see you again?" I said.

"You'll no doubt hear from us soon, though I'm not sure if our next tour will have an Earth stop."

"Venues here not big enough?"

"Not for what we're planning," said Skark, grinning. "You two look fabulous. Assure me you'll get out of this town. You're the only fashionable ones around."

"We will," I said.

Then the band was out the door. A few moments after that, I felt the rumble of the Interstellar Libertine passing over the school.

"Are you still taking pictures?" Sophie said to the prom photographer, who was starting to pack up his equipment.

"I'm on the clock for one more minute."

"We're coming right now," said Sophie. "Don't put away your camera."

The photographer waited. We took our positions.

And if you look closely enough at that prom picture—Sophie and I pressed against each other in front of a metallic blue background covered with stars, underneath a canopy of gray and purple balloons, between a pair of snowflake-covered columns—you can *just barely* make out a cop's hand entering the frame.

EPILOGUE

When questioned about where we'd been, Sophie and I told everybody the truth—aliens had abducted her, I went after her upon finding some sympathetic musicians at the In-N-Out drive-through, and it took about a week to track her down and bring her back, more or less. Everyone thought we were lying, and the cops ended up chalking up their missing-person case to us being a teenage couple who had run off together for a few days and didn't want to tell anybody where we'd gone.

After the initial interrogations, it took a few weeks for reporters to stop knocking on our doors and for UFO conspiracy theorists who had read about the story on the Internet—"High School Lovers Embark on Martian Romp"—to stop calling our houses, fishing for more details of where we'd been and what we'd seen.

Then things finally quieted down, and Sophie and I finally started enjoying the summer. As girlfriend and boyfriend.

Though not at first.

Her parents weren't exactly *pleased* with our burgeoning relationship, but because we were neighbors, there was little they could do to prevent us from seeing each other aside from grounding her, which they did, a hard-line detention period that ended on the last day of June.

My grounding was equally long, but less severe in its tone. My parents arrived home from Southeast Asia the day *after* I returned from space. They were sunburned, beset with stomach ailments, and exhausted, their suitcases full of knockoff luxury goods purchased in Ho Chi Minh City.

They found me sitting in the living room with a cop, once again repeating my story for his notebook: "That's right. There were two aliens in the band, and one human."

"And a ram . . ."

"The ram wasn't a musician. Well, actually, that's a good question. He could have been, but I never saw him play anything. I've told you this before. Are we done? Because as far as I can tell, I didn't do anything wrong except miss school."

"And lie to the police."

"I'm telling the *truth*."

"Bennett, what's going on here?" said my mom, the sight of the cop causing her to drop a tin of ceremonial tea she had carried with her from the highlands of Vietnam. For days afterward, the house smelled like lotus blossoms, which was pleasant.

Because my parents hadn't been around for my absence, they were in a strange position when it came to punishing me—after all, the house was fine, the cops weren't pressing charges, and both Sophie and I had the same story about where we'd been. Since they hadn't had to deal with the *anxiety* of me being gone, it was hard for them to dole out an appropriate punishment for something they hadn't experienced.

"You're grounded until the end of June," said my dad.

"And every chore we can think of, you're doing," said my mom.

The penalty seemed fair, and I was pleased my release date corresponded with Sophie's, which meant we'd have July and August together.

After a month and a half of carving hedges into geometrically perfect squares, folding mountains of laundry, washing every window in the house, shampooing carpets, filling bird feeders, cleaning the bathroom tiles with a toothbrush, and raking the dirt around the cacti in our backyard twice a week, I was free to be with Sophie.

I had plenty of time with her, due to the fact that I was unable to find a summer job since everybody in town thought I was a kidnapper. Since Sophie and I had disappeared at the same time, it was just as logical that she had abducted *me* as I had abducted her, but nobody even *considered* that possibility, because she was attractive and going to Princeton, and I was—for all intents and purposes—now a townie.

I applied for a job at the movie theater, a couple of pizza

places, a crafts store, a day spa, and, finally, a septic tank cleaning company.

"You're that crazy boy from the newspaper, aren't you?" said the owner of the septic company during our interview. "The one who says he was abducted."

"I'm not crazy."

"I'm afraid your presence might upset some of my clients. But thank you for coming in."

Not even qualified to siphon human waste from metal vats. I pretty much knew that no matter where I applied, I wouldn't get the job, so I stopped trying and just hung out with Sophie. We walked around and talked. We listened to music in my room. We tried to avoid her dad, who still held me responsible for her disappearance and stood angrily in the doorway watching me whenever I was over at her place, which was unpleasant. We hung out on my porch, talking about things that had nothing to do with our abductions. She had been a riddle to me for eighteen years, and now I wanted to know everything.

It was July 10 when I walked to the mailbox and found a thin envelope stamped in the upper left with the Princeton logo. I opened it in the driveway and discovered that I had finally made it off the wait list and straight into the rejection pile.

After careful consideration, we regret to inform you that Princeton University will not be able to offer you admission to the class of . . .

I stopped reading, ripped up the letter, and tossed it in the trash can, which was conveniently located next to me on the curb. After that, I went inside and watched the entire second season of *Cupcake Wars* on the Food Network, which I had never watched before. I don't even have a sweet tooth. I had no idea what else to do.

The next day, while we were watching *Pretty in Pink* on my couch, I told her. It took me until the end credits to get up the will to do so, because I knew that saying it out loud meant when the summer ended, we wouldn't be together anymore. That, and I couldn't do it during the climactic prom scene. It wouldn't be right.

She rubbed my arm and kissed my neck and told me everything was going to be okay, which is how it went for the rest of the summer. With no job, no college prospects, and no idea what I was going to do next, I gave my full attention to making out with Sophie as much as possible.

On the day she left, at the end of August, I had to see her in the morning, because I knew that her parents wouldn't want me around while they finished packing the car for the cross-country drive to her college. We'd already agreed that this was the end—she needed to get on with her future and have the freedom to date whatever geniuses and sons of industry and well-dressed European students she met in the dorms, while I had to start looking around for a damp, dark room in which to spend the next few years wallowing in depression and watching daytime television, because I had no idea what else I was going to do with myself. No college, no job, no girlfriend. Maybe I would take up Internet poker, or start sniffing glue.

Sophie and I were sitting on the edge of my porch near my telescope when we said goodbye.

"I can't believe you're leaving," I said.

"You can visit whenever you want."

"I would, but I have no money and my truck is in a junkyard in Roswell."

"And you might strangle someone in the admission office."

"That would be the main reason to go, aside from seeing you."

Sophie checked the time on her phone and put it back in her pocket. She tapped the dirt in front of her with the heel of one of her zip-up riding boots. No matter the moment, she always looked cool.

"I'm glad you saw me through the telescope that day," she said.

"I wish it was strong enough that I could see you on the other side of the country."

"What about your rule against stalking?"

"I'm reconsidering it right now."

Sophie leaned in and kissed me. Every time, it gave me the same feeling that it did on the rock in the desert. My vision still blurred and I always saw stars, morning, afternoon, or night.

She stood up from the porch. She didn't have to tell me—I knew it was time for her to go, and I knew we were breaking up. I walked her back to her driveway. I was glad it was far away.

Her parents were waiting in the car when we got there, all

her suitcases crammed inside. I kissed her until her father's honking became unbearable.

"I wish we still had the bus," she said. "I'm bringing more stuff than I thought I would. It would make this move easier."

"And then I could have used it to store the cans and bottles I'll be collecting in my new career as a homeless man."

"*HA . . . hehhhhhh.* At least you'd be a cute homeless man."

She took her arms from around my body and walked to the car. Her father was grinning at me from behind the wheel, delighted that I was no longer going to be in his daughter's life. I might have seen him high-five her mom.

Sophie got in the backseat and rolled down the window to stick her hand out and wave goodbye. The window shot right back up, nearly cutting her arm off in the process. I could read her father's lips saying he was turning on the air-conditioning, and with that, the car pulled out of the driveway. I walked out into the street to watch it go . . .

. . . and immediately regretted letting her leave, *especially* knowing that she was now single once again.

"Sophie, *no!*" I yelled, running after her. "I changed my *mind.* I don't *want* you to have new experiences and expand your horizons. Come *back.*"

But by the time I made it to the middle of the road, the Gilkeys' car was already speeding away, Mr. Gilkey's round face grinning at me in the rearview mirror. He might have even flipped me off, but I couldn't be sure, because my eyes were wet.

And there you go. Sophie's gone, and I have fully slid into the I-am-a-complete-piece-of-crap existence that goes along with being simultaneously a local pariah and the only kid around who isn't going to college, or the workforce, or the military, or anywhere at all.

Anyway, at least now I've gotten this story down on paper, in case thirty years from now somebody discovers me in my childhood bedroom, holed up like Howard Hughes, my fingernails overgrown, hair down to my ankles, surrounded by filthy blankets, having forgotten how to speak because nobody has talked to me since Sophie and I said goodbye. This story can explain how I got that way. I've got my guitar—and any guitar worth its wood needs a few tears on it.

Shit . . . I just broke a string.

MORE EPILOGUE

Hey. So I'm picking up this book again, after quite a bit of time. I can't believe I even brought it with me. Things have changed since the peak of my depression—to say the least— and I thought I should finish it out to reflect new developments.

As October started, with Sophie gone a month, I found myself in the same place I'd spent the previous four years—in my bedroom, with my guitar, writing songs. But at least I knew how to finish them now. I just pictured myself onstage in a tight jumpsuit, and that generally worked.

Unfortunately, *imagining* myself performing was as close as I was going to get to utilizing my new songwriting confidence. There weren't a great multitude of musicians in Gordo who were into dance-rock, and I wasn't sure when I was going to be able to leave my town, if ever.

My photograph—the unflattering *Most Awkward* picture from the yearbook—had been in the newspaper so much during the Sophie saga that I couldn't walk into the supermarket without seeing shoppers whisper about me or having little kids point and ask their parents if I was the man who'd gone to space.

If I wanted to attend college, I was going to have to restart the whole application procedure—figure out which schools I wanted to go to, get new recommendations from my teachers (which might be difficult, given the fact that they thought I was a criminal), write new essays, wait for responses. And if I was honest with myself, I knew that I didn't *want* to go to some backup school. I wanted to go to Princeton. I wanted to be with Sophie.

I thought about her constantly. She sent the occasional email talking about the autumn weather or how the leaves were changing, but I got the sense that she was holding back on saying too much about the school in order to spare my feelings. I didn't ask her if she was dating anybody new; she didn't ask if I had taken to wandering the desert, waiting to be attacked by coyotes in order to end my misery in a manner that didn't technically count as suicide, which had crossed my mind. We wrote less and less as the days went on, with her life moving forward and mine still a corpse.

It was Halloween when I walked downstairs from my room after waking up at my now-customary two in the afternoon— depression!—and found my parents standing at the front door, dressed as Robin Hood and Maid Marian, about to go to a costume barbecue before starting the night's parties. I hadn't been invited to any parties.

"Look who's finally decided to show himself," said my mom. "What time did you go to bed last night?"

"Sorry, I was working until dawn. I tried not to be too loud."

"The new music sounds good," she said.

I'd finally started playing my music in the house whether my parents were home or not. After I'd performed for a crowd of thousands and thousands at Dondoozle, it didn't seem like such a big deal to have people hear what I was doing. I also had the ability to actually *finish* songs now, some of which I thought were pretty good—though if I didn't get out of New Mexico, they were all going to end up rotting in my head, unheard by anyone.

"If you get a job, you'll be able to buy better equipment," said my dad.

"I'm looking for a job," I said. "I've tried everywhere."

"Then you'll have to start trying other towns," said my dad. "We can't have you here doing nothing forever."

"Now's not the time to discuss this," said my mom. "Bennett, your father and I need to head out, but there's chicken salad in the fridge, so help yourself. Also, a letter came for you in the mail. . . . Did you apply for a credit card or something?"

"No. Why?"

"It's from Bank of America," said my mom. "It's probably

junk, but it had your name on it. Don't sign up for any credit cards without talking to us first."

My parents left, and I looked at the envelope on the counter. Nothing came to the house specifically for me anymore. I used to get *Rolling Stone* magazine but I had to let my subscription lapse because I couldn't afford it. There were a couple of months when I would get weird letters from UFO hunters asking for information about what had happened to me, but pretty soon those stopped too. I could feel myself slipping off the grid, becoming nothing.

The envelope didn't seem junk-mail-ish—there was nothing on it advertising interest rates or special offers or anything like that—so I sliced open the top with a butter knife and read the letter inside.

What I saw made me sit down.

It was a *Welcome to Bank of America* package informing me an account had been opened in my name. There were only a few sheets of paper—the first was the boilerplate describing the benefits of being a Bank of America customer, the second was a receipt describing how the account had been opened (*c/o The Perfectly Reasonable LLC / The Sophie Album*), and the third was the *number* stating exactly how much money I now had at my disposal.

I had never seen so many zeros. The universe was a big consumer market, and apparently the record was a hit.

I looked in the envelope to see if there was anything that I had missed, and discovered a creased magazine page. I opened the page, which contained a list showing the Perfectly Reasonable holding the position of ninth-best band in the universe, just behind Radiohead.

I don't know how the band had managed to exchange their earnings from space into dollars down here. Maybe there were wire transfers from space that only financial institutions knew about—somebody had to keep banks in business—maybe the band bought gold wherever they were and exchanged it for cash, maybe they showed up at some Belgian outpost with a suitcase of diamonds and told the teller to turn it into a number. However the band had opened my account, the end result was that I was now *rich*.

"Thank you," I said to space. "Thank you thank you thank you."

I had an idea. I picked up the phone and dialed Information. *"What city?"*

"Princeton, New Jersey."

"What listing?"

"Princeton University Admission Office, please."

"Do you want to dial the number yourself or be connected? It's a fifty-cent charge for being put through."

"You can just put me through. I think I can afford it."

I heard the clicking sound of the operator connecting me, and then a ringing phone.

"Undergraduate Admission Office."

"Hello, my name is Bennett Bardo. I was on your wait list to get in before I got rejected at the start of the summer, and I was just wondering if there's anything I could do to make you change your mind."

"I'm sorry to hear you were rejected, but the semester has already started and the class is full."

"There's no way to get in?"

"We'd be happy to have you apply again, but I'm afraid there's nothing else you could do at this time."

I was waiting for that.

"What if . . . I donate a building?"

"I'm sorry, I don't have time to joke around."

"What if I'm not kidding?"

There was silence on the other end.

"Please hold."

It would have been tacky to put my name on the new auditorium, especially as a current student, so I asked the Princeton administration to call it the Perfectly Reasonable Center for the Performing Arts. They thought it was a strange choice, yet inoffensive enough that they went with it, so long as I used small letters on the facade.

The plan was for the building to be constructed in a corner of the campus near the Engineering Quadrangle. I asked the university to build it with brick because I wanted it to fit with the classic, tree-lined aesthetic of the rest of the grounds, which I adored so much. Inside, it looked like an empty ballroom; while seats could be set up for more formal gatherings—quartet recitals, poetry readings, violin concertos—the main idea behind the center was that it would be a place where bands could play.

But I'm getting ahead of myself.

After springing my pickup truck from the junkyard where it had sat since that night at In-N-Out, I retrofitted it with forty thousand dollars' worth of aftermarket parts so it would never break down again, and then I drove across the country to my new school, staying at a couple of fine hotels along the way, ordering room service each night.

Oddly enough, on the day I pulled up to Princeton in my truck, Sophie was the first person I saw. She was running in the street outside the main gates, waving a piece of paper above her head and screaming, *"Oh my God."*

I pulled up next to her.

"Why, hello," I said.

She launched herself through the driver's-side window to hug me.

"Bennett."

"Let me guess—you got your royalty check from the band."

"Yes. Oh my *God."*

"What are you going to buy?"

"Looking at this, either an island or a city, I'm not sure yet. This is *incredible.* Is the money real?"

"It's real," I said. "I've already started spending it. You may even start noticing a few improvements around campus soon."

"You bought your way in, didn't you?" she said.

"Gloriously so."

"Good move. Rich snots here do it all the time."

"You want a ride?"

"Yeah, to an ATM."

"Not to a mall?"

"Don't joke about that. I never want to see a mall again."

She climbed in the truck.

"This is *nice*," she said. "Is this the same truck you had before?"

"Same truck, but the interior is all new and the engine could be in a race car. I couldn't leave it behind. I made it across the country in two days."

She looked at the shining, newly installed stereo, then back at me. She raised an eyebrow.

"New sound system . . . ," she said.

"Try it out."

She pressed the power button, and all at once, the voice of the Phantom rang out of the speakers.

Sing once again with me . . . Our strange duet . . .

"I *knew* you were listening to *Phantom of the Opera* by choice," she said.

"It's hard not to," I said.

"It sounds amazing."

"No more cassettes."

"I'm glad you're here," she said. "I can't *believe* this."

"What city are you going to buy?"

She looked down at her check again, shaking her head.

"It seems like with this, my options are pretty open," she said. "Maybe Barcelona? Rome?"

"I hear Stockholm is nice, and it might be more manageable because it's smaller. A starter city."

"You're right," she said. "I'll get used to paying the mortgage somewhere like Stockholm, and then move up to something like Paris or Tokyo."

She hugged me again.

"It's amazing that you're *here*. Where are you living?"

"The dorms," I said. "I brought flip-flops for the shower and everything. I may be extremely wealthy, but I'm a man of the people."

"What about your guitar?"

"Yeah. I brought my guitar. I also brought all my new guitars."

"What did you have to do to buy your way in?"

"Donate a building. Part of me wanted to buy the whole place and rename it Bennett College, but it turns out there already is one in North Carolina."

Sophie fell silent, pondering her riches.

"I guess I can change my course of study to something impractical now," she said. "I'd been doing finance, but now I have all the money, so it's hard to see the point."

"You could always endow a department and create your own major," I suggested.

"I've always liked history," she said. "Think they'll let me dig up famous figures and clone them so I can ask questions?"

"I don't see why not. Who would you pick?"

"Maybe Hannibal of Carthage. I mean, anybody who can lead a battalion of elephants over the Alps to fight the Romans seems like a guy who would have some interesting ideas."

"I love that Hannibal's your number one."

"I'm sure a lot of people would just want to clone Einstein or something, but I'd rather hear about the elephants than theories about gravity. I'm done with facts about space."

Outside the truck, elm trees and brick buildings rolled past. My tires kicked up flame-colored leaves. I could smell the earthy eastern air. Sophie leaned over and embraced me—surprisingly firmly, I might add. I guess she was still kickboxing.

If there is a way for a person to be happier than I was in that moment, I don't know what it is.

My new roommate's name was Li. He was from Hong Kong, and he played the cello in the university orchestra.

"Do you . . . have any interest in dance-rock?" I asked during our first conversation. He said he did, so I asked if anybody else in the orchestra felt the same way. He said he would check with the other members, and that's how I ended up with a band consisting of a drummer, a French horn player, a pianist, two cellists, and me on guitar. I called the group the School Dance.

Because of the time necessary for the construction of a

building, it was a couple of years before I finally got the chance to play the venue that my money had built, so I spent my time honing my skills at local clubs and dances, and—more than anything—being a college student.

Though I'd had to buy my way in, once I arrived at Princeton I focused on proving that the admission office had made a mistake by rejecting me in the first place, and studied like a madman. I declared a major in astrophysics, which might not have been the most practical course of study, since I didn't know what I was going to do with my degree, and math was always a horrible weakness of mine. But due to the fact that I didn't have to worry about money, I figured I would do something that interested me, and if I failed a class, I could just take it again. No rush. Whenever my classmates insisted that long-distance space travel was impossible, I kept smugly silent, because I alone knew the truth. I still didn't understand the mechanics of *how* it was possible, but I guess that's what you get when you have a bassist from New Jersey try to explain the folding of space-time instead of somebody more qualified.

Perhaps the strangest thing about my college experience was that Sophie and I naturally fell into the roles of good friends, and that was all. We dated for a few months when I first got to Princeton, but then she wanted to look around and see other people, and when I was honest with myself, I knew that I wanted the same thing.

Allow me to explain.

In Gordo, I had been attracted to Sophie because she had

seemed so unbelievably *interesting* compared to the other students, but at Princeton, *everybody* seemed interesting. During those few months when Sophie was at college and I was rotting away in New Mexico, she had gotten used to dating stimulating people from around the world, and while we cared for each other immeasurably, the reason we had both wanted to go to Princeton was to *get away* from our hometown and become more well rounded. It seemed counterintuitive to only see each other. I think we both secretly thought we might get together again down the line, but after working so hard to win our freedom from New Mexico, we wanted to run with it.

In my first two years of school alone, I dated a Lebanese anthropologist, a Croatian flautist named Lika, and the Argentinean national equestrian champion. As Cad had promised, the dregs of the Spine Wine I had consumed lingered in my body for a couple of years, which meant that I was able to understand everything foreign students said in their native languages, even if I couldn't speak their languages myself. It was a good parlor trick—more than once, I found myself in a bar while, say, a girl from India named objects in the room in her native tongue and I instantly pointed them out. But eventually my abilities started to fade, which was probably for the best. No need to have more strange chemicals in one's tissues than is absolutely necessary.

Sophie dated guys who were equally intriguing—a member of the Danish royal family, one of Picasso's great-grandnephews, a baseball player who had been drafted by the Cubs—though I tried not to pay too much attention to her conquests because I occasionally got the urge to kill them, open-minded as I was.

But Sophie was my best friend at school, and when I finally got up onstage with the School Dance at the newly completed Perfectly Reasonable Center for the Performing Arts as a junior, she was standing in front of the stage, just as she had been for all our gigs. I even wore a yellow jumpsuit with a lightning bolt for the occasion, because it just seemed *right.*

The Perfectly Reasonable would have been proud of the auditorium. The walls were swathed in purple satin, and there was an enormous wet bar at the back. In honor of Skark, I'd asked the administration to track down the highest-quality disco ball they could find for the room's centerpiece. The one they found was less a *ball* than an antique Venetian chandelier shaped like a sphere that was taken from an opera house and had a sophisticated pedigree that would have no doubt delighted Skark.

The building was full for my band's performance, a ninety-minute sweating, shouting, dancing mess in which I rattled off twenty new songs. Ever since I had gotten to college and met musicians who were able to help me bring my concepts to life, I had been writing songs at a tremendous rate, at times finishing two or three a night, so I was always able to give the crowd something new. And the band had actual *fans*—not just kids who happened to be at parties we were playing, but people who would show up at our gigs whether they were students or not.

For the encore of every show I would ask the audience to shout out anything they wanted to hear, and we would do our best to accommodate them. There were songs that people asked for all the time—"Night Fever" by the Bee Gees, "Girls Just Want to Have Fun" by Cyndi Lauper, "Burning Down the

House" by Talking Heads—but this time there was a request from the back of the room that I'd never heard.

"Play 'Sophie and Me Up in Those Trees.'"

Which was a song I hadn't played since the Dondoozle Festival.

"Now *that* is a deep cut," I said.

"I don't think I know that one," said Li, turning to me.

"No reason you would. I'll do it solo," I said, taking off my electric guitar and putting on an acoustic. Nobody there would have any reason to shout it out aside from Sophie, who I saw had her neck craned and was standing on her tiptoes as she scanned the back of the room, thinking the same thing I was.

As I played the song—*You're swinging up there and I'm looking up at you, can't wait to come home to a tree house made for two*—I stared at the back of the crowd to see if I could locate the source of the request, but the lights were too bright and the auditorium too large.

> *And Skark was up in the vines*
> *Singing about old times. . . .*

I added the line because I knew the audience was probably too buzzed to care about the lyrics, and I wanted to see if anything would happen if I threw his name out. I didn't get a response, but—though there was no way to be sure about this—I thought I saw a tall figure pause by the emergency exit and look back at the stage just before ducking his head and walking through the door.

I peeked at Sophie, who shrugged. Wouldn't put it past him to show up.

Sophie and I escorted each other home that night—we lived in the same upperclassman dorm, which meant we were always walking together. Outside, there was the kind of chill in the air I had known I'd love even before arriving on campus—naked trees, mitten-wearing couples holding hands, clouds drifting in front of a huge yellow moon—and when Sophie gave me a look, I gave her my scarf, which is what often seemed to happen.

"I know you have the money to buy your own scarf," I said.

"But if I bought my own, it wouldn't be one of yours."

"That's my point. Even though you're no longer my girl-friend, you seem to think you still have full scarf privileges."

"If an ex-boyfriend and ex-girlfriend are on good terms, the ex-girlfriend gets lifetime scarf privileges. It's just the rule."

"I'd like to read that rule book."

"The library has an ancient copy in its archives. I'd show it to you, but any man who touches it is doomed to years of date-lessness. It's cursed."

"I must have accidentally read it in high school."

A sharp breeze blew across campus, and I zipped up my jacket to cover my neck. A food wrapper bounced along the ground in front of me, pushed by the wind, and I bent over to pick it up, because litter had no place in my version of college.

I was about to drop the wrapper in a trash can when something printed on it caught my eye—it was the In-N-Out logo. I held it up to Sophie.

"What's strange about this?" I said.

"There's no In-N-Out on the East Coast."

"No, there is not."

We looked up at the sky to see if we could spot the Interstellar Libertine, but all we saw was the normal stars blinking warmly.

"Do you ever wish we still had the bus?" she said.

"There's nowhere I'd rather be than here."

I listened to the quiet campus.

"I think you're supposed to end that sentence by saying *here with you.*"

"I thought transitioning to friendship meant I didn't have to finish sentences anymore," I said.

"At least do it jokingly, for old times' sake. You can't just cut me out of a good moment."

"I will put you back in the moment if we can also make out, for old times' sake."

"*HA . . . hehhhhhh. Snort.*"

"You've added a *snort* to your laugh?" I said.

"I don't know where it came from," she said.

"In the wake of this new snorting development, I'm withdrawing my make-out offer."

"Good, because it was never under consideration," she said. "Particularly because of that goober on your face."

"You're lying."

"I'm not. It's like a little intruder below your nose. Don't get defensive. It's cold outside—no need to be ashamed."

"Where?"

"Right there. Below your left . . . nostril."

I wiped my face. Definitely a goober.

"Told you," she said. "On your nostril."

"Nostril," I said. "Another terrible word."

"Not as bad as *oyster.*"

"Good one. Which reminds me, I've been hating *pamphlet* recently."

"Squat."

"Emission."

"Great one. Why is that so awful?"

"I think it's because of the *sss* and then the *un.* There's something about them together that doesn't work. And the context is kind of unappealing. *Emiss-ing.*"

For a moment, she looked lost in thought.

"I've got one," she said.

"Try me."

"Polyp," she said.

"That is *horrible,*" I said. "What is it?"

"It's a bump that grows in your colon."

"Tough to match, but I've got the best one ever," I said.

"Give it."

"I don't think you're going to be able to take it."

"I can handle anything."

"Here it comes."

"Bring it."

If Skark had visited campus to pay his respects to the temple his band's success had built, I was glad he'd left quietly, because I was done with visiting space. At the moment, the only stars I wanted to see were the points of light haloing from sidewalk lamps, the only nebulae I cared about were the clouds Sophie and I were exhaling in the cold night, and even if the Earth was zipping around the sun at a speed I hadn't *quite* been able to figure out from my astrophysics classes, it was nice to feel completely still.

"You're killing me," said Sophie. "Come *on.*"

"*. . . Girdle.*"

"*HA . . . hehhhhhhhhh . . .*"

Best thing in the universe.